EVIL PRINCE

CHICAGO MAFIA DONS

BIANCA COLE

CONTENTS

Book cover design by Deliciously Dark Designs

Photography by Wander Aguiar

BLURB

He's evil incarnate, cloaked in a beautiful disguise.

My father uprooted our family, forcing me to relocate to America. If that wasn't bad enough, he's making me marry the son of a psychopath. Maxim Volkov. Heir to the Volkov Bratva.

I'd rather die than be shackled to a man so evil. A man who has no soul. His piercing blue eyes are as cold as his stony heart. And he's not exactly thrilled, either.

My life has never felt so hopeless. Maxim makes it clear I'm to be his slave. A wife to tend to his every whim and desire. The thing is, I've got darkness inside of me too.

He may think he's the monster in this union, but violence is a part of my soul, and I won't bow down to his command. Maxim has finally met his match. Let chaos reign until death do us part, preferably his…

AUTHOR'S NOTE

*H*ello reader,

This is a warning to let you know that this may be my darkest book yet, which means there are some sensitive subject matters addressed. If you have any triggers, it would be important to proceed with caution.

As well as an evil anti-hero who doesn't take no for an answer and who becomes very possessive of the heroine, who is equally dark and messed up, this book addresses some sensitive subjects, a full list of these can be found <u>here</u>. As always, this book has a **HEA** and there's no cheating.

If you have any triggers, then it's best to read the warnings and not proceed if any could be triggering for you. However, if none of these are an issue for you, read on and enjoy this dark romance and slip into chaos with Maxim and Livia.

LIVIA

*T*he unending deep blue sea stretches for miles around me, making me feel like I'm drowning, even though I'm standing on the deck of my family's yacht, clutching onto the railings.

The soft waves crest against the side of the yacht, so at least I have something to be thankful for, that the Atlantic is being kind to us for now. It should be beautiful, as I love being out at sea, but I find it hard to appreciate the beauty right now when I know where my journey will end.

Italy is hundreds of miles away in the distance, the home we're leaving behind. Chicago seems like a such a dark, unhappy place from the searches I did on the internet, full of concrete buildings and no nature at all, except for some man-made parks. I love my hometown of Catanzaro in southern Italy, because it's steeped in history and surrounded by the unmatchable beauty of the Ionian coast line.

My father's greed is tearing us away from our home and everything we know.

"Are you out here sulking again?" Rizzo asks, approaching from behind.

I don't turn around to face my brother. "Don't tell me you're happy about moving to Chicago?"

He leans against the railing next to me, shaking his head. "No, I'm angry." He glances at me. "Father doesn't care what we want, though." He moves his attention to the horizon. "At least you aren't being shipped off to some mafia academy."

I sigh. "You'll be fine. It's only for eight months."

Our father is enrolling Rizzo in an academy for mafia heirs, almost an entire day's drive from Chicago, in Maine, once we reach the shores of America.

It's hard not to wonder what he expects me to do in Chicago. In Catanzaro, I had a part-time job working for a small boutique art gallery in the center of the city, even though my father thought it foolish for me to work when our family is so rich. I doubt I'll be offered any freedom once we're in America, since we're entering a war zone.

Father has been obsessed for as long as I can remember about getting vengeance on the people responsible for his parents' murder. The Morrone family, who fled Italy twenty years ago, now live in Chicago and control some of the territory. His hope is that the Bianchi family will unseat the Morrone family and steal everything they've built, righting the wrong they did to us.

It's no use trying to reason with him that vengeance never brings you peace.

"At least you'll be away from the shit show our father is cooking up." I meet my brother's piercing gaze. "You'll be safe in Maine."

His jaw clenches. "Yeah, and what about you?"

I shrug. "Who knows what plans he has?"

Rizzo's eyes flash with guilt as he rubs a hand across the back of his neck. "I hate that we won't be together. How am I supposed to protect you?"

I smile at him, but it's forced. "Don't be silly. I'm a big girl and can look after myself."

His jaw clenches. "How long do you think it will take for him to slip back into his old ways?"

A lead weight sinks into my stomach as he's voicing my own concerns. There's no doubt that with Rizzo gone, my father will slip back into his abusive ways, but eight months of beatings from him will be nothing compared to what we endured as children. "It's only eight months," I say, infusing my voice with lightness. I ruffle my brother's well groomed hair, which I know he hates. "I'll survive."

"Oi," he says, grabbing my hand. "Don't do that."

I stick out my tongue at him. "Sorry, bro."

He releases my hand, shaking his head as a small

smile twists onto his lips. "Did you know a Morrone attends the Syndicate Academy?"

My brow furrows. "No, which one?"

He sighs. "Camilla Morrone. She's a senior too."

I stand taller and glance at my brother. "You're worried about her being there?"

Rizzo shrugs. "Do you think she'll even know our family? She wasn't even alive when her father killed our grandparents."

I shake my head. "I doubt it. Just keep your head down, and you'll be fine."

"It's pretty fucked up that they have an academy for heirs of criminal organizations. It's dangerous to bring children from different families together like that."

I have heard terrible rumors about the academy that Rizzo is going to join. It's brutal, but I know it's nothing my brother can't handle. He's tougher than most. "It's unconventional, but you'll be fine."

He turns to me. "What are you going to do in Chicago? Maybe you can find a job at an art gallery."

"Unlikely. For one, art galleries in America aren't like they are back home. Second, I'm pretty sure father won't have me running around the city if we're entering a war zone."

"True." Rizzo turns around and leans his back on the railings. "So you'll be a prisoner, then?"

I roll my eyes. "I'll spend my days plotting my escape like Andy Dufresne in The Shawshank Redemption."

He laughs. "Don't tell me you're going to tunnel out of the house with a rock hammer?"

I shrug. "Desperate times."

We both laugh, and I feel my worries ease as we talk together. A calm silence falls between us, punctuated only by the sound of the engine and the rolling waves.

Our dark childhood brought us closer than most siblings, particularly siblings of criminal families. We endured things that children shouldn't have to, always fighting to survive together. "I know you worry, but I've survived his brutality before. I can do it again."

Rizzo sighs. "You shouldn't have to, though."

"I know."

He stares across the sea again. "Sometimes I wish I could squeeze the life out of him and be done with it." There's a haunted look in his eyes. "Even after everything he's done, I don't have it in me to kill my father." He laughs. "Pathetic, isn't it?"

I shake my head, but I've had the same sick fantasies and never acted on them. Although, in my fantasies, I don't strangle my father to death. In my fantasy, I torture him, and make him hurt for as long as possible, the way he made the three of us hurt. I make him bleed so damn much that it's running like a river from my dreams.

I swallow hard, pushing away the twisted thoughts in my mind. I scare myself with how dark my mind can get.

"It's not pathetic," I say, placing my hand over his.

"It's natural. Even though we both hate him, there's no getting away from the fact he's our flesh and blood."

He sighs. "Mother is going to struggle in Chicago."

"I know, but I'll take care of her." I notice his pained expression. "We'll all be okay."

He clenches his fists by his side. "I don't know what Father is thinking, dragging her across the Atlantic in her condition. She's been bad for months, and this is only going to make her worse."

He's right. Our mother suffers from bipolar disorder, and has been on medication ever since I can remember. However, the past few months, she's been more unstable than ever. I fear this move is only going to send her spiraling into places she can't recover from.

"I have to make sure that doesn't happen." I give him a stern look. "After all, I've got nothing else to do in Chicago, so I might as well spend my time helping her."

Someone clears their throat behind us, forcing us to turn around. It's my mother's maid, Alba.

"Is everything okay, Alba?" I ask.

She nods. "Yes, your mother is asking after you both. I said I'd find you."

Rizzo and I exchange glances, surprised that our mother would ask to see us. Half of the time, she doesn't even acknowledge our existence. "Of course, we'll get to her now," I reply.

Alba smiles and walks away, leaving us alone.

"Why the fuck would she be asking for us?" Rizzo asks.

"Let's find out." I nod my head toward the sitting room, and we both head inside.

My father is in a heated discussion with his consigliere, Marcello. We slip past unnoticed, heading up the stairs toward our mother's room. The door is shut and I can hear soft music playing on the other side.

I reach for the door and knock.

"Come in," Mother calls, her voice lighter than usual.

Rizzo opens it and steps in first. "You asked for us, mother?"

She smiles widely, which is unusual. "Yes, I'm having a good day today." She shrugs. "I think it's the sea air. I thought we could have some dinner together." She nods her head toward the balcony where a table is already set up and patio heaters surround it.

"Oh, that sounds nice," I say, smiling back at my mother.

We've been around her episodes enough to know that when she's like this, it could take one wrong word to send her spiraling back into darkness.

Rizzo smiles. "Sure, sounds good."

My father hates that my mother is so weak, as he calls it. He doesn't believe in mental health issues, even though she's been diagnosed with bipolar for years. We all know there's no cure for it, other than trying to ease the symptoms of her disorder with drugs. However, my father doesn't help her mood. He's a bastard to her, and sometimes I think he's the reason she's so unstable all the time.

She claps her hands, practically jumping a foot in the air. "Perfect. I had the cook prepare all our favorites. It's going to be just wonderful having dinner together tonight. Isn't it? Oh look, the stars are out. How beautiful." She rushes toward the doors, still speaking at a fast pace.

My stomach churns, as this is one of her manic episodes. "Do you think she's taken her medication?" I whisper to Rizzo.

He sighs. "Who knows? But asking her could set her off balance."

I nod in response as we follow her out onto the balcony, where she's still jabbering. I assume to us, but neither of us were listening since we were still in her room.

"Sit down. Sit down," she says, overly animating her gestures.

We're used to her mood swings, but often she doesn't want to be around us, whether she's overly happy or down in the dumps. I sit in my seat and grab the napkin off the plate, placing it on my lap.

Rizzo sits by my side and does the same.

My mother drops into her seat and sighs. "Isn't it lovely to be together, the three of us? After all, now we're moving somewhere we don't even know. All three of us need to stick together." There's a manic look in my mother's eyes. One that scares me a little. "It's such a shame, Rizzo, that you didn't get to finish school, but I've found you a tutor for your last year and you can take your exams still."

Rizzo and I exchange glances.

"Mom, hasn't dad told you?" I ask.

Rizzo kicks me under the table, and I know it's because telling her might be the catalyst for a downward swing, but she has to know.

"Told me what, dear?" she asks.

I swallow hard. "Father already enrolled Rizzo in an academy in Maine for his senior year."

Her brow furrows, and she shakes her head. "No, that can't be right. Maine isn't anywhere near Chicago."

I place my hand over hers and squeeze. "It's a day's drive, but it's only for eight months. You'll still have me."

Her thoughts are racing at one-hundred miles an hour. I can see it behind her eyes. "That bastard," she says, shaking her head. "If it isn't enough tearing my home from me, he tears my son from me, too."

Her eyes well with tears, and I know she's about to shift into a depressive mood. The tears fall and her entire demeanor changes. Her shoulders slump, her neck droops and her cheeks flood with tears.

"I'm sorry, mom. I had to tell you."

Rizzo shakes his head. "Could have waited until after dinner."

My mom holds her hand up to me. "Don't you dare apologize to me, Livia. This is your father's fault." She stands and moves slowly back toward the bedroom.

We both watch as she disappears inside and slumps onto the bed.

Rizzo sighs. "Couldn't you have waited?"

"What was the point?" I shake my head. "We both know something we said would have changed her mood."

His shoulders slump and he pulls off the lid off the food in front of him, smiling when he does. "She still thinks I'm ten years old."

I lean over to see what food she had cooked for him, laughing when I do. It's a cheese and tomato pizza in the shape of a dinosaur. "Yeah, shall we stay here and eat?" I ask, lifting my plate to reveal spaghetti shaped in a smiley face.

Rizzo glances into the room where our mother has passed out on the bed. "I guess so." He grabs his knife and fork and tucks into his food.

We eat in heavy silence, both of us aware that the lives waiting for us on the other side of the Atlantic will be drastically different from what we've been used to.

2

MAXIM

I wonder if I'm staring into a mirror when I sit opposite my father. Our eyes are so similar, although his are more gray than blue. We have similar features and the same dark hair, even if I style mine differently, keeping it shorter. However, I know that it's not a mirror because the man sitting opposite me is so fucked in the head, he actually tried to kill his daughter, my baby sister.

My fists ache as I clench them beneath the table, wishing I could take out my fury on him and pummel them into his face repeatedly.

It's been a month since that fated day, and he shows no ounce of remorse. I always knew he was damaged, but I never knew the extent of his depravity, not until that day. Many believe me akin to my father in my ruthless, psychotic tendencies, but I'd never hurt my flesh and blood. Viki and I may not always see eye to eye, but there's one thing I'm sure of; I'd die trying to protect my sister.

"Are you going to speak or just glare at me?" Father asks.

I narrow my eyes. "Since you called the meeting, I was waiting for you to speak."

He grunts and stands from his chair, walking over to the dresser beneath the window of his office to pour himself a scotch. "It's time for you to do your duty for this family."

A shiver races down my spine, as that's not the first time he's said those words to me. It's feels like fucking déjà vu. About a year ago, he told me about his intention for me to wed Maeve Callaghan before she disappeared, landing us in this shit show of a war we're fighting. I sense he's about to tell me he's found me a new wife.

"There's an Italian family making moves on the Morrone territory here in Chicago." He turns around to face me. "Their daughter, Livia, is to be your wife."

I raise a brow. "Italian?" My father hates Italians, so I find it hard to believe he'd agree on an allegiance with them.

"Yes, they want to remove Remy Morrone from power, which aligns with our aims." He cracks his neck as he takes his seat opposite me again. "The Bianchi family has an old feud to settle with the Morrone family, and I have every intention of helping them settle it."

I sit forward, leaning my elbows on my thighs and steepling my fingers as I observe my father. "I think I'd prefer to decline after what happened last time."

His jaw clenches. "You'll marry her. This isn't a discussion."

I raise a brow. "Last time you arranged my engagement, we ended up in a war unlike any we've ever seen."

Father growls, eyes flashing with untamable rage. "This is entirely different." He cracks his knuckles, danger sparking in his pale blue eyes. "You'll marry her because it's our only way out of this war."

I know my father well enough to know that if I push him on this, he'll snap. Instead, I lean back in defeat and give him a sharp nod.

His jaw clenches. "Good." He knocks back the rest of his scotch, as always, never offering me a drink when in his office.

At twenty-two years old, the last thing I want is to be married to some bitch I don't even know. I'm in the prime of my youth, and I won't allow my vows to change my life. I do what I want, when I want.

"Do you wish to see a photo of her?" Father asks.

I shrug. "Sure." I might as well know what I'm dealing with.

He grabs his iPad and flicks through, pulling up a photo of my soon to be wife. "Here." He passes it to me.

I take it and look at the photo, feeling a pulse of

desire in my groin at the beautiful little Italian girl on screen. My father chose this photo because she's only wearing a bikini, lying on a sun lounger and smiling at the camera. The hue of her dark hair complements her sun-kissed skin and her piercing green eyes.

She's curvy, with full breasts and a beautiful figure. I can't deny that if this photo is an accurate representation of my fiancé, she's far more beautiful than Maeve.

"Not too shabby, hey?" my father questions.

"She's beautiful." I meet my father's gaze. "But does she like being told what to do?" I don't have the time or patience for a woman who defies me.

My father shrugs. "One thing you'll learn is that every woman can be forced into submission." His eyes glint with a wicked light. "Even the toughest ones."

I clench my jaw. "Was mother one of the toughest ones?"

His countenance changes at the mention of his late wife. "Your mother was the smartest, toughest woman I ever knew." He snatches the iPad out of my hand, setting it down on his desk. "The one woman I accepted deserved as much respect as I did."

I watch as he slumps back into his chair, shutting his eyes. Her death tore him apart, especially as he couldn't have prevented it. She was far too young when she died at thirty-two years old.

My parents were high-school sweethearts, and they had me when they were both only eighteen years old, fresh out of school.

"If you ever found a woman like your mother, you'd be a very lucky man."

I sigh as my memories of her were happy indeed. Our lives were very different when she was alive. It became darker and more twisted the moment she lost her life to cancer. Father changed. Her death derailed him and he spirals further into insanity the more time that passes. It makes me wonder if she was like his anchor, keeping him sane the way an anchor keeps a ship grounded. Many times I've considered how disappointed she'd be if she could look down and see what has become of our family.

He claps his hands, startling me. "I almost forgot. We have a rat in the basement." His eyes light up. "Do you fancy helping me make it squeal?"

I swallow hard, searching my father's pale blue eyes. There are times I fear I've fallen as far off the rails as he has, but then he always shocks me with his psychotic tendencies.

Ever since he tried to kill my sister, I've struggled to look at him in the same light. However, I know that refusing to help him torture a man who has betrayed our family he would construe as weak, so I plaster on a fake smirk. "Sounds good."

"Great." He stands and leads the way toward the exit of his study. "I think I'll let you take the lead on this one. After all, you're about to become your own man."

I clench my jaw, knowing that responding to him will only result in an argument. Instead, I lead the way out of the study and down the hallway toward the entrance to the basement. As I descend into the dank space, the scent of death overwhelms me. It's a scent I've known since I was little.

The first room on the right is where Father holds the prisoners, so I enter to find Kirill, one of our long-standing boyevik, for the Volkov Bratva. I don't know what Kirill did, and I know not to question my father when we're about to make a kill.

It's his number one rule when it comes to bratva business, always present a united front. It's become increasingly hard ever since we disagreed about his actions involving Viki. She shouldn't have jumped into bed with our enemy, but it's clear she loves Rourke Callaghan. It wasn't much more than a year since he was going to force me to wed Rourke's sister, so I don't see the difference.

"What do we have here?" I ask, stalking toward Kirill, whose eyes shoot open the moment he hears my voice.

"A dirty little rat," my father replies.

I smirk as I stop a foot away from him, narrowing my eyes. "And what do we do to rats?" I glance back at my father, who is now looking a little manic.

"Make them squeal."

Kirill makes a muffled plea behind the rag shoved in his mouth.

"Sorry, I can't hear you." I lean closer. "What was that?"

His muffled pleas become louder, more frantic, as I glance at my father.

"I really can't understand what he's saying, because I don't speak rat," I snarl, sliding my hand into my pocket to grab a switch knife. "I guess I'll have to open you up and find out what secrets you hide instead."

The fear in the man's eyes calls to a sick part of me. And then I notice the wet stain forming over his crotch, forcing me to step back.

"Fucking pathetic," I say, walking slowly around the chair he's strapped to. "Only cowards piss themselves before they die."

My father watches in delight, smirking from ear to ear. "Exactly. Anyone cowardly enough to betray our trust doesn't deserve to live." His eyes narrow. "We know all about the hedge fund you have open on the side, using our organization's cash." He steps closer, eyes blazing with power and rage.

It's rare to detect emotion in my father's eyes, but when it's just the two of us, and a man we're about to kill, he lets down those carefully constructed shields. "You'll burn for this, Kirill, mark my words." My father's attention moves to the electronic torture device nearby. "Burn from the inside out." His smirk widens.

Unfortunately, he can't help himself when it comes to torture. He may have said I could lead, but it only takes a short while for him to become too tempted by inflicting pain. My preferred method of torture is with a knife, but he loves to get creative with his methods.

"Have some fun, son," he says, nodding toward the knife. "And then I'll finish him with that." He nods at the device.

I don't have to be asked twice as I step toward the man shaking like a leaf in the chair. The Volkov Bratva doesn't give second chances. In fact, if we find out you've wronged us, you don't even get the chance to plead your fucking case.

I slide the flat edge of the knife over his collarbone, nicking his skin as I do.

The coward shudders, pupils dilating so much I can hardly distinguish the surrounding brown. Predatory instincts kick in as adrenaline filters into my blood-stream, sharpening my senses. Father taught me to thrive off of fear from a young age. He made sure the name Maxim Volkov was almost as feared as Spartak Volkov the moment I turned fourteen, the same year my mother died.

I cut a path into his skin beneath his collarbone, a thrumming buzz pulsing through my veins the moment I see the blood dripping down his skin. As I carve him up like a fucking butcher, it feels like I'm watching from above. It's always like this, anytime the violence takes control. Somehow, I've learned to detach myself from the act and thrive off of it.

Kirill's head lulls as his shirt soaks through with blood. His eyes are lucid but full of pain, as he admits defeat. There's no way he's getting out of this, so all he can do is hope it doesn't last too long.

I make three move horizontal cuts down his shirt, tearing it apart. The Volkov Bratva sigil sits pride of place tattooed on his chest, as it does on all members, including myself. I glance at my father. "A rat like this doesn't deserve to have our sigil on his chest, even when he's dead," I sneer.

My father's face lights up. "Too true, Maxim. Cut it off of him."

I make an incision around the crest of our family. Kirill's eyes widen at the sudden change in depth of cut as he squeals behind the gag, writhing in renewed agony. The amount of blood would be horrific to most, but I've become so accustomed to bloodshed, I hardly bat an eyelid. Once I've cut an incision around the tattoo, the real pain begins.

My father passes me a scalpel, which I run across the flesh between the incisions, cutting his skin off of his chest. Kirill passes out completely, his head lulling lifelessly forward as I pull the flesh from his body. Once I'm done, I toss it aside and glance at my father. "Your turn."

The smirk on his face is what I fear the most. I've learned to enjoy torture. After all, it's how he taught me, but he delights in it in a way I can't quite comprehend. As if he lives for this kind of shit. And yet, every time I torture someone, I feel the grasp on myself slipping as if I'm drowning a little more every time I cut open another person.

My father yanks his head back hard, forcing him to

awaken. "Time for a barbeque, Kirill." He affixes the paddles of the electronic device to his cut up chest, struggling to get them to stick with the amount of blood. Once he does, he affixes a strap around his head and two around his wrists.

This isn't the first time my father has opted to use this device, and every time is as disgusting as the first. It's not only watching the person be practically fried alive, but the smell that really gets to you. Father gives me a smirk, but I can't return it, not right now. And then, he turns it on to the highest power.

Kirill's body spasms out of control, his eyes so wide they look like they're trying to pop out of the sockets. The blood and gore I coaxed from his body only adds to the depraved image, but I force myself to keep watching.

Never look away when you watch a traitor die.

My father's words to me when he made me take part in my first torture at fourteen years old. After three painful minutes, Kirill's heart finally gives out, his entire body smoking from the electric coursing through his veins and heating his blood. If there's one thing I can say for him, he had some fight.

Father turns around and claps me on the back. "How about we go get some dinner?" he says, as if we didn't just murder a man in our basement.

"Sure," I reply, despite not wishing to spend any more time than necessary with the man that tried to murder my sister. If I put one foot wrong, he might do the same thing to me. I don't trust the man who raised me, not anymore.

3

LIVIA

 My palms sweat and my heart pounds in my ears as I make my way toward my father's study.

We've been in Chicago for three weeks, and I've seen him twice. My mother's bipolar disorder is worse than ever, as Rizzo and I suspected it would be. After all, she at least had a semblance of a life in Catanzaro, like I did. Now what does she have?

Nothing.

She barely leaves her room, and her appetite is worse than it's been for years. I see the untouched trays the staff bring down, and know if I don't do something soon, her health will be in danger.

I come to a stop outside of my father's study, wishing he hadn't summoned me here. It can't be for a good reason. Whenever he wants to see me, it's always bad. I knock on the door, waiting for his response.

"Come in," he calls.

I swallow hard. "You wanted to see me, father?" I ask as I push the door open to his study.

I miss Rizzo, as he left two weeks ago for the Syndicate Academy. Although we talk on the phone, I've never felt more alone than I do here in Chicago. It sounds like he's enjoying his time at his new school, though, which I'm thankful for. When he can, he rings daily to check up on me and mom, because he fears my father will soon slip back into his old ways. Up to now, I've had nothing to report, since my time in Chicago has been uneventful and boring.

Although I've had fantasies of fleeing this godforsaken place and running back to Catanzaro, the only thing that keeps me here is my mother. If I were to leave her alone, I'm not sure what she'd do. I miss my life back home more than I can put into words.

My father looks tired as he glances up from his desk. He has dark rings around his eyes and his usual neat gray hair is messy and displaced. "Yes, please take a seat." He gestures to the cracked leather chair opposite him.

I sink into it, shuffling in discomfort under his piercing, brown-eyed gaze. It's always the same when we're alone, as we have nothing in common. Sometimes, he feels like a stranger rather than my father.

"I have an important matter to discuss with you," he says, pinning me with his dark stare. "The war here in

Chicago is more intense than I realized, and we need an ally in the city."

I tilt my head. "I'm not sure how I can assist with that."

His jaw clenches. "You'll marry Maxim Volkov in a fortnight, giving us an ally in the Volkov Bratva."

It feels like time stands still as I stare blankly at my father, wondering if I heard him right. I may have only been in Chicago for three weeks, but I have done my homework on the families that control the city. Two psychopaths who delight in blood and gore run the Volkov Bratva. Maxim Volkov and his father Spartak are renowned for their brutality.

"No way," I say, shaking my head.

My father's eyes flash with rage as he clenches his fists on the desk. "This isn't a discussion, Livia. It's already done."

I shake my head. "What the hell is wrong with you?"

"Nothing." His eyes narrow. "You've known for a long time that me and your mother would select your husband."

"Does mother even know about this?" I ask.

He growls. "You know your mother isn't in any condition to make any rational decisions, Livia."

"Then don't bring her into this." I cross my arms over my chest. "It was your decision to sell me to a psychopath. I know about Maxim Volkov's violent tendencies, particularly with women."

My father holds my gaze, but he doesn't look remorseful. "He won't hurt you, as you're to be his wife."

"Like it ever stopped you?" I laugh. "That's the most stupid thing you've ever said, father."

He slams his hand down on his desk. "Don't speak to me like that." He points a finger at me. "Go and wash and get dressed, as Maxim and his father are joining us for dinner in two hours." His eyes narrow. "I want you presentable."

My stomach sinks at the thought of meeting my fiancé tonight. Father hasn't even given me a day to process the news, thrusting me straight in front of the wolves. "You're a disgrace," I say, shaking my head. "You couldn't even give me time to get used to the idea, could you?" My voice rises as I notice the rage flaring to life in my father's eyes. "Instead, you tell me one minute and then thrust me in front of this man like a piece of fucking meat."

My father stands and moves faster than I've seen him move in a while, rushing for me in a fit of rage. This time, he doesn't punch me. Instead, he slaps me hard across my face. Probably ensuring he doesn't leave a bruise on my face when my new fiancé meets me.

I place a hand against my stinging flesh and glare at him. It's not unusual for him to hit me, but for the past two years, I've grown used to my younger brother protecting me and making it impossible for him to do so. Rizzo scares my father, because he's stronger than him and younger. Not to mention, I think he has a darkness inside of him too, one he tries to hide.

Father used to beat both of us pretty badly until one day Rizzo found the courage to hit him back hard. Ever since, he hasn't touched us. With Rizzo gone to the academy, it was only a matter of time before he raised a hand to me again. I know my mother's mental state is because of my father's abuse, but she won't leave him— perhaps she can't.

"You don't have your brother here to protect you now, Livia," he snarls, lip curling in a disgusting smirk. "I won't stand for you disrespecting me."

Two weeks.

That's how long it took for him to slip back into his ways once Rizzo left. I swallow hard, realizing that if I marry Maxim in a fortnight, my mother will be alone with this monster. He won't have me to take his frustration out on, and I'm not sure my mother can withstand his brutality.

I glare at my father, feeling the darkness that lives beneath my skin rising to the surface. He fears my brother, but little does he know the depraved thoughts I have in my head probably far surpasses anything in Rizzo's. It's a sickness feeding on my thoughts, dragging me into the abyss.

The mental images that flash through my mind as I stare into his dark, soulless eyes are beyond sick. I imagine taking a knife and slowly opening him up, cutting him apart piece by piece and slowly removing each of his organs, delighting in his blood on my hands. The desire to watch him hurt the way he's hurt mom, me and Rizzo over the years and get payback as I torture him painfully is intense.

I'd delight in watching him bleed. I'd delight in seeing the fear in his dark eyes as I finally snap and make him pay. The sharp pain of my nails digging into my palm draws me back to the present. I glance down to see I've pierced the flesh as blood drips onto the floor.

It should be his blood.

"Don't stand there, Livia. Get ready now," he barks, nostrils flaring.

I turn around to stop myself from doing something I'll regret and leave his office. My mind is reeling as it's not the first time those sick mental images have come to mind when I'm around my father.

There's this unbelievably deep rooted desire to murder him. A desire to make him pay for all the pain he inflicted on the people I love. I bring my fingers up to the stinging skin of my cheek, a reminder of the pain he still inflicts. Not only physical, but emotional pain when he dragged us from our home in pursuit of some ancient vendetta he can't let go.

Mother won't survive this. If she's left alone without me or Rizzo, she'll do something stupid. I bite the inside of my cheek, trying to take my mind off of her for a moment. There's only one thing that can bring me back down from the cliff-edge when I'm like this. I glance into the kitchen, thankful to see it's empty. My father keeps the drugs in a cabinet on the far wall, so I head toward it, my head pounding against my rib cage.

I've run out of the pain meds I bought in Catanzaro, but father always has a stash of fentanyl that the doctors prescribed him after someone shot him in the hip. I know it's a stupid way to cope, but if I don't take something, it feels like I'm going to go insane. Quickly, I riffle through the cabinet searching for the drugs. My stomach churns as I find three packets at the bottom, grabbing them and stuffing them into my jacket pocket.

I glance over my shoulder, making sure no one is around. Quickly, I stow everything away where it was, except the missing fentanyl, and shut the cabinet door. My stomach churns as I rush toward the fridge and open the door, grabbing a milkshake out and shutting it, just in case anyone sees me come out of here empty-handed. My father would kill me if he knew about my habit.

Despite him being prescribed the drugs for his hip injury, he rarely takes the medicine. Instead, he likes to medicate with scotch, leaving me his stash. I head up the stairs and into my room, pulling out the medicine and staring at it. Two hours isn't long enough for the effects to wear off. I grunt and tear at my hair, wishing my father wasn't such a fucking asshole.

All I want right now is to take the pills and curl up in a ball and fall asleep, as it eases the pain and depraved thoughts. The pills are my only escape from myself.

I throw the packets of pills into my nightstand, knowing that I can't risk it right now. If my father found out I'm taking drugs, he'll kill me. Instead, I grab a couple of oxycodone instead and take them, knowing they're nowhere near as strong, but it should help tide me over. No one knows about my dependance on painkillers, not even Rizzo. He would go mad if he found out.

I stand and walk toward my bathroom, turning on the faucet in the shower. My stomach churns as the twisted visions of my father lying on the floor of his study in a pool of blood won't go away, no matter how badly I wish them away.

I can't marry a man like my father, because I know it's only a matter of time until I'll snap and kill him. If rumors are true, I fear Maxim is worse than my father. The drugs infect my bloodstream, giving me a slight buzz, but since I've been taking fentanyl, only that really works. I force my mind to go blank as I wash myself, getting ready to meet my fiancé.

My father doesn't deserve the title. If he were a true Father, he would never marry me off to someone like Maxim. Let alone not even tell me until the night I meet him.

4

MAXIM

*M*y father stops in front of an unremarkable town house in a pleasant part of the city. "Is this where they live?" I ask, glancing out of the car window at it.

This isn't what I'm used to when it comes to other powerful families. Normally, their homes are their first show of wealth and power, and this shows neither.

"I believe it's a rental until their permanent home is ready," my father answers, adjusting his tie. "I want you to be on your best behavior." He pushes the gearstick into park and glares at me. Since this new alliance between the Bianchi family and our family is top secret, Father drove us here. It's odd seeing him drive, as I'm so used to us being chauffeured around by Gregor or Yury.

I smirk. "I always am." It's ironic really, because he never fucking is.

He shakes his head. "I mean it, Maxim. Don't fuck

this up." He gets out of the car, and I do the same. "There's a lot at stake."

I sigh heavily, adjusting my tie as we walk up the steps to the front door.

My father pushes the doorbell and waits, tapping his foot impatiently as he does.

A lady opens the door, wearing a maid's uniform. "Hello, you must be Mr. Volkov," she says to my father.

My father grunts in response.

"Please, come in." She steps aside, opening the door wider.

We both walk into the town house, which despite being small, is opulently furnished. The lady shuts the door. "Mr. Bianchi and his daughter are waiting for you in the study. Follow me." She leads the way down a small corridor to the third door on the right, knocking hard.

"Yes," a voice calls.

"Sir, Mr. Volkov and his son are here."

"Let them in," he replies.

My father gives me a warning glance as the maid opens the door for us.

Father walks in first, and I follow close behind.

Vito Bianchi stands and walks over to greet us, but his daughter remains seated. A sign of disrespect and that she's about as thrilled as me by this new arrangement. "Spartak, thank you for coming tonight." Vito smiles, but it doesn't reach his eyes.

I hate men like him. Men that feel they have to put

on an act, when really we're all here for business. The marriage is a business transaction, and that's all. My father grabs his outstretched hand in a firm grasp and shakes it, making Vito wince as he reclaims his hand.

"My pleasure," Father says, eyes darting toward Livia, who still hasn't bothered to glance our way, let alone move from her seat. "I assume this is my son's future wife?"

"Livia," Vito barks, eyes flashing with rage. "Come and greet our guests."

Her jaw clenches and so do her fists as she stands, turning and walking stiffly toward us.

I study her intently, noticing subtle differences to the picture my father showed me. In this light, her eyes appear almost pale green rather than vibrant, and she has thick red lips which are pursed in irritation as she sets her gaze on me. It's a rather different expression than the smiling girl in the photo Father showed me earlier, and yet that photo didn't do her beauty justice.

I can tell she's not wearing any makeup, and yet she's utterly stunning. I guess I could have ended up with far worse from an arranged marriage.

Once she reaches her father's side, she doesn't say a word. Instead, she glares at me with unguarded anger. It's sick that my body responds to her heated gaze, especially since she's obviously less thrilled than I am about this arrangement. I wasn't too pleased when Father told me two days ago, but as I stare at my future wife, I'd say I'm coming around to the idea pretty quickly.

"Livia, this is Mr. Volkov and his son, Maxim," her father urges.

She glares at him. "I know who they are."

Her father's fists clench as if he is holding himself back from hitting her. It makes me wonder if he does beat his daughter. "Manners, Livia. I brought you up to be polite." My father's an asshole, and although he spared Viki's skin from the same marks of abuse I now wear, he did hit her at times but not regularly like he me. Although he wasn't a saint when it came to her. My stomach churns as I remember the way he threw my sister off a cliff when she was ten years old because she didn't want to do a bungee jump.

"It's nice to meet you," she says, with absolutely zero sincerity in her voice.

I can't help but smile at the bratty tone, knowing that I'll enjoy making her submit once she's mine.

My father turns to me, a small smirk on his lips. "You're going to have your hands full breaking in this one."

I meet Livia's gaze and smirk. "It seems like it."

Vito turns stiff, nostrils flaring at the way my father talks about her. If he's offended, he doesn't voice it, though, which is wise. "Livia, fetch Mr. Volkov and his son a drink. What can she get you?"

"Scotch," I reply.

My father's brow furrows. "Vodka for me."

Livia turns away from us and storms toward the dresser on the other side of the room, where decanters are filled with alcohol. I can't take my eyes off of her as she pours our drinks, slamming the decanters down. Something tells me she won't be easy to handle on first impressions, but I like a challenge.

"Please, gentlemen. Have a seat," Vito says, signaling to the sofas positioned in front of a fireplace.

I sit down in one of the seats, crossing one leg over the other. My father does exactly the same.

Livia approaches and slams the drinks down on the coffee table, spilling some as she does. Without a word, she sits down next to her father, who gives her a stern glare.

"So, Livia," my father says, drawing her attention to him. "How's your fitness levels?" His eyes are assessing as they roam over every inch of her body, as if he's undressing her with them. My father can come across as a real pig at times, but I know that's not what he's assessing. He wants to know if she's fit and healthy enough to provide the Volkov bratva with its next heir.

Her eyes narrow. "I hate fitness," she replies.

"You wouldn't tell from your figure," my father says, brow furrowing. "Any infertility problems we should know about?"

Livia scoffs, eyes widening. "What the fuck?"

"Language," Vito growls, glaring at his daughter. "As far as we're aware, Livia is fertile and has regular periods. She is, of course, entirely untouched."

My father's nostrils flare. "Oh good, a virgin," he muses, glancing at me knowingly.

Livia turns a deep shade of red as we talk about her like a fucking prize breeding bitch. "You're all fucking sick," she says.

Her father this time doesn't contain his rage, flattening his palm and slapping it across her face hard. "You'll not disrespect me or my guests in my home, Livia." His eyes are practically glowing with anger now.

I clench my jaw, feeling a little irritated by his heavy handed approach. Granted, I enjoy inflicting pain on women, but not the way he did. That's the coward's way to get a woman to do as she's told.

Livia holds a hand to her face, keeping her eyes down on the ground.

"She needs disciplining a little," Vito says, shrugging. "After that, she'll make a perfect wife."

I think Vito underestimates the fire inside his daughter. I saw it when we first walked in here, that desire to rebel. A desire to make the people that hurt her hurt. She's got a darkness inside of her, like all of us do.

Her jaw clenches, but she keeps her gaze averted.

"We've got no problem with teaching discipline, do we, Father?" I ask, smirking at her as she tenses.

Her eyes move to meet mine and I'm surprised to see such confidence blazing in those pale green irises. "I'd like to see you try," she says.

My father holds a hand up. "Perhaps we should give your daughter a taste of our methods now. Let her prepare for what she's in for when she becomes Livia Volkov."

Her lip trembles as she glances at her father, begging him to say no, I'd assume.

He ignores her and nods. "Do what you like." He stands and walks toward the door. "I'm going to check on dinner, which will be ready in ten minutes. I'll return then."

"Father," Livia pleads, her hands trembling now.

Vito glares at her. "It's about time someone taught you a lesson." He walks away without a glance backward, leaving his daughter in the wolves' den.

My father stands and gives me a nod. "Since she's your fiancé, I'll let you take care of this." He sits down on the sofa next to her. "But I'm going to watch while you teach her a lesson."

Livia shakes as I stand and unbutton my jacket, throwing it to one side.

"Stand up," I order.

Her nostrils flare. "Make me."

"Wrong answer, printessa." I grab hold of her hair and yank her to her feet, making her yelp. "I'm going to make you wish you never spoke back," I growl, grabbing hold of her hip with my free hand and forcing her to turn around. "Bend over."

She shudders, glancing at my father, who's perched on the sofa, smirking at her. "I'd do as he says if I were you, little girl."

Instead of bending over, she straightens her back and stares forward.

"Resistance is futile," I whisper into her ear before roughly bending her in two.

I weigh her down with my weight, hitching her skirt up over her ass. She turns rigid in my arms the moment I reveal her black lace thong.

My father nods in approval. "Prekrasnyy zhopa."

"It is a lovely ass," I say, flattening my palm against it. "Ripe for a beating." I bring my palm back and give her a firm, sharp smack.

Livia squeals, trying to escape from me.

I do the same on her other ass cheek, repeatedly, until her skin is tinged bright pink. My cock thickens in my pants as I continue to make my mark on her skin, feeling satisfied when I notice the handprint my last spank left on her flaming red ass. However, it's not enough. I scan the room, searching for a more vicious implement to use that will brand her for longer. A hand is fine, but it won't leave as good welts as a riding crop.

Someone clears their throat behind us. "I'm sorry to interrupt, but dinner is ready." It's the maid who answered the door to us earlier, and she doesn't know where to look as I loom over Livia's bare ass.

My father chuckles. "Saved by the bell. My son was only getting warmed up." He throws me a knowing glance and stands. "You'll have plenty of time once you're married." He claps me on the shoulder.

I grab a fistful of her hair and force her upright,

pressing my body against hers. "I can't wait to make you scream for real, printessa." And then I release her and walk away before she can say a word.

My cock is painfully hard as I adjust myself in my pants, knowing that I'm going to enjoy breaking my wife more than I expected. Perhaps an arranged marriage won't be as bad as I thought.

5

LIVIA

*J*rush down the corridor toward the bathroom, unshed tears prickling my eyes. There's no way in hell I'm letting those two assholes make me cry. I will not do it.

How could my father let them do that to me?

It was fucking humiliating. I had to get away from those two psychopaths. All my life, I thought I knew what evil was. The two men who my father invited to dinner bring a new meaning to the word. They're sick and depraved, and I know I've hardly seen anything yet.

The moment I looked at them, they set my nerves on edge and my heart pound—not in a good way. Both Maxim and his father stare at me as if I'm a fine steak they're considering consuming. Their questions and gazes are assessing in the worst kind of way, as though I'm a prize mare they're about to buy. I guess I am.

The thing I hate the most, though, is the fact that they scare me. It's been a long time since I've felt genuine fear. My father made sure both me and Rizzo grew up fast, fearing nothing, and yet Maxim Volkov scares me. My ass stings from Maxim's heavy-handed assault. Although my father has bashed me about for years, this was entirely different.

I get a feeling that by the time I'm married to that son of a bitch, I'll be having the same sick and twisted visions I have about my father. I'll be imagining myself carving him up with a knife. There's no doubt he's attractive, but there are more things to life than looks, and I'd take an ugly, but kind husband any day over the devil in a beautiful disguise.

I rush into the downstairs bathroom and run the faucet on the tap, splashing the cool water over my face to stop myself from crying. As I stare into the mirror above the sink, I don't know who I am anymore.

It feels like I'm a ghost floating through my life. For years, my only purpose was to look after my mother, and go to my job at the art gallery. Now it feels like I won't have a purpose at all, and that scares me the most. This man will be determined to break me, but perhaps he underestimates how black my soul is, too. I have no allegiance to him, even once we're married, which means if he hurts me, I'll hurt him.

As I stare at myself in the mirror, the desire to head upstairs and take a fuck load of pills washes over me.

Father would be pissed, because I'm supposed to be joining them for dinner right now.

How can I sit there after what they did to me?

I shake my head. That's exactly why I have to sit there. I can't let them break me. I turn off the faucet and head out of the bathroom, stumbling straight into a solid wall of muscle. My stomach dips when I glance up to see Maxim smirking at me. His pale blue eyes assessing me in that same predatory manner.

I take a step back, putting distance between us. "Why are you down here?" I ask, narrowing my eyes.

His smirk widens. "I wanted to make sure you didn't get lost, since you're my fiancé now. Your father asked me to go find you."

I glare at him, knowing without a doubt I hate this man. "I think it's unlikely that I'd get lost in my home." I cross my arms over my chest. "So, cut the bullshit and tell me why you followed me."

His nostrils flare, but his icy blue eyes remain lacking of any emotion. I notice the way he freezes, turning unnaturally still, like a puma ready to pounce on its prey. "Listen to me very carefully, Liv."

I cringe at him calling me that, shaking my head. "Don't fucking call me that. My name is Livia."

Maxim moves quick, taking me by surprise. One minute, he's three feet away, the next he has me pressed against the bathroom door with his hand tight around my throat. I struggle to breathe, planting my hands against the sturdy wall of muscle and trying to push him away. He's too powerful.

"I will call you what I damn well like," he snarls, his face coming closer to mine than I'm comfortable with. "You're going to be my wife, which means you'll obey me, no matter what." His ice-blue eyes hold no emotion. If he's angry, I can't detect it behind his shields. "That spanking session was fucking child's play compared to what I'll do."

I don't allow him to see my fear, even though my heart is racing beneath my skin, pounding so hard it's as if the organ is attempting to break free of my body and flee the devil before me. "There's no chance in hell I'll ever obey you," I spit, managing to speak despite his hold on my throat.

"I'm not happy about this fucked up arrangement either." He moves his face to within an inch of mine and his scent floods my senses. It's musky and woody, with a hint of scotch. "Do you think I want to get married to someone I don't know at twenty-two?" He searches my eyes, still holding onto my throat in a firm grasp.

It's hard to believe that anyone can make this man do anything, and yet I know Maxim answers to Spartak. "Then why are you marrying me?" I rasp.

He releases my throat, but doesn't move away from me. His tall frame crowds me against the bathroom door, making me feel claustrophobic. "Because it's my duty to my family, and…" He pauses, eyes drawing down the front of my conservative dress in a slow, demeaning manner. "And I rather like the idea of fucking you into submission," he murmurs, a sick smirk twisting onto his lips.

"Over my dead body," I reply.

His nostrils flare. "If you prefer it that way, I think you'd be a good fuck, dead or alive."

My stomach churns with nausea at his perverse comment, but the worst part of it is, I don't think he's joking. The man is psychopathic and I don't know what he's capable of, or how deep his depravity runs. "You're sick," I say.

His lips are so close to mine they're practically touching, and I sense he's going to kiss me at any moment. The air crackles with intent, making my skin crawl. "Such a pretty little virgin you are," he breathes, tickling my face as he speaks. And then, he kisses me with such aggression it feels like an attack rather than a kiss.

I set my hands on his chest again, pushing as hard as I can, but he doesn't move. Instead, he grabs my hips and pulls me harder against him. A dizziness descends over my mind as he thrusts his tongue between my lips, filling me with an odd thrill at the intimacy of that act coupled with my revulsion.

My heart pounds. My body shakes. I need to escape him, fast.

I bite his tongue, making him yelp as the metallic taste of blood fills my mouth. He pulls away from me, eyes blazing now with unconfined rage. "You fucking bitch," he growls, placing a finger against his tongue, which is bleeding. "Did you just bite me?"

I stand as tall as I can, although he's a full foot taller than me. "If you think I'm some hussy you can order around, forget it." I step toward him, baring my teeth. "I'll fight you every step of the fucking way."

His eyes turn ice cold again, and he steps closer until our chests press together. "Sounds like fun, printessa." He grabs hold of my throat and squeezes so hard I can't breathe. "I do like a challenge and breaking you will be so fucking satisfying."

I shudder as he licks a path right up the side of my face, making a mix of desire and disgust morph into the most confusing sensation I've ever experienced. No man has ever touched me before, let alone kissed or licked me, since my father made sure I remained untouched because of my value to the family.

I know the small amount of desire I feel is born out of my lack of experience and has nothing to do with the man who is touching me.

He turns to walk back down the corridor.

"You better watch your back, because I wouldn't mind breaking you too," I seethe.

He laughs and continues walking. "Stop sulking and come to dinner, darling." His tone drips with sarcasm as he glances back at me once more before turning the corner toward the dining room.

I'm going to fucking murder that man. I can feel the darkness inside of me rising to the surface, and I'm desperate for something to take the edge off. My palms sweat as I stare after my future husband, knowing that I can't take anything if I join them for dinner. If I don't join them, my father will find me and drag me in there. Perhaps I'll have to try my father's method and drink it away.

I clench my fists and march after my fiancé, knowing that if I don't walk in there with my head held high, they'll believe they've broken me. And I won't let anyone break me, especially not some stupid Russian heir who thinks the world revolves around him. Father never would have got away with this shit if Rizzo had been here.

My heart pounds unevenly as I stop outside of the shut dining-room door, hearing their muffled voices on the other side. I can't believe my father left me alone with them, and yet nothing he does should surprise me. He barely even warrants the title of father, considering the way he's treated me and Rizzo over the years.

I open the door and straighten my back, walking in with all the confidence I can muster, even though those two assholes have seen my half-bare ass. My father sits in his usual seat at the head of the table furthest from the door, and Spartak sits opposite him.

I don't say a word as I walk in and sit down to the

left of my father, the only place available set for dinner, directly opposite Maxim. I can feel his gaze burning a hole into me, but I don't meet it. The bastard doesn't deserve my attention, so I have no desire to give it to him. My ass stings on these hardwood dining chairs, but I try to ignore it, grabbing a jug of wine and pouring myself a large glass.

"What plans do you have exactly for taking over the Morrone family's territory?" Spartak asks, clearly focusing on how they can help each other in this war, rather than on me, thankfully.

Father clears his throat. "My men are on their way here as we speak." He runs a hand across the back of his neck. Those dark rings around his eyes seem worse than ever. "Once they arrive, I intend to hit Remy hard when he least expects it." His eyes narrow. "After all, he's never going to see me coming."

Spartak smirks, but there's no delight or emotion in his eyes at all. They're blue like Maxim's, but paler, with a hint of gray. Merely looking at him too long makes a shiver travel the length of my spine. I may have called Maxim the devil in disguise, but I sense the real devil is the man who fathered him. After all, Maxim had to learn how to be a twisted little bastard from someone.

"So, printessa," Maxim says, his voice hard as stone. "Tell me what interests do you have other than being a brat and getting spanked?"

I clench my jaw and look him square in the eye. "I like torturing men like you," I say.

His eyes flash with what looks like excitement. "Is that right? And what, may I ask, is your preferred torture method?" He tilts his head.

My stomach churns as I have tortured people in the past. When I was growing up, one of my father's favorite ways of punishing us would be to beat us until we were black and blue and then force us to torture his enemies to make us strong. It's sick that I loved the way it felt to drag a knife across a man's skin and watch him bleed, always imagining it was my father. "A knife," I say simply. "It's the best implement, in my opinion."

Maxim's smirk drops and his eyes narrow. "I agree, but I don't agree with a woman doing the torture."

"Why is that? Too afraid a woman might be better at it than you?" I ask, lifting my wineglass to my lips and knocking the contents back in one. All this talk of torture makes the darkness that resides inside of me rise to the surface, which I don't need right now.

He grins, barring his teeth at me like a wolf. "Because a woman's place is on her knees, pleasing her husband."

"Fuck you," I breathe, glaring at him with such hatred. "I'll never be that woman."

"We'll see," Maxim says, swirling the scotch in his glass. "I sense I have more experience in breaking women than you have with resisting submission."

I realize at this point that both my father and Spartak have stopped talking, and they're watching us.

My cheeks heat and I grab the jug of wine, filling my glass to the brim again.

It's official. I hate the man I'm betrothed to. My fiancé is a cocky, twisted son of a bitch and I'll die before I bow to his command.

6

MAXIM

"*M*axim, where are we on the deal with the New York Bratva?" Father asks, drawing everyone's attention to me.

I shrug, glancing down at the paperwork in front of me. "Andrei's dragging his heels with no solid reason." My eyes narrow as I've never trusted Andrei Petrov. "He's unreliable and dangerous."

My father nods. "I agree. Our alliance suited us before, but he's too ambitious for his own good. Now we're at war. He may try to use it to his advantage."

Timur, my father's sovietnik, clears his throat. "Does that mean we're pulling out of the deal with him?"

Father contemplates the question for a few minutes. "Yes, I believe it's time we cut ties with him. After all, he tried to unseat Mikhail Gurin in Boston." He shakes his head. "I've known for a while. It's only a matter of time until he turns his sights on Chicago." His gaze lands on me. "Cut him off, Maxim."

"Is that wise, brother?" Artyom, my uncle, questions. As always, he loves to challenge my father, as they have had a tenuous relationship all their lives. He's only eighteen months younger than my father, and has always resented that the crown automatically went to his older brother. It's a dangerous game he's constantly playing, pushing a man as unpredictable as my father.

I clear my throat, glaring at my uncle. "It's the only option. Andrei is too aggressive in his expansion."

Valeri, my cousin, nods. "I have to agree with the others, Father. This isn't the right time to risk alliances with men like Andrei." Unlike my uncle, Valeri is more willing to accept my father's rule. Adrik, his brother, is the black sheep of the family and, as always, hasn't shown up to this meeting.

"It's settled then." He glares at his brother. "The majority agree." Father glances at the six other men at the table. "Daniel, Roman, Vitaly and Artur, I'll leave it to you to instruct the men under you that if anyone sees Andrei in our territory, to report straight to me."

The four brigadiers bow their heads in response to their pakhan's order.

He glances at Timur, and then at Osip, his obshchak. "You two need to make sure all our associates and enforcers know of this change."

"Sir," they reply in unison, nodding their agreement.

"On other business, do we have any news about the Morrone family's movements?" Father's gaze is on Timur, who he trusts to work as his spy.

Timur nods. "It's not good." His brow furrows. "There's news that relatives of the Morrone family have moved from San Diego to Chicago. They're consolidating forces to help them in the war."

My father growls softly, eyes flashing with rage. "Remy," he snarls, nostrils flaring. "When will he learn that it's futile to take on the Bratva?"

Osip cuts in, "When he realizes you too have a new ally. After all, he won't know about the Bianchi family. How can he? It's only the people in this room that know about your deal with Vito."

The mention of Vito makes me tense, as I've struggled to keep his daughter out of my mind ever since our first rather heated meeting. It's been a week since I met my wife to be, and it has surprised me often I think about her. From first impressions, it's clear that she has no intention of making this easy for me.

Osip's comment calms my father's rage, as he always knows the right thing to say. He's smart, calculating and has worked for him since I can remember. His dark brown eyes observe my father carefully, waiting for his response.

"You're right, as always, Osip. He may have a new ally, but so do we." His eyes narrow. "I wish to send a message to him he can't ignore." His attention moves to

Timur. "Get me all the intel you can on these relatives of his."

Timur nods. "Of course, sir."

He turns his attention to the rest of the men at the table. "Is there anything else to discuss?"

All of them remain silent.

"Good, then you're dismissed. I expect reports on the tasks I have given you within a week." He gives me a pointed glare, which tells me not to leave. He's dismissing everyone but me.

I clench my fist under the table, wondering why he'd need to speak to me alone. Ever since he shot Viki, I hate being alone with him and having to play the part I've always played. The day he pulled that trigger, something shifted in our relationship. A fundamental change that can't be reversed. It's not as if it was ever a truly strong relationship anyway, considering the way he toughened me up as a child, but there was always respect on my side. He lost it the moment he shot his flesh and blood.

Once everyone has exited the room, he turns to me. "I heard you visited Viki at the Callaghan residence on Monday." His pale blue eyes look gray in this lighting. "Is that true?"

Fucking Timur.

I've been visiting Viki ever since he shot her, but I was sure that no one was following me. It appears I must have gotten sloppy or complacent, perhaps both.

Sighing heavily, I narrow my eyes at him. "Yes, she's my sister."

He slams his hands down on the table. "She's a traitorous little slut is what she is."

I clench my jaw, wanting nothing more than to slam my fist into my father's face. It's a mental vision that I often struggle to wipe from my brain, but one that can never be reality. To strike my pakhan would in his eyes be as bad as betraying the bratva, and after he shot my sister, I have no idea what he's capable of when it comes to me.

"She's family. Just because she fell in love with a Callaghan, doesn't mean she's a traitor."

"Fell in love?" He scoffs, shaking his head. "Pathetic. Rourke only married her to spite me. He doesn't care about your sister."

"I have to disagree." I stand tall, squaring up to him as best I can. "I've seen how he treats her. The guy loves her."

"We're at fucking war with them, Maxim. You can't visit their home, for fuck's sake." He shakes his head. "Do you know the shit the men are saying behind your back?"

I narrow my eyes. "What are they saying?" My tone is lethal, as if people are talking shit about me, then I won't hesitate to put them in their place.

"They're saying you're a rat, my own fucking son." He paces toward me, stopping a foot away. "You can't go to the Callaghan residence anymore. If you want to see your sister, you find a neutral place and you make sure no one follows you. Do you understand?"

I'm surprised he doesn't ban me from seeing her entirely, but perhaps he senses that I'd ignore him, anyway. "Fair enough," I say through gritted teeth.

"Good," he says, running a hand through his tousled dark hair. "Now, you can go."

I turn around and walk away from my father without another word, feeling chaotic. As I reach the door, he speaks, "Are you ready for the wedding next Saturday?"

I stop and glance at him over my shoulder. "Yulia is handling everything."

"Don't let me down, son."

I shake my head, clenching my jaw. "Of course not." I don't enjoy following his orders anymore. Once he was a man I admired, despite all the shit he put me through, now he's nothing more than a pathetic little man who shot his daughter.

I head out of the boardroom of my father's enterprise, feeling on edge. I have one more week until I see Livia Bianchi again. One week until I will shackle her to me forever.

My wife. My captive.

They're the same. Livia will soon learn the true meaning of submission.

My FATHER SITS by my side in the back of the town car, staring blankly at the privacy screen.

Today is the day my life will change forever. Livia Bianchi is about to become my wife within the next hour.

I'm surprised that I don't feel more dread about it. Instead, there's a thrill at the prospect of breaking her resolve and making her bend to my will. When my father first told me about the arrangement, I wasn't happy, but now I've met her, I'm open to it.

The way she bit me when I kissed her was sexy. I do love a woman who isn't afraid to put up a fight. It makes the end result all the more satisfying. When I watch her come apart beneath me, it will be worth every drop of blood she draws from my body. I'm not afraid of pain and in time she'll come to love it too, crave it even.

"How are you feeling?" he asks.

I glare at my father. "Great." I run a hand through my hair. "Tell me again why my sister can't attend my wedding?"

He bares his teeth at me, which is a severe warning to back off. "Because the Callaghans are our enemy and they can't know about our deal with the Bianchi family yet." He shakes his head. "Honestly, people would think you were a fucking idiot rather than the future pakhan of the Volkov Bratva at times, Maxim."

I know he's trying to get under my skin with that comment. "Viki wouldn't have said a word if I'd asked her not to," I reply, watching the buildings rush past the window.

"So Naïve." He shakes his head. "He's her husband, who you claim she loves. Of course she'd tell him."

It may be naïve, but I'd hope that although we've never been overly close that she'd keep this secret if I'd asked her to. However, I didn't even get the chance to tell her. She'll no doubt find out later down the line from someone else, which irritates me. There's enough tension between us as it is.

"Is this deal with Vito that lucrative?" I ask, glancing at my father. "Couldn't a more established ally in North America proven better for our family?" It's a question that has been on my mind since the day that my father announced I was to marry Livia.

There's a calculating smirk on my father's face, which tells me there's an underlying motive to his choice. "Do you know anything about the Bianchi family or their assets?"

I shake my head. "No."

"Then don't question my choices about something you don't even understand." He crosses his arms over his chest. "They're our portal into Europe, Maxim."

I look at my father, brow furrowing. "Europe?"

He nods. "You know how badly I've wanted to break ground in Europe. They hold the keys to a well placed port in Catanzaro." The look in his eyes is almost manic. "Vito agreed to move our products through it at a very favorable price for help in this war and a union between our families."

"Why didn't I know about this?"

Father chuckles. "You aren't pakhan yet, Maxim. You have a lot to learn, and until then, I make the deals." He sits back in his seat. "I don't have to run them by you."

"Does Timur know?" I ask.

"Of course," he says, smirking at me in the most irritating way. It makes me want to punch it right off his face, but I know better than to raise my hand to my father. I'll fucking lose my hand if I do. I may be my father's son, but it doesn't mean his brutality stops at me. I've too frequently been at the wrong end of his rage and it's never nice. It's why I have so many tattoos to cover the numerous scars I sustained growing up.

Instead of responding, I turn my attention out of the window at the same moment Gregor, my driver, pulls up to the curb outside the church. Thankfully, the wedding is a minor affair with only the handful of people who know about our deal with Vito. I hate the idea of a big wedding. The faster this is over, the better.

Because then I can turn my attention to the task that I've been unable to stop thinking about since the day I set eyes on Livia Bianchi, making her mine. I intend to break the fight in her and force her into submission, no matter how much blood, sweat, and tears it takes. Although the tears will all be hers.

"It's time," Father says, getting out of the car.

I follow suit, adjusting the jacket of my tuxedo as I stare up at the church.

I can't wait to make Livia my willing little slave. It'll be so satisfying to watch her break as she becomes my captive of her own free will, no matter how long it takes.

My cock hardens in my pants at the mere thought. I've been unbelievably insatiable these past two weeks, jerking off like a pubescent teen in anticipation of making her mine.

To my surprise, I've never been more ready for anything in my life.

7

LIVIA

*R*izzo rushes into the back room of the church, eyes wide. "What the fuck is he thinking?"

I smile the moment I see him, knowing his presence today is the only thing that can make marrying Maxim bearable. "I don't know," I say.

"I swear to God when I see him, I'm going to—"

I set my hand on Rizzo's arm and shake my head. "You'll do nothing."

Rizzo's brow furrows. "What do you mean?"

"I've accepted my fate. It's why I didn't tell you about it. I didn't want you to worry." I search his blue eyes, smiling wistfully. "How did you find out?"

"I had to hear through the gossip at school. Everyone knows."

My stomach churns. "They do?" I ask, knowing that this union between our families was supposed to stay secret. No one is supposed to know about the Volkov and Bianchi alliance, which suggests someone close to either Spartak or my father has leaked it.

He nods. "Yes, everyone. Do you know how embarrassing it was to have to hear about my sister's wedding from another pupil?"

"I'm sorry," I say, hanging my head. "No one is supposed to know." I swallow hard. "If everyone at your school knows, that means the Morrone family knows?"

"Of course, Camilla Morrone is in attendance there."

"Shit." I run a hand over the pleats of my wedding dress, fumbling with them. "You should warn father."

Rizzo snarls, lip curling. "I'd rather fucking kill him."

I sigh. "Okay, warn Maxim and his father, then. It would be a good way to start our alliance, don't you think?" I glance at myself in the mirror. "I'm resigned to my fate. If it wasn't Maxim, it would have been some other asshole."

"How is mother handling it?" he asks.

I raise a brow. "She's not. She refuses to leave her room." I feel a knot form in my throat. "She told me there's no way she's attending."

He nods in response and silence falls between us.

"How did you get time off school?" I ask.

"When I heard the rumors, I went straight to the principal and asked for a few days' leave to attend." He shrugs. "He granted it, since it's an important family event."

"Well, since you're here, will you walk me down the aisle?" I ask, knowing the last person I want on my arm as I walk toward my uncertain future is the man who orchestrated this. The man I've hated for so long, I can hardly remember a time when I thought of him as a loving father.

"Won't that piss Father off?" he asks.

I shrug. "I don't really a give a shit. I'm making enough sacrifices for his God damn organization, so I'll have who I want walk me down the aisle."

Rizzo beams at me. "Sounds like a plan."

Someone knocks at the door. "Who is it?" I call.

"Your future father-in-law," Spartak replies, his voice sending shivers down my spine.

"What do you want?" I ask.

Rizzo's eyes widen when he hears me speak to him like that.

Spartak chuckles. "To check on the bride." He opens the door, even though I haven't asked him in.

He stops when he sees my brother. "And who exactly is this?" His eyes narrow.

Rizzo stands tall, glaring at him. "Rizzo Bianchi, her brother."

He tilts his head. "I thought you were supposed to be at the Syndicate Academy." Spartak glances at me. "Did you tell him?"

I shake my head, opening my mouth. Before I can

speak, Rizzo cuts in. "No, she didn't. I had to learn about it from other students. It's the fucking gossip of the damn century right now."

Spartak's jaw clenches. "How the fuck did anyone find out?"

Rizzo shrugs. "Beats me. I don't know who started the rumor, but Morrone's youngest is in attendance."

"Blyad!" Spartak says, no doubt swearing in Russian. He storms out of the room, leaving us alone.

"Your future father-in-law is charming."

I sigh. "You haven't met my fiancé yet."

His expression turns furious. "I'll kill him if he harms you."

The door opens again, and this time it's our father standing there. He looks furious when he sees Rizzo. "What the fuck do you think you're doing here?" He charges toward him, forcing Rizzo to clench his fists and stand tall, ready for a fight.

Father backs off when he sees the look in his eyes, glancing at me. "Did you tell him after I explicitly told you not to?"

I grind my teeth together. "No. He heard from school."

"I had to hear from a stranger rather than my family that my sister is getting married." He steps closer to my father, fists still clenched. "Tell me why I shouldn't beat the shit out of you right here and now?" he snarls.

My father glares at him, but I know he's too much

of a coward to stand up to Rizzo. "Your sister needs to do her duty for this family."

"Family," Rizzo scoffs, shaking his head. "What family?"

"Rizzo, it's okay," I say, walking forward and setting my hand on his shoulder. "I'm doing this."

Father looks relieved at my attempt to calm him, which only makes me sick. "It's time, Liv. Take my arm."

I shake my head. "No, Rizzo is walking me down the aisle."

He opens his mouth to argue.

"And before you say a word, I'm sacrificing enough by marrying this fucking psycho, so you'll not stop my brother from walking me down the aisle."

He shuts it, glaring at me. "Fine." He glances at Rizzo. "No funny business."

Rizzo's body tenses, fists still clenched as he watches our father slip away. "I hate that son of a bitch."

"Tell me about it," I say, hooking my arm into his. "Shall we?"

He looks dejected. "I'd rather steal you away from here. Maxim isn't the man I would have wished to marry my sister."

It's a nice thought, running from this, but we know that there's no escape. "Don't worry, I'm tougher than I look." I smile, even though deep down my gut is churning. "He won't break me." I mean that, as I'd rather fucking die than break for that cocky son of a bitch.

"If he does, he'll wish he was never born."

I squeeze his arm and shake my head. "You're so dramatic, baby brother."

"I'm serious." He leads me out of the dressing room, pausing a moment. "By the way, even though I'm furious about this, you look absolutely stunning." He kisses my cheek. "I wish you were marrying someone worthy of you."

I wrinkle my nose. "Is anyone really worthy of me?" I say, lightening my voice.

He laughs. "I doubt it." He glances at the double doors into the church. "Fuck it, here goes nothing, then?"

I nod as he pushes open the doors and the band switch from the song they were playing to the wedding march. Thankfully, because only a handful of people were supposed to know about this union, there's only about ten people in attendance, which suits me. I hate the idea of hundreds of people staring at me.

"You're shaking, Livia," Rizzo whispers into my ear. "It's not too late to say fuck you and storm out of here."

I raise my brow. "You know that's a complete and utter lie."

Maxim stands at the end of the aisle with his father by his side, a cocky smirk plastered on his too perfect face. A man so evil shouldn't be so damn beautiful. His pale blue eyes almost glow as the light outside penetrates the stained glass windows around the church, bathing the entire room in an almost mystical glow. He's wearing a dark navy blue tuxedo with contrasting black lapel, paired with a white dress shirt beneath. There's no denying that he's as handsome as a male model, especially in that suit, but he's as rotten as the dirt beneath my feet. Evil to the very core.

My father sits at the front, watching me and Rizzo like a hawk. As we come to a stop a few feet from Maxim, a shudder races down my spine at the way his gaze drops down my dress as if he's undressing me.

Rizzo notices it too and turns as stiff as stone against me, glaring at him.

"Who gives away this woman to this man?" The officiant asks.

Rizzo glares at Maxim. "I do, unwillingly, I might add." The look he gives Maxim would intimidate most men, but Maxim isn't most men.

The officiant clears his throat as my fiancé takes my hand off of Rizzo, smirking at him the entire time. It's a miracle that Rizzo doesn't lose it and punch him in the face. He's always had a hard time containing his rage. Thankfully, he steps back and returns to sit in the same pew as my father at the front, but a few places away from him.

The rest of the fucked up ceremony goes by in a blur. I feel like I'm watching it from above, as Maxim smirks the entire time through, like the jerk he is. It's only when the officiant's last words are said that I'm pulled right back into my body.

"I now pronounce you husband and wife. You may kiss the bride."

A lead weight sinks into my stomach as Maxim advances toward me. The last time he kissed me, it was fucking awful. Okay, that's not entirely true. I felt desire toward him, but I hated it at the same time.

He wraps a powerful arm around my back, yanking me against him. "I can't wait to officially make you Mrs. Volkov tonight," he breathes.

And then his lips descend on mine with that same aggression as before. I resist, trying to pull back, but he won't let go of me. Instead, he forces his tongue into my mouth, clearly undeterred by the people watching.

A fluttering ignites in my stomach as he strokes his tongue in forceful lashes against my own, stoking something foreign inside of me. I consider biting his tongue again, but know it would cause a scene in front of my brother that I'd rather avoid. Finally, he releases me and I wipe my mouth, feeling utterly sickened by the man I now have to call my husband.

He grabs my hand and yanks me down the steps from the altar, smirking at my brother as he leads me away.

Spartak approaches, brow raised. "Where do you think you're going?"

"Home to consummate the marriage," Maxim says.

My stomach dips at the thought.

"No, we've agreed to head to Vito's new home, which they've moved into for the reception." He shakes his head. "Have some restraint, Maxim. You're acting like a horny teenager."

I laugh at that, which results in Spartak giving me a stern look that could almost stop my heart from beating.

"You won't be laughing tonight, little girl," Spartak says, turning around and marching out of the church. I'm almost surprised he made it in and out of here without bursting into flames.

"He's right, you'll be screaming all night long," Maxim murmurs into my ear. "The question is, will it be from pain or pleasure?"

"Fuck you," I breathe, feeling that dark hatred clawing its way to the surface.

He laughs. "No, I'll be fucking you tonight."

My stomach churns as he yanks me out of the church and onto the sidewalk, where a town car is waiting for us. I can't think of anything worse than losing my virginity to this monster.

Maxim's driver gives him a nod, opening the door for us to slip inside.

"After you, printessa," Maxim says, stepping to the side.

I glare at my husband before slipping into the town car, as far as possible from the door.

Maxim won't keep his hands off of me once we're alone. The thought of which makes my skin crawl. Perhaps I should have taken fentanyl to get through this shit, but the last thing I want is for this bastard to learn my weakness. If I'm going to survive in this psychopath's world, I need to have my wits about me.

Maxim slides in next to me, and as I expected, gets as close as he physically can. He places his hand on my thigh and squeezes hard. "Well done for not biting my tongue off in the church," he says, sarcasm dripping from his voice.

"Only because my brother was watching, and I didn't want him to knock you out."

He places his free hand against his heart. "How sweet of you to think of me." His eyes narrow. "Your brother is nothing but a child and if he'd tried, he'd probably be dead and bleeding out on the altar of the church right now."

My stomach twists with nausea at the terrible mental image and the coldness of his tone. There's no joke in his voice. He's deadly serious. Those pale ice-blue eyes hold absolutely no emotion as he watches me like a hawk. "You're a sick bastard," I say, searching those alluring yet cold eyes of his. "You stay away from my family, do you understand?" My hands tremble slightly as I hold his gaze. "I don't care what the fuck you do to me, but you keep Rizzo out of it."

He tilts his head slightly, assessing me. "Deal, print-essa, but only because it's our wedding day, and that's my gift to you." He moves his hand to my throat and squeezes firmly. "I give you my word I won't harm your little brother."

A flood of relief races through me as my shoulders

slump and he releases my throat. Maxim Volkov is capable of violence far beyond my imagination and I won't allow Rizzo to be dragged into this shit. I may have to live with him, but my little brother doesn't have to be a part of this.

The town car moves through the streets toward our new home close to the church, as a tense silence falls between me and my new husband. I wish I didn't fear him as much as I do, but it's hard not to. He's evil incarnate and I know his darkness is only going to draw my own to the surface. I'll fight him with all I've got, and yet I still fear it won't be enough. I fear he's going to enjoy the fight.

"That's more like it," Maxim says as we pull up the long, winding driveway to my father's new mansion. "The other place was fucking embarrassing."

I narrow my eyes. "Right, because size is all that matters?" I ask.

He raises a brow. "Yes, and you'll find that out later, too."

"You're a cocky pig," I spit, baring my teeth at him.

All he does is smirk. "I know, but it's warranted, believe me." He grabs hold of my hand and forces it over his crotch, making me feel the semi-hard length of him in his pants.

My stomach tumbles as I try to pull away, heat pulsing through my veins and traveling up my neck. "Let go of me."

He chuckles, his cock turning harder beneath my

hand as he rubs it up and down his cock, which, unfortunately for me, is big. "What's wrong, printessa? Never touched a cock before?"

I swallow hard and use all my strength to yank my hand away, slipping free as the vehicle comes to a stop. As fast as I can, I jump out of my side of the car and away from my husband.

A car pulls up behind and Rizzo jumps out, eyes fixed on me. He marches toward me, noticing my distress. "Are you okay?" His jaw clenches. "What did he do?"

I shake my head. "Nothing."

"Don't lie, Livia. I know you well enough to know when something's wrong."

Maxim approaches, hands stuffed casually into the pockets of his suit pants. "My wife is perfectly fine, Rizzo. She's not your concern anymore."

Rizzo stiffens, turning to face Maxim, who's a little taller than him by about two inches. I always thought my brother was tall, but Maxim and his father both exceed him in height. They both have to be about six foot five tall. "If you hurt her, I'll—"

"You'll what, Bianchi?" His eyes narrow and he stands straighter, lethal danger sparking in his eyes. "Kill me?" He asks, shaking his head. "We're allies now in this war, so quit with the threats. Your sister belongs to me. Get the fuck over it and man up." He grabs my hand and yanks me with him, heading toward the house.

I glance over my shoulder at Rizzo, giving him an apologetic look, even though none of this is my fault. It's my father's.

"Thank you for not hurting him," I say, quietly.

Maxim doesn't acknowledge me, pulling me through the doors of my parents home. My mother, to my surprise, is standing in the hallway, greeting the few guests. When she sees me, she beams and rushes over. A sign she's in the middle of one of her more manic episodes.

"Sweetheart, how did it go?" She glances at me and then at Maxim, without giving me a chance to speak. "Everyone said it was a quick affair. I'm sorry I wasn't there, but I didn't feel up to it earlier."

I grab her hand and squeeze, trying to slow her down. "I know, it's okay," I say, smiling. "Mom, this is Maxim. My new husband."

She smiles at him but there's no hiding the mania in her eyes. "Oh, it's lovely to meet you. Please look after my little girl. She needs to be taken care of after everything she's been through." Her eyes shift to my father, and I wince, wishing she hadn't said that. Maxim doesn't need to know about my abusive childhood, as it's another weapon for him to use against me.

Maxim looks a little confused as he stares at my mother. "Of course, it's lovely to meet you, too."

I'm surprised he's so polite, but thankful for it.

"If you'd excuse me, I need to speak with my

father," he says, giving me a peck on the check for appearances before slipping away.

"What can I get you to drink or eat, sweetheart?" Mom asks, glancing over at the buffet table set up on the far side.

"Don't worry, I'm not hungry right now." I notice father enter the hall and his demeanor changes from calm to furious within seconds of setting his eyes on my mother. He's embarrassed of her, and he won't be happy that's she out of her room.

"Excuse me for a second, mom. Rizzo probably wants to see you. He's over there." I point to Rizzo, who notices and gives me a nod.

"Oh, of course." She rushes off, allowing me the chance to stop my father in his tracks.

I march up to him, crossing my arms over my chest. "Don't you dare say a fucking word to her. Do you hear me?"

My father's nostrils flare. "You don't tell me what to do, Liv."

"She's in a stable place right now, a little manic, but we could pass it off as excitement over her daughter's marriage." I set my hands on my hips and stand as tall as I can. "Leave her alone. It's my wedding reception and I want her here."

He grunts, searching my eyes. "If she makes a scene, I'm dragging her back to her room."

"Leave her alone," I reiterate again, before turning away from him in search of my brother.

Rizzo is by the buffet table with Mom, picking at the food. He's smiling, which makes a change. "How about some arancini?" he asks, placing some on a plate and passing it to my mom. It's one of her favorite foods.

"Oh, yes, I love arancini, don't I?" She takes the plate and eats, which is a good change. Perhaps it helps that Rizzo is here, even if it's only for a couple of days.

She's been so down in the dumps since we arrived here, I thought she'd never snap out of it.

"How is it?" I ask.

She hums with her mouth full, nodding.

"I better get some then," I say, despite the queasiness that came over me ever since being in the back of that car with Maxim. I grab a plate and load it with pizza, arancini, and pasta, hoping it will settle my stomach.

Rizzo follows. "You dealt with father?"

I nod in response. "He shouldn't bother her." I glance around the room, wondering where Maxim disappeared to. "Maxim looked a little shocked by her mood."

Rizzo looks furious at the mention of my husband. "I don't like him at all, Livia."

"Me neither," I say, laughing. "At least you're not married to him."

It appears my lighthearted approach doesn't rub off on him, so I nudge him in the ribs. "Chill out and stop worrying. I'm going to be fine." I don't even know if that's true, but I can't have him worrying about me. "Seriously."

"It's my job to worry about you."

I shake my head. "Not anymore, it's not. Maxim's right." I hate to admit it, but he is. "Let's stop thinking about it and enjoy our time together as a family." I nod at my mom, who is happily picking at her arancini. "The three of us."

Rizzo smiles and nods in agreement. "Sounds good."

I wish we were here together under different circumstances. Maxim has already made it clear what he expects of me. A slave to tend to his every whim and desire. He's going to have a shock, as submission goes against the very grain of who I am.

Let the games begin.

8

MAXIM

*A*s the reception winds down, and the few guests being to leave, I can't keep my eyes off of my wife.

I've kept away from her the entire three hours we've been here, allowing her time to be with her family. Her mother is clearly not right in the head. I don't know what condition she has, but it's not something my father was aware of. All I can hope is it's not genetic, as that was my father's first concern. I need a strong and reliable heir with Livia who can guarantee the future of the Volkov Bratva.

My father approaches me. "I'm heading home." He follows my gaze, which is still fixed on my wife. "I suggest you do too."

I nod in response, knowing it's time for me to take my conquest home and stake my claim on her. "I will."

He claps my shoulder and walks away, heading toward Vito.

Livia sits on a plush dark brown sofa next to her mother, and Rizzo sits opposite them on a matching armchair.

I clear my throat as I approach. "I'm sorry to interrupt, but I should get Livia home."

Her mother's brow furrows. "What do you mean? Livia is home."

Livia's face pales, and she squeezes her mother's hand. "Mom, I got married today, so I'm going to be living with Maxim from now on."

Her shoulders dip and countenance changes. "You're leaving me alone with him?" she asks, her voice suddenly an octave lower and slower than it was a moment ago. Clearly, she has some kind of depressive disorder.

Livia's expression is pained as she gives her brother a pleading look.

Rizzo stands and grabs her hand. "Come on, Mom. Let's get you to bed." He pulls her to her feet. "It's been a long day and I'm still here."

Her mother walks away, lead like a puppet from the sofa by her son. I watch as my wife stares after them, looking concerned. When she tears her attention from them, she jumps to her feet and nods. "Okay, let's go."

I raise a brow. "You seem awfully eager, darling."

Her jaw clenches as if she's only now remembering

how much she dislikes me. "There's no use putting off the inevitable. The quicker it's over, the better."

My brow furrows. "I'm not sure what you expect to be over after tonight, but fucking you is going to be one of my most frequent past times, so you'll have to get used to it."

Her eyes narrow. "I'll never get used to it."

"Never say never, printessa." I grab her wrist and yank her against me forcefully, making her steady herself with a hand on my chest. "By the time I'm through with you, you'll be begging me for it."

"I'll die before I beg you for anything," she snarls, pulling her hands away from me and taking a step back.

I shake my head and grab her wrist again, heading out of the house without a word to our host. Something tells me he has never treated his children right, considering the way they both avoid him. I watched them, and it's as if their family comprises of the three of them, and Vito is an outsider.

Livia doesn't wait for me to tell her to get into the back of the car, opening the door and sliding in before I can even open my mouth. She'll regret changing out of her long, flowing bridal gown which made access to her body more difficult.

I slip in after her and get close, setting my hand on her bare thigh.

"Do you have to be so touchy all the time?" she asks, glaring at my hand.

I chuckle. "It's a husband's right to touch his wife, you know?" I inch my hand further up her thigh, allowing it to slip under the skirt of her dress.

Livia freezes like prey in the jaws of a predator, her chest rising and falling with harsher movements as she breathes erratically. I can practically smell her fear, and it's intoxicating. I keep moving my hand, knowing that at any moment she'll retaliate.

"Stop," she snaps, grabbing my hand once it's an inch away from her panties. "Get your hand off me." Her pale green eyes fix on me with a fire that makes my skin burn.

"Or what?"

She glares at me for a few beats before yanking my hand out of her skirt and bending my fingers back enough to ache in warning. "I'll break your fucking fingers."

I smirk. "Are you sure you're strong enough?" I have to call her bluff, otherwise she'll think she has the upper hand.

"My father taught me how to break fingers when I was twelve years old," she deadpans, no hint of uncertainty in her voice as she stares at me blankly, barely blinking.

I narrow my eyes, trying to assess how true that statement is. I've got to admit, the more time I spend with Livia Bianchi, the more of an enigma she becomes. "Is that right?" I glance at our entwined hands and the way she's bending mine back, wondering if she really would snap my bones. "Please let go of my hand, printessa."

She does as I say, releasing my hand and turning away from me to look out of the window. "Don't touch me again."

"I'm afraid when you said *I do* earlier today, touching became obligatory." I clench my fists, knowing I'll have to wait until we're in my bedroom, where I can tie her up, before I touch her again. After all, I don't want to call her bluff and end up with broken fingers. The embarrassment of being injured by my own wife I wouldn't be able to overcome. I'm kicking myself for not bringing the handcuffs in the car. "You'll have to accept it."

Livia meets my gaze. "I'll accept it when hell freezes over. I went along with my father's plan to unite our families, but I never said I'd let you touch me."

It's hard not to admire her tenacity. "A marriage isn't official until we consummate it, Liv."

She snarls, hearing me use the nickname she hates. "I told you not to call me that."

"Why?" I ask, genuinely intrigued by what is wrong with the name Liv.

"My father calls me it, and I fucking hate it."

I watch her as she crosses her arms over her chest, glancing out of the window again. There's a deep hatred inside of her for her father, one which I can relate to in some ways. I've always feared my father since I was little, but I had a certain amount of respect for him, respect which died the moment he pulled that trigger and shot Viki. "I guess you aren't too fond of dear old dad, hey?"

Her nostrils flare as she returns her attention to me. "No." She faces away, and that's when something inside of me snaps.

I grab her throat hard, squeezing enough to cut off her airways. Livia's eyes widen, but she doesn't panic, taking as much oxygen into her lungs as I allow her. "Let me get one thing straight. You're married to me now, which means you're my slave, my captive." I narrow my eyes, tightening my grasp dangerously around her throat, hoping for some kind of reaction. "A wife's duty is to please her husband. You'll do what I want, when I want." Her skin turns pale, warning me I'm being too rough. She doesn't cry out or try to remove my hand from her neck, as if she has a death wish. "Don't keep pushing me or you'll regret it," I warn, releasing her.

Livia gasps for air, but she doesn't bring her hand up to her throat. She's oddly desensitized to my violent tendencies, which makes me wonder what kind of violence her father subjected her to. It's the only explanation for that hatred she has for him.

I expect some kind of smartass retort, but she doesn't say a word for the next ten minutes of the journey. I also give up with small talk, realizing it won't get me anywhere.

My driver, Gregor, pulls up in front of the Volkov

residence. I'm lucky that I have my apartment within the town house with a separate entrance. Father allowed me to move into the apartment on the top floor the moment I turned eighteen, giving me a freedom he never would have afforded Viki.

I get out and walk around, opening Livia's door, holding my hand out to her. Naturally, she ignores me and gets out without my help. I set my hand on the small of her back and steer her toward the side entrance of the house, which leads straight up to the penthouse apartment.

"Why aren't we using the front door?" she asks.

"Because I live in a self-contained apartment on the top floor, which has its own entrance."

Livia's throat bobs as she stares through the doorway into the apartment, where there is the choice of a lift or stairs.

I normally opt for the stairs as I know it helps keep me fit. "Come on," I say, forcefully pushing her through the doorway and shutting it behind us. "Do you want to——"

Livia is already marching up the stairs away from me before I can ask if she wants to take the lift.

"Stairs it is, then…" I mutter, marching after her.

She's fast, but I'm faster as I reach her after two flights.

"Where do you think you're going so fast?" I ask, watching her as she charges up the stairs like a woman on a mission.

"Away from you."

I chuckle. "Not working out too well for you, is it?" I fall into step beside her effortlessly.

She tries to speed up, but I match her pace.

"I'm curious what you intend to do when you get to the apartment? Are you going to jump off the balcony to avoid me?" I ask.

"Probably beats the alternative."

"You wound me, Livia." I hold a hand to my chest mockingly as we take the last flight of steps to the locked front door of my apartment.

She glares at me as I pull out the key. "Wouldn't have got far without this, though. Would you?" I slide the key into the door and open it, and Livia attempts to rush past me.

I don't allow her to, grabbing her hips hard from behind and pulling her tight against my body. "Not so fast, printessa."

"Stop calling me that," she says.

I bite her earlobe hard enough to give her shock. "I'll call you what I like, baby," I murmur, my fingers digging into her hips hard enough to bruise. "You're using all your energy before the fight even starts."

Her shoulders slump, proving I've struck a chord with her. "I know, but that's because you make me so angry."

"Anger can be fun in bed, you know?"

She stiffens. "No, I don't."

I bite her shoulder, making her yelp. "Then I'll

teach you." I remove my hands slowly from her hips and place one hand in hers, firmly grasping her fingers to ensure she doesn't break mine. "Come with me. Let's get a drink."

I'm not a fool. Livia is a virgin, and she's going to be so damn uptight it'll be like trying to fit a fucking freight ship through a canal route. A drink or two will help take the edge off, as I fear my attempts to loosen her up physically may not work as well on a girl so hellbent on hating me.

I let go of her hand once we're in the kitchen, heading toward the cabinet where I store my alcohol. "What do you want?"

Livia rubs a finger over her forehead. "Not sure alcohol is a good idea. My head is killing me. Do you have any aspirin?"

I shrug. "Alcohol is as good a painkiller. Tell me your poison."

She sighs heavily, looking overly disappointed at me not giving her aspirin. "Vodka, I guess."

I grab two tumblers, pouring her a vodka and myself a scotch before approaching her and placing the tumbler in her hand. My finger brushes against hers and I feel a shot of electricity pulse through my veins. I don't miss the way her lips part in reaction too, as she inhales sharply. However, she's quick to recover as she brings the glass to her lips, downing the drink in one before slamming the tumbler on the table. I notice her eye the bottle of vodka out of her reach.

"Do you have an alcohol problem I wasn't aware of?" I ask, raising a brow.

"I need something to get me through this night." She crosses her arms over her chest, glaring at me. "Top me up."

I raise a brow and push the bottle toward her, allowing her to help herself.

Livia pours a large glass and downs it again, before grabbing the bottle.

I grab her wrist, forcing her to drop it. "No more. I'm not fucking you completely off your head." I yank her out of her seat, pulling her body against mine. "I'm going to make sure you won't ever be able to get this night out of your mind," I say, sipping my scotch, which I hold in my free hand. "I'm going to make sure that every waking thought you have after tonight will be about me fucking you." I push her against the kitchen island. "You'll want me so fucking bad, but you're so stubborn you'll never admit it, suffering in silence while you finger yourself and think of me multiple times a day."

"That's never going to happen," Livia says, searching my eyes with heated rage. Rage that sets my soul on fire. I know I can't wait any longer as I set my whiskey down next to her, crashing into her as my lips press against hers.

She fights it, pushing against my chest as my tongue eases through her lips. Her teeth nip me in warning, but I ignore it, stroking my tongue against hers in sensuous movements, stoking the fire she can't understand to life deep inside of her. Before I know it, she's fighting for dominance. Her hands grip the back of my neck, clawing her nails into my skin as she tries to wrestle my tongue into submission. She fails. It's hectic and frantic and so fucking hot.

I wrap my arm around her back and lift her onto the kitchen island, knowing that I'm playing with fire, taking this further without first restraining my firecracker of a wife. My cock doesn't give a shit. I'm harder than I've ever been, as I lick a path down her neck, nipping and sucking at her flesh.

Livia's nails dig into my scalp as I move lower. "What are you doing?" she asks, watching me with both intrigue and irritation in those beautiful, pale green eyes.

"I'm going to taste my wife and make her scream my name," I say, as I part her thighs and push her skirt up her hips, revealing the sexiest pair of white lace underwear and a suspender belt holding up her stockings. An odd choice for a girl who doesn't want to be touched. "Fucking beautiful," I say, before pressing my mouth to her lace clad arousal, licking her through the fabric.

Livia's hips jerk toward me, but she continues to glare at me like she wants to burn me at a stake. It's oddly arousing. I rub my hand across my straining crotch, and use the other hand to undo her suspenders, sliding her panties down to her knees.

I'm surprised she doesn't cover herself up. Livia is certainly not a shy, timid virgin. She's fucking gutsy, and it's something I think I could come to admire about her. I stare at her beautiful pussy nestled between her thick thighs, glistening wet with arousal. It looks like I affect her after all.

"I thought you said you hate me, baby, but your pretty little cunt is dripping wet," I murmur, letting my fingers edge closer across her inner thighs.

"I do hate you," she says, eyes so bright they look like they're glowing. "Any virgin would be wet from being touched for the first time, no matter who was doing the touching."

"I'm not so sure." I raise a brow. "I'd say deep down under all that rage you want me as badly as I want you."

"No chance," she says, shaking her head.

Even as she refuses to accept the truth, her pussy gets wetter as I caress her inner thighs. The sight of her so damn ready for me makes me groan as I bury my tongue between her legs, tasting her sweetness for the first time.

Livia whimpers, her hips pushing toward my face in search of more pleasure as I drag the flat length of my tongue right through her, stopping a breath away from her sensitive clit. And then I slowly draw the tip of my tongue right around it, worshipping it as she gushes more.

Her hands tighten on the edge of the kitchen island

as I slide a finger into her virgin entrance. It's so damn tight, which means we've got a long way until she's ready for me. And yet, I don't know if I have the restraint when it comes to her. I bite her inner thigh, hard enough to leave a mark on her skin.

Livia squeals, eyes blazing with fire as she glares down at me. "What the fuck was that for?" Even as she fights it, I notice the way her pupils dilate further.

I smirk at her. "Pain can elevate your pleasure if you're open to it." I sink my teeth into her left thigh, leaving a matching mark on the other side.

Her thighs quiver in response as her brow furrows. "Does that mean I get to hurt you, too?"

Normally, I don't let women hurt me, but when Livia bit my tongue the day we met, it made me so hard. I enjoyed it almost as much as I enjoy inflicting pain. "Perhaps." I place a firm hand on her stomach and push her down so she's lying on the kitchen island. "Just relax and enjoy it."

Although she's glaring at me hatefully, she doesn't protest as I return my attention between her thighs, turning her into a hot mess of need right on my kitchen counter. This is the fantasy I've been longing for since the day I first set eyes on her.

9

LIVIA

I hate the moan that escapes my lips, grinding my teeth together to stop myself from making anymore sound.

The man between my legs is a monster, and he's playing with fire. Every intimate lick of his tongue sets my soul on fire, and yet it also coaxes that deep darkness to the surface. I can't believe he wouldn't give me an aspirin, as it might have helped keep that sick and twisted part of me at bay.

I have a desire to both hurt and fuck this man between my legs. I want to inflict pain on him and have my way with him all at the same time. It's a conflicting sensation.

"Fuck," I breathe, knowing that I'm on the edge of coming undone.

I should be embarrassed. After all, I've never come in front of anyone before. And yet, I'm not. I sit up and look at Maxim between my legs, feasting on me like a wolf tearing apart his kill. He's not gentle, using his teeth, lips, and tongue to turn me into a puddle on his kitchen counter.

The pain, as he said, is as good as the pleasure. Another testament to how fucked up I really am.

I grab hold of his hair violently and sink my fingernails into his scalp, which makes him groan.

He doesn't stop though, sending me right to the edge. "Oh fuck," I cry, as the most intense orgasm I've ever had hits me. My vision darkens around the edges as I watch him lick the gushing liquid flooding from my pussy. He grazes his teeth repeatedly over my clit, dragging out the intoxicating pleasure that's rolling over me in waves. I shudder on the kitchen counter, wishing I hadn't allowed this bastard to make me come apart so easily.

He wipes his mouth and stands in front of me, looking immensely pleased with himself. "You taste so fucking sweet, printessa."

I narrow my eyes, waiting for his next move.

He yanks me off the kitchen island, pulling me into his powerful body. Suddenly, his lips are on mine and his tongue sliding into my mouth, allowing me to taste myself on him. It's oddly arousing, and I hate it. I hate experiencing any kind of intimacy with this man.

I bite his tongue, which doesn't deter him as he groans into my mouth, deepening the kiss. His fingertips claw at my hips so hard it feels like he's trying to break me apart. The only kisses I've ever experienced were quick pecks on the lips, but Maxim thrusts his tongue into my mouth like he's trying to fuck me with it.

His tongue retreats and I bite his lip. He groans and pulls back, shaking his head. "How am I going to trust you to suck my cock if you're constantly biting me?"

I wrinkle my nose at the thought. "Don't put that thing anywhere near my mouth or you might lose it."

He sighs heavily. "So I can lick you to orgasm, but you won't touch my cock. Is that what you're saying?" His icy blue eyes give away nothing of what he's thinking right now.

I nod. "Exactly."

His eyes darken, and he grabs my wrist, yanking me off the kitchen island. "Wrong answer."

I swallow hard as he drags me through his apartment, stopping in front of a door. He pushes it open to reveal a large bedroom, which is so cold and unwelcoming, it makes me shudder. There's no color at all, it's just gray walls and gray bedding. The only warm color is the mahogany wood bed.

Maxim drags me over to the bed and forces me down onto it. "Don't move."

I glare at my husband and then eye the door, wondering if I can still escape him.

"Don't even think about it." He holds a key. "It's locked."

My brow furrows, as I must have been so distracted

by the coldness of the decor in his bedroom that I didn't notice him lock the door behind us.

After a few moments, he walks away and disappears behind a door to the left. I hear him rustling about in there, and then he returns, holding a few objects that make my heart rate spike. "Don't come near me with those," I say, eyeing them warily.

"If you don't give me any choice, baby. What's a man supposed to do?" He tilts his head to the side, those cold, calculating eyes assessing me.

I get off the bed, knowing that I'm not letting him restrain me without a fight. It's my worst nightmare. Why the hell didn't he give me some aspirin? I could have taken a fuck load and lay there not feeling anything while this son of a bitch had his way with me. Instead, I want to make him hurt. I want to fight him until he's bloody.

"Liv, we both know this won't end well for you if you try to fight." He chucks the items he found onto the bed and advances toward me. "You may have the tenacity to fight me, but I'm stronger."

I clench my jaw, my fingernails digging into my palm until they hurt so badly I feel them pierce through my flesh. "I hate you." It's a pathetic comeback, but I have nothing more. I'm backed into a fucking corner by this man with no soul and there's no escape.

He chuckles. "Join the club. Many people do."

My breathing becomes labored as my vision blurs a little. I hate being so out of control, so helpless.

Maxim comes toward me, but I don't have the strength to move. It's as if my body has surrendered itself and my brain is screaming at it to move. He grabs my hips and yanks me against his solid body, placing a hand around the back of my neck and squeezing. "You'll submit to me. I don't care how long it takes, Livia."

My nostrils flare and my teeth ache from clenching my jaw, but I can't find the words anymore. I'm like a rabbit caught in headlights, frozen in fear and unable to get myself out of danger.

He wraps an arm around my back and lifts me over his shoulder, carrying me to the bed. The moment I'm on my back, he slides handcuffs around my wrists, fixing them to the solid wood bedposts. I glare at the man I forever tied my life to earlier today, feeling my stomach churn with sickness.

The sickness is born in both a deep hatred for this man and disgust at myself for how wet I am right now. My thighs are slick with arousal as he fixes my wrists to the bedpost with metal clipped cuffs. Once they're secure, he moves to my ankles and does the same, forcing my thighs permanently open for him, so I'm splayed out like a fucking starfish.

Every muscle in my body tenses when he pulls out a switchblade from his pocket. "What are you going to do with that?" I hate that my voice trembles, revealing my fear.

Maxim shakes his head. "Relax I'm going to fuck

you, not kill you." He grabs hold of the fabric of my dress and slices it from my body, leaving me in nothing but my suspenders and matching bra, since he left my panties and stockings in the kitchen. His eyes flash with heat as the ice in them melts. "So fucking beautiful," he murmurs, making heat race to the surface of my skin, covering my entire body.

No one has ever called me beautiful. Yet Maxim can't seem to stop calling me that. I shudder under his heated gaze, waiting for his next move, which I know won't be good.

"As much as I want to lick you to climax again, which I intend to do shortly. I need to feel that hot little mouth wrapped around my cock, baby." He grabs another device and my world spins. I know nothing about sex other than what I've seen in porn, and I've never seen what he's holding, but it's easy to imagine what it's for.

"I promise I won't bite," I say, not wanting that thing affixed to my mouth.

Maxim shakes his head. "I'm sorry, printessa, but you're unpredictable. The gag is an insurance for my cock."

He places the device into my mouth and affixes the straps around the back of my head, making me feel utterly humiliated as my mouth hangs open.

I watch as he removes his jacket and throws it on a nearby chair, unbuttoning his shirt to reveal his heavily inked body. My thighs tremble at the utter perfection of every dip and line of his muscles, and the way the tattoos sprawl over his skin like a living, breathing piece of art. There's no denying how beautiful my husband is, even if he's a twisted fucker. I guess I could have had it worse, as he could have been ugly and evil.

Maxim smirks as he notices me gawking at him. "Like what you see?"

I narrow my eyes, hating that he's asking me a question I can't even answer with this fucking gag in my mouth. It makes my jaw ache as it keeps my mouth hanging open and stretched wide. Instead, I shake my head.

He sighs and drops his fingers to the button of his pants, making my mouth water in anticipation. I've never seen a man naked before, and for some sick reason, I'm excited to see all of him. His pants pool at his ankles and he steps out of them, standing in a pair of tight black boxer briefs that frame the enormity of him. My stomach tightens as I stare unashamedly at the bulge at his crotch, wondering how the fuck it's supposed to fit inside any part of me.

"How about now?" he asks, as he drags the waistband of his boxers down and his thick, hard, and veiny length bobs free from the fabric, slapping his abs as it does.

My mind short wires as I stare at it, making it impossible to even shake my head in reply. I feel my pussy getting wetter looking at him, which is fucking sickening. I know it's because at twenty years old, I'm a horny mess of a virgin who has barely ever been kissed by a man, let alone touched. It could be any son of a bitch standing there naked, and I'd be gushing with need. It makes my desire to hurt him stronger, and yet he's made sure that's impossible.

"Looks like you're getting wetter looking at me," he says, walking closer and rubbing his fingers through my soaking wet entrance. "It's time for you to taste me."

I shuffle as much as the restraints allow as he straddles my neck, making me feel claustrophobic. And then he pushes his hips up so he's practically dangling his cock over my face. I have no control as he sinks down, thrusting his huge cock through the gag and right into the back of my throat. It makes me gag instantly, saliva spilling out of my mouth as I panic, clawing at my own palms so hard that blood drips from them.

Maxim notices and pulls back, eyes narrowing. "Relax, Livia. I'm not trying to kill you with my cock. Breathe through your nose and stop tensing up, or it'll be worse for you."

I shut my eyes and focus on breathing through my nose, trying to calm the storm tearing its way through me. As I do as he says, Maxim continues his assault on my throat. This time, I try not to focus on the act and listen to the rhythm of my breathing through my nose. It's all I can do, as Maxim has me entirely restrained. I have no control at all in that moment, but it feels like a part of the darkness inside of me melts away, which makes no sense.

I lean into the relief of it, allowing it to overwhelm me. For a moment, the need to hurt, to lash out, and harm aren't there. It's as if I've left my body and I'm floating above it. All the while, Maxim grunts and groans above me as he fucks my throat like a wild animal.

I watch him, the way his muscles strain beneath the ink over his skin. Looking closer at his tattoos, I can see the many scars that they're hiding. They've got a strange beauty, and it makes me wonder if perhaps our childhoods weren't so different.

The desire to reach out and touch his skin overcomes me, and yet, I can't. The restraints make it impossible.

"Fuck, Livia," he groans, eyes rolling back in his head. "You're fucking amazing at deep throating my cock," he growls, before pulling out suddenly. "So fucking good I almost came." Maxim unfastens the gag and chucks it away, making me feel relief that I can finally talk.

"Why didn't you?" I ask.

His brow furrows. "Because when I come, I'm going to be buried deep in that virgin cunt of yours," he murmurs, pressing his lips to mine and kissing me deeply. He groans into my mouth, sucking on my tongue like he's starving for me. Maxim's fingers travel to between my spread thighs and he growls. "You're fucking dripping, baby." He pulls back, searching my eyes. "I know you won't admit it, but I know how badly you want my cock."

I shake my head. "I'd say you're delusional." It's a fucking lie, as my body is aching with the need for this man I hate. A man who takes what he wants and doesn't care about the consequences. "Just get it over with already."

He smirks, and it's an evil one that makes my stomach dip. "No, princess. You don't get to feel me inside of you yet," he breathes, his normally cold eyes flashing with unmatched fire. "I'm going to make you come so many fucking times, you won't remember your own name. By the time I slide inside of you, you may actually beg me for it."

"In your dreams."

Maxim kisses a path down my neck, trailing lower to my nipples, which are hard and sensitive. I jolt as he gently runs the tip of his tongue in a circle around each one before sucking on them, all the while he holds my gaze with those beautiful blue eyes of his.

I shudder as he licks right down my abdomen, getting lower and lower until he's a breath away from where I need to feel him.

Fuck.

When did I start needing anything from this man?

He teases me, placing kisses against my inner thighs next. All the time, his gaze holds mine as if waiting for me to snap and beg him for it. I clench my jaw, knowing that no matter how badly I want to feel his mouth on me, I won't beg him for it.

This man may have the upper hand with sex, but I won't break that easily. I'd rather die than give him the satisfaction.

10

MAXIM

*M*y wife is one of the most stubborn women I've ever met.

As I coax her third orgasm from her, she still won't beg me for my cock. She's either got willpower of steel or she really isn't bothered whether I fuck her. Normally, women would be gagging for it by now, but all she does is moan as she comes apart and then returns to glaring at me as I start all over again.

"Are you enjoying this, printessa?" I ask, searching those green eyes which now look more vibrant, more wild.

She shakes her head. "Not particularly."

It's a fucking lie and we both know it. However, patience isn't my forte. I grab her thighs and push them as far apart as the restraints will allow, kneeling between her legs and positioning the head of my cock with her tight virgin hole.

"What are you doing?"

I rub my finger over her clit and she jolts in response, nipples hardening. "It's time for me to claim what's mine."

"Fuck you," she spits, trying with force to shut her legs.

I hold them open. "No, I'm going to fuck you until you can't take it anymore," I breathe, rubbing my finger through her wet folds. "I'm going to break you in half and make you come apart all over my cock."

Her jaw clenches as she glares at me with a heat that only makes me harder. "If I wasn't restrained, I'd claw your fucking eyes out." She writhes against the chains holding her to the bed, leaving marks on her soft skin where the metal digs in.

I chuckle. "You're very violent, aren't you?" I ask, rubbing the head of my cock through her still soaking wet entrance.

She spits in my face, which only serves to spur me on. Her fight makes this more intoxicating.

"Wrong answer, baby." I thrust my cock through her tight, unwilling entrance with such force she's screams.

A sound that makes my balls draw up, proving how twisted I am. I've accepted I was broken beyond repair a long time ago. All I can do is revel in my depravity.

The resistance I'm met with doesn't slow me down as I break through her virginal walls and slide all the way inside. As I pull out, I notice a little blood coating my dick, which drives me wild. I'd wondered if perhaps her father was lying that she's a twenty-year-old virgin, since there's no real way to prove it, but damn it, this girl really was.

I lean down and risk a kiss, my tongue sliding into her mouth. I'm rewarded with a sharp bite, which makes me groan as I bite her back harder. Our tongues and lips and teeth go to war as I fuck her, feeling her muscles relax around my cock as her body gets used to the invasion.

I sense the hatred and fighting only turns her on more. A woman after my own fucking heart.

Her hard nipples graze against my bare chest as I bite her lip hard enough to break the skin. She bites mine back, breaking the skin too. The metallic taste of blood fills my mouth as we continue to fight each other. She hates that she's enjoying it and it only makes her fight harder, and I regret not letting her remain unrestrained so she could hurt me the way she wants.

Perhaps that's something I should fix right now. I break away, panting for oxygen. "I'm going to remove the restraints from your hands, because I like it when you fight, printessa." I reach for the restraint on her left wrist and flick open the cuffs, followed by her right.

All the while, she glares at me with a deep, dark hatred mixed with lust and desire. "Your funeral."

I smirk as she claws at me hard, digging her nails into my chest and scrapping them down the length of my body. I glance down, admiring the sharp red scrapes she left in my skin. The sting makes me swell harder inside of her. "Keep doing that and I won't stop fucking you until we both pass out from exhaustion." I grab her hips so hard I know I'll leave bruises on her skin, which earns me a sharp hiss of pleasure as her nostrils flare. She holds my gaze as I move inside of her, my cock throbbing as her pussy clamps around me so tightly it's like she's trying to break it.

Livia slaps me hard across the face, which takes me by surprise. "I'll never take this without a fight," she snarls, glaring at me as her pupils dilate with pleasure.

"Good," I growl, grabbing her wrists hard in one hand and her throat in the other, as I continue to pound into her. "You fighting me makes me harder than I've ever fucking been." My hips roll with violent, vicious thrusts as I make my wife mine, even if she's as stubborn as a fucking mule.

Her pussy clenches around me, warning me she's on the edge of coming undone. Looks like my pretty little wife enjoys being choked. I release her throat and her wrists, which lands me a hard punch in my chest. "Get the fuck off me, you bastard," she cries. She lands two more hard punches, one to my gut, the other to my throat.

I take the pain, shaking my head and smirking at her manically. What she doesn't realize is every time she hits me, it makes the darkness inside of me rise to the surface. "I don't think you want that at all, not when you were about to come apart all over my cock."

Her eyes narrow. "That's bullshit."

I pull my cock out of her, which makes her involuntarily whimper in protest. The moment that sound leaves her lips, she sinks her teeth into the busted flesh as her cheeks deepen from pink to almost red.

I move my attention to her ankles, unclasping the restraints.

She tries to escape the moment they're off, scrambling off the side of the bed.

As much as I'd love the thrill of chasing her through the apartment, feeding off her fear, I grab her by the ankles before she can escape and yank her back onto the bed. Her chin slams into the hard mahogany as I drag her up the side of the bed, but I don't care. It's self-inflicted. I seize her already bruised thighs and flip her over face first on the bed. "There's no escape, printessa. I'm going to fuck you from behind," I say, using my weight to hold her against the bed.

She remains flat, her legs clamped shut hard. I'll give her one thing. She's got some serious restraint considering she was on the edge of coming apart moments ago. Few women could resist the need to come apart with such determination.

I dig my fingers into her inner thighs and prize them apart forcefully, groaning when I see the mess her pussy has made on the bed. She's so fucking aroused. It's insane. I grab her hips and yank her onto her knees, moving her around like a fucking puppet. Livia may fight, but she's half my size and no match for my strength.

Her back arches, even as she tries to crawl away from me. I spank her ass viciously with the flat of my palm, wishing I'd kept my belt close at hand to bring it down on her perfect ass. If her father abused her as a child, there are no signs of it on her skin, like me. She's scar free, but I know that doesn't mean he didn't beat her. Vito doesn't strike me as a man that has the capability for the extent of brutality that my father does. Granted, Father never left scars on Viki. As they would have made her less valuable, so perhaps that's why she's so blemish free, so utterly perfect.

Livia jerks forward, whimpering, as I continue to spank her ass until it's red. Her arousal drips down her thighs, making a mess of the bed. I can't hold out any longer as I position myself at her entrance and thrust forward with all my strength.

Livia squeals, clawing at the bed sheets as if it were my body she's trying to tear apart. Suddenly, she gets her leg free and kicks me right in the gut, making me grunt. "Get off me, you fucking bastard!" she shouts, getting about a foot away from me as my cock slips from her soaking wet pussy.

I don't let go of her, my fingernails digging so hard into her hips I pierce the skin. She half-moans and half-screams as the pain turns her on. With all my strength, I drag her back and impale her on my cock.

"Stop fighting it. You're my wife, which means you're mine. Do you understand?" I growl, sounding more like a fucking caveman than the prince of the

Volkov Bratva. It's what this girl does to me. Turns me into a mindless fucking heathen with no control. Her feisty, fighting attitude is dangerous. I thrust my cock so deep inside of her in this position that it feels like I'm going to split her in half.

Livia moans, spurring me on as the violence of my desire for her reaches a peak. I don't want to want my wife this way. I hate that I do, and yet my body loves it. It's a conflicting sensation. I grab hold of her neck from behind and yank her back against me, forcing her back to arch almost unnaturally.

"When are you going to accept that you want this?" I murmur into her ear.

"Never," she replies.

I bite her earlobe, which makes her pussy tense. She's on the edge of no return and I can't wait to feel her come apart on my cock. I'll make her orgasm for me for the fourth time tonight. My thrusts turn erratic and uncontrolled as I wrap my arm around her throat, squeezing. "It won't change the truth, printessa. You're about to come like a dirty little virgin who gets off on pain, choking and rough sex," I whisper into her ear.

That's all it takes to have her come apart. She screams this time, forgetting her desire to prove she doesn't want this. "Fuck, yes!" she shouts. Despite my stranglehold on her throat, she's coherent.

Her muscles flutter around my cock, drawing me deeper than I believed possible. I freeze behind her as she coaxes my release, forcing me to fill her with my cum. I sink my teeth into the juncture between her neck and her shoulder hard, groaning as I release every drop deep into her virgin cunt, marking her as mine.

Livia is still trembling in my arms as I release her throat and allow her to collapse face forward on the bed. She doesn't say a word, panting for oxygen as she lies buck naked, my cum dripping from her pussy onto the bedsheets. I ease the duvet over her and then lie down by her side, which makes her roll away from me, turning her back.

I allow it to slide, doing the same wordlessly. There's nothing to say. I've made her my wife. It's time to sleep and I'll allow her to escape her reality while she does. In time, Livia will come to accept her position as mine, but deep down, I hope she never loses that desire to fight me.

She's shackled to me now in a way there's no escape from. Although, she has seen nothing yet. The question is, will she survive once I unleash the true darkness inside of me on her?

11

LIVIA

*D*arkness surrounds me as I stare into the abyss, waiting for the pain to follow.

I gaze into the pitch black, anticipating those dark, soulless brown eyes to appear. His anger to hit me and tear me apart far worse than his fists could do. My heart stutters, as it's different this time. The dark eyes are replaced with ice-blue eyes, glaring at me with a twisted mix of lust and rage.

"Admit it, printessa." His bitter voice licks over me, sending shivers down my spine.

"Admit what?" I ask, my voice quiet as if I'm speaking underwater.

He advances toward me, his features becoming sharper, more defined. I shudder at the stony look in his eyes, waiting for him to speak. Once he's a foot away from me, he stops and clenches his fists by his side. "You're as sick and twisted as me," he murmurs, a manic spark lighting up his eyes. "The darkness inside of you will never go away."

A lump wedges in my throat as blood trickles out of his eye sockets as he glares at me.

"You want to kill and maim me like the monster you are," he continues, advancing forward.

Suddenly, I'm holding a knife that I slash right through his throat.

He laughs as blood trickles from his throat and he chokes and coughs on it, the blood splattering over my face.

"No!" I shout, dropping the knife with a sharp clang. "I'm not like you and never will be!" I scream, feeling like my body is being torn in two.

Sharp pain coils through my shoulders, and that's when I'm pulled out of the dream. Pulled back to my horrific reality as I stare into those same crystal blue eyes. "You were having a nightmare," he says, no emotion in his voice as he releases my shoulders. "I kept trying to wake you, but…" He trails off and shrugs. "I guess we all have demons."

I glance around the room, noticing that between the crack in the thick curtains, it's light outside. "What time is it?" I ask, sitting up and rubbing my eyes.

He sits back as well and stretches his arms over his head, drawing my attention to his muscled, tattooed body. "Eight o'clock."

I bite my sore bottom lip, wondering what the fuck I'm supposed to do now, stuck in Maxim's apartment. "I think I'll visit my mom today."

Maxim raises a brow. "You won't be leaving this

apartment, Livia." The sternness of his voice sets me on edge.

"Why the fuck not?" I ask.

He swings his legs out of bed and walks toward the bathroom buck naked, turning as he gets to the door.

My stomach dips when I see his cock is hard, standing upright.

"Because we're at war and someone betrayed our trust by telling the whole fucking world about the alliance between my family and yours. Which means you're in danger until we figure out who fucked with us." He cracks his neck and then disappears into the bathroom, without allowing me to say a word. I hear the shower turn on, but he keeps the door open.

I clench my fists, digging my fingernails into the palm of my hand. Maxim Volkov is a cocky son of a bitch who I have no intention of taking orders from. I'll fight him tooth and nail if he keeps trying to control me. I may have vowed to spend the rest of my life with him until death do we part. All I can hope is it's his death that parts us, sooner rather than later.

My nightmares have always been a problem, but the only person who is ever present in them is my father. It appears I have a new tormentor, one that I both hate and desire at the same time.

Maxim calls from the bathroom. "Are you coming?"

I glare at the doorway. "No, thanks."

He leans against the doorframe, cock in his hand as

he strokes it lazily. "Don't make me drag you into the shower."

"Fuck off." I shake my head. "If I'm not going anywhere, there's no need for me to get out of bed." I pull the duvet tightly around me and turn my back to him, which results in a soft, beastlike growl from my husband.

I don't react as I hear his soft yet firm footsteps pounding toward the bed, holding the duvet with all my strength. It doesn't help though as he gathers me in it and lifts me off the bed as if I weigh nothing at all.

"I won't stand for disobedience," he snarls, carrying me into the bathroom.

I fight against him, but it's hard when he has me immobilized in a duvet. "Let me go."

"When hell freezes over," he purrs.

I grind my teeth. "Why? Because you won't be able to get out?"

He chuckles at that. "Exactly. Do you think it's wise to fight the devil?" He drops me to the floor in a heap of duvet in the center of the bathroom, which is ridiculously large.

"I think it's wise to fight oppression." I give him the finger.

He merely smirks. "You're going to have to do better than that to offend me."

I stand and walk up to him, slamming my clenched fist hard in the center of his chest.

He groans, but doesn't retaliate. Instead, he pulls me

hard against his naked body and whispers into my ear, "You know how to make a man harder, don't you?"

I grimace. "You're a sick fuck."

"Why thank you." He digs his fingers into my already abused hips and yanks me toward the shower. "Get in."

I cross my arms over my chest and glare at him. "Make me."

His eyes flutter shut, and he releases a long breath. When they snap open, they're full of dangerous intent. "Wrong answer." He comes for me, grabbing me by the waist and hoisting me into his arms as he carries me over the threshold and into the huge double shower. "You'll learn life is easier if you do as you're told."

"I'm not a slave," I grit out, hating the way the sight of his beautiful body makes me feel.

"We'll have to agree to disagree on that matter." He pushes me around and slams my body front first against the cold, tiled shower wall. "Wife, captive, it's all the fucking same in my eyes." He spanks my ass so hard it feels like he's trying to leave his handprint permanently on my skin. "Everyone can be forced to bow, Livia. Everyone."

"Not me," I reply, hating the vulnerability in my voice.

He laughs wickedly. "There's not a fucking person alive that doesn't have a weakness." He presses his powerful body against mine, letting me feel his hard cock against my ass. "Once I find out yours, it'll only be a matter of time until you crumble."

"Good luck," I rasp, wishing his body didn't make mine react. The dampness between my thighs is as disgusting as the ache deep in the pit of my stomach.

I feel Maxim's rough hands part my cheeks and the tip of his cock press against my wet entrance. My body stiffens as I glare at the tiles in front of me, wanting to hurt the man behind me. If I let him take what the fuck he wants, then perhaps he's right. I'm a slave to tend to his every whim and desire. While he's distracted, I twist around and land a hard punch to his jaw.

He growls, grabbing his face as I slip around him and out of the shower.

I get about three feet before I'm yanked backward.

"Not so fast." He digs his fingernails into my bruised hips, making me squeal. "Do you want me to restrain you like last night?"

"I want you to get the fuck off me!"

He slides a finger between my legs and dips it into my pussy, making me squirm. "Such a naughty little liar you are," he murmurs, his breath hot against my ear. "Don't you mean you want me to fuck you?"

My muscles flutter around his finger as he lazily fingers me. I hate the way my body reacts to this man, and yet I'm powerless to stop the reactions. A part of me wants to drown in my hate for him and kiss, bite and scratch him as he has his way with me, just like last night. The sane part of me wants to stab a knife through his heart and flee the fucking country, return to Catanzaro, and never look back.

"You're an evil son of a bitch," I rasp, hating the desire in my tone.

He rubs his finger over my clit, and my toes involuntarily curl as I lean into him. I never knew pleasure could be so confusing. "Stop fighting this, baby," he whispers into my ear before licking a path down the side of my neck. "Give me what is mine," he purrs.

"I belong to no one," I grit out, biting the inside of my cheek to stop myself from moaning as he rubs my clit faster. Before I know it, my thighs are trembling and I'm on the edge of coming undone like a desperate whore. And then he removes his hand, leaving me panting and aching. I want to complain, but I know that would give him too much satisfaction, so I bite my tongue instead.

"Are you done now?" I ask.

"Not even close," he breathes, yanking me back into the shower and lifting me so my back is against the wall.

Out of instinct, my legs wrap around his muscled hips, drawing his cock closer to me. A war rages inside of me as I stare at the thick, length ready to slide inside of me and quench that ache. I hate him and I want him all at the same time. I want to dig my nails into his skin and watch him bleed while he fucks me like an animal.

Those ice-blue eyes search mine as he holds me

there, immobile and weak. "I want to fuck you while you fight me, printessa."

I clench my jaw. "You're messed up," I breathe, but I don't mean it, because if he's messed up, then so am I. That's exactly what I want as well. That raw, dark hatred spurring the both of us on as we fuck like beasts.

"So are you, baby. I see it in your eyes." He positions the head of his cock at my entrance, watching my expression carefully. "I see the pleasure you get from fighting while we fuck and inflicting pain as well as receiving it. The pain, the fight, and the hatred turn you on."

I glare at him, hating that this man knows that. A part of me that no other person has ever had insight into and this evil, calculating man has seen right through me in less than twenty-four hours of marriage. "I don't know what you're talking about."

"Deny it all you like," he says, eyes so intense it looks like he's staring right into my soul. "I know the truth." He pushes forward, making me squeal at the sudden invasion of his huge cock. Every inch buried inside of me in one quick, violent thrust.

I claw my nails into his scalp and pull him toward me, biting his lip hard enough to break the skin. "You're a fucking bastard," I hiss.

He groans and fucks me harder, pressing his lips to mine and forcing his tongue through them. "And you love it," he murmurs against my mouth, his hips pistoning harder and faster.

A soft moan escapes my lips as I claw at him, desperate to make him hurt.

He growls as I move my hands to his shoulders and drag fingernails down his scared, tattooed back. "That's it baby, hurt me." His hips move harder and faster as he fucks me against the wall, my back aching as he slams me into the tiles.

I press my lips to his, biting them in desperation to taste that metallic tang in my mouth. The raw, earthy taste when I make him bleed makes me wild. He bites me back, groaning as our blood mixes, flooding our mouths. "You love it so much, don't you, baby?" he asks.

I shudder as I watch a droplet of blood run down his chin, unable to answer him in this haze of sick, fucked-up pleasure.

Suddenly, he pulls his cock out and drops me to my feet, pushing me front first against the tiles instead. The water cascades over us as he quickly fills me again, grabbing my wrists and forcing them over my head. "You need to learn how good it is to submit, printessa," he breathes into my ear. "How freeing it could be for you."

I shudder, eyes fluttering shut as both shame and desire morph into one.

Maxim takes away my control and every time he does, I feel that darkness slip away for a moment. As if he's the cure to the sickness that lies in wait. I've known for a long time that the more I bury the darkness, the harder it'll try to claw its way to the surface. It's why I'm so reliant on the painkillers. They take away my feelings, drowning them deeper beneath the surface where they can't escape.

He's ruthless and brutal as he takes me hard against the tiled wall. His body slamming against mine as if he's trying to break me apart. "I'm going to fuck you so hard you can't walk," he growls. The violence only gives us something in common.

We're the same. Two dark and lost souls finding a momentary relief in each other. Something I never believed possible when I first met this man and yet despite my hate for him, he brings me a kind of solace. Even if it's temporary.

I relax into it, allowing him to take what he wants.

His strong hand remains clasped around my wrists, keeping me captive. His other hand moves from my hip to my throat as he clasps it firmly, blocking my airways. "That's right, relax into it," he encourages, his hips slamming into me harder.

I jolt as he releases my throat, allowing me to take a deep gulp of oxygen.

His hand moves to my ass, and he spanks me hard and fast on each cheek before parting them. "I could get used to watching you take every inch of my cock, baby."

"Well, don't," I grit out, despite myself. "As this is the last time."

He laughs and spanks me even harder. "It most

certainly isn't the last time. I promise I'm going to fuck you every morning and every night for the rest of our lives," he breathes, biting my earlobe so hard I'm sure he broke the skin. "Some days I'll spend the entire day buried in you."

My stomach twists with a mix of hope and disgust.

What the hell is wrong with me?

I don't reply to him, because deep down I want it too. As when he's inside me, the darkness quietens. Especially when he allows me to hurt him. It's like an outlet for the pain, inflicting it on him. None of this makes any sense.

He spanks me again, and I can feel myself on the edge of no return. My thighs quiver as he holds me firmly against the wall. "That's it, printessa," he groans, his thrusts becoming frantic. "Make that pretty little pussy come on my cock," he orders.

The dominance in his voice is arousing as he smashes into me harder. Our bodies coming together in a violent clash of skin against skin. I let my head fall back against his shoulder as the intensity of my orgasm hits me. My knees buckle as he holds me up firmly, his powerful body anchoring me.

Maxim grabs a fistful of my hair and forces my head around, capturing my lips in a desperate kiss. My body shudders as I come apart, coating his cock in my arousal. He groans, thrusting once more as his cock swells inside of me, coating my insides with his seed. It should disgust me, but in that moment I can't think past the haze of pleasure that's settled over my mind.

Maxim holds us there for a short while, both of us panting for oxygen beneath the spray of water. After a few minutes, he slides out of me and leaves the cubicle, grabbing a towel and wrapping it around his waist as he walks back into the bedroom.

My stomach dips as I realize I allowed him to take total control of that situation and liked it too much. As I stand motionless under the spray of warm water, his words repeat over in my mind.

There's not a fucking person alive that doesn't have a weakness. Once I find out yours, it will only be a matter of time until you crumble.

I'll never let him break me. If he unearths my weakness, then he won't survive it. My weakness is also my strength, and that's something that scares me.

Maxim better hope he never uncovers it, or chaos will reign.

12

MAXIM

*A*drik notices me as I approach his table at the back of our club, Podolka. "To what do I owe this pleasure, cousin?" He has his arm slung over a drunk prostitute's shoulder, as always.

I shrug. "Needed a drink and I knew you'd be here." I sit down at his table, not waiting for an invitation. After all, this is my father's club.

He chuckles. "Married life not suiting you?"

I roll my eyes. "Marriage isn't going to change my life. I won't let it."

He raises a brow. "That's what they all say." He knocks back a glass of the finest scotch we sell, slamming the tumbler down. "Want a drink?" He pushes the bottle toward me, which I know he hasn't paid for.

Adrik is useless most of the time. A drunk who can't be bothered to pull his weight and work hard for the

Bratva, but since he's family, it's often brushed under the carpet. "Sure." Any other member of the Bratva would be dead and buried for the shit he pulls.

He pours me a glass and slides it over.

I bring the glass to my lips and take a sip, enjoying the burn as it slides down my throat. It takes my mind off of the scratch and bite marks all over my body. It's been five days since we got married, and the more we fuck, the more pain she inflicts on me.

Livia is an enigma, and the longer I know her, the more confusing she becomes.

"So, what's your wife like?" Adrik asks.

"You might have seen for yourself if you showed up to my wedding," I reply, glaring at him over the rim of my tumbler.

His father, Adrik, and Valeri, were all absent at the wedding. No doubt a fuck you to my father, as they don't agree with this alliance. They believe the Bianchi family has nothing to offer us, but that's because only Me, Timur and my father know the true extent of their power and the doors they can open for the Volkov Bratva.

"Sorry, I had a prior engagement," he says.

I shake my head. "Cut the bullshit, Adrik. I know your father ensured none of you attended." I knock back the scotch and grab the bottle, topping my glass up. "He always has to make a public show when he doesn't agree with Father."

He sighs. "Yeah, that's because he's a sore loser and he hates that your father wears the crown."

Someone clears their throat behind us, drawing our attention. "Brother, cousin," Valeri says, looking a little irritated as he glares at Adrik.

Valeri is the polar opposite to Adrik. Loyal to the Bratva, but also loyal to his father. He's the golden child out of the two.

"What are you doing here?" Adrik asks.

He shrugs. "Father asked me to come and keep an eye on you."

Adrik clenches his fists on the table. "What the fuck for?"

Valeri sits down next to me, smirking at his brother. "You didn't show up to the last two meetings. He's worried about you."

Adrik scoffs. "Worried my ass." He gives me a pointed look. "The bastard is only worried about me spoiling his reputation."

The prostitute, who appears to be close to passing out, slumps against Adrik. "Are we going to get out of here?"

Adrik pushes her away, shaking his head. "Nah, change of plans. You can fuck off."

I shake my head, watching as she glares at him angrily before pushing herself up and stumbling away. "When are you going to stop messing around with hookers?"

"When pigs fly." His brow furrows. "You still haven't told me what your wife is like?"

Valeri leans forward. "Oh yeah, congratulations on your nuptials, cousin." He smirks at me. "Taking one for the team marrying an Italian, hey?"

I try to ignore the dig. "Why does her nationality matter?"

"Haven't you heard Italian women are fucking crazy?" Valeria asks, amusement dancing in his dark brown eyes. "I bet that's why you're here instead of at home, escaping the crazy bitch."

I grab hold of Valeri by his tie and pull it so hard that it tightens around his neck. He falls forward, almost tumbling off his chair. "Don't you ever talk about my wife in that way again," I snarl, surprising myself with the viciousness in my voice. "She's a Volkov now. The princess to the fucking throne by my side, and you will show her some respect."

Valeri's face pales as he tries desperately to loosen the fabric around his throat.

"We fucking get it, release him for fuck's sake, Maxim." Adrik pleads, clearly concerned for his brother's safety as he turns gray.

I can't have my cousins disrespect me. As the heir to the throne of the Volkov Bratva, I need to keep them in line. Once my father steps down, I'll take his place and these two clowns will linger like my uncle, waiting like vultures ready to pounce if they see the opportunity. That's why I won't ever give them one.

I release him and he gasps, yanking the tie off entirely. He coughs, bending over and retching. "Seriously?" he asks, glaring at me.

I knock back my scotch and shrug. "She's Livia Volkov. My wife. What did you expect?" I narrow my eyes. "You disrespect her, then you disrespect me."

He holds his hands up. "Fair enough."

Adrik raises a brow. "Looks like she's under your skin, Max."

I growl softly, as I hate being called Max. "Don't call me that."

He chuckles, shaking his head. "So easy to piss off."

I clench my fists beneath the table. "Tell me, Adrik, do you want me to choke you with your tie next?"

"Chill out, cousin. I'm only jesting." He sighs heavily. "When did you two become such fucking bores?"

Valeri and I exchange glances. "We're not bores, we've just grown up, Adrik." I cross my arms over my chest. "I suggest you do the same."

Valeri nods, agreeing with me. "Yeah, you're a year older than Maxim, but you act like a fucking kid."

He waves his hand in response. "Whatever. Drink and chill out. Even adults can have fun in a club."

I grab the bottle of scotch and pour myself a third glass, bringing it to my lips and sipping the smokey, forty-year-old whiskey.

Adrik smirks as I drink. But this is exactly why I came here tonight. I need to drown the need and desire I have for my wife before we tear each other apart. If we don't stop, we might fucking kill each other, and I get the sense we'd both enjoy it. There's always been a part of me that's broken. I never expected to find a woman with the exact same screws loose.

"Seriously though, is she hot?" Adrik asks, questioning me again about my wife.

"That's none of your fucking business," I say, knowing that if I admit how attracted I am to my wife, I open myself up to ridicule. "She's perfectly adequate."

Valeri cuts in. "We'll soon see for ourselves, anyway. It's your father's birthday in two weeks, and I assume you and your wife will attend the party."

I clench my jaw, realizing my father will be forty-six in two weeks. "Of course." I'd forgotten all about it.

"Have you heard from Viki at all?" Adrik asks, a clear look of concern in his eyes. They were always close when we were kids, even though they drifted apart as Adrik plowed himself full of booze daily. But I know he cares about her.

I shake my head. "No, not a word." I can't admit that I've been meeting her secretly, even if that's the rumor going around. It's best I deny it, to ensure no one calls me a fucking rat, especially after news of my wedding got out.

Adrik runs a hand through his messy, dark hair. "I hope she's alright with that fucking Irish bastard."

"When I spoke to her in the hospital, she said he loved her." I shrug. "Maybe she's doing better than you think." I know she's fine, as Rourke worships her.

"I still can't believe your psycho of a father shot her," Valeri adds.

I give him a stern glare, even though I'm in total agreement over how much of a bastard he is for shooting my sister. "Careful, Val, you don't want to disrespect my father, too."

He laughs. "It's not disrespectful. It's the reason he's so feared."

He's right, but I don't laugh with him. Instead, I knock back the rest of my drink. "Well, this was fun, but I ought to get going." I stand.

My two cousins stand too, out of habit rather than genuine respect. Valeri is three years older than me, and although he'd never say it to my face, he resents the fact that I'm next in line for the throne.

"Pakah," I say in parting.

My two cousins dutifully repeat the Russian farewell, as I turn and leave them behind.

I glance at my Rolex, noticing it's only ten o'clock, which is fucking early. Normally when I come out to Podolka, I stay until the early hours of the morning, and yet ever since I've arrived I can't forget the one thing I came here to forget. My wife.

I know she's at home alone, waiting for me to return. No doubt dripping wet in anticipation. This is the latest I've stayed out since we married less than a week ago. It seems the novelty is yet to wear off, so I need to fuck her out of my system like a crazed animal. Perhaps then I can finally stop thinking about her.

THE APARTMENT IS dark when I return.

"Livia," I call her name into the darkness.

There's no reply. My brow furrows as I switch on the kitchen light, noticing a half-eaten lasagne left out. I groan, hating how messy my wife can be. She never clears up after herself, which is a habit I'll need to address at some point.

I grab the plate and throw away the food in the trash, pausing when I see an aspirin packet. I pick it up, recognizing it as the same aspirin I keep in my drug cabinet. Livia must have taken them, but I'm surprised she would have finished an entire packet in just five days, unless she has some kind of chronic pain issue I don't know about. I drop it back into the trash and chuck the plate in the dishwasher.

And then, I search for my wife. When I come to the doorway of our bedroom, I pause. Livia is curled in a ball on the center of the bed, her chest rising and falling in frantic breaths.

I push open the door and advance toward her, making sure my footsteps are light. When I get to her, she's fast asleep. I gently rock her shoulder, trying to wake her.

She doesn't stir at all.

"Livia," I say her name, softly at first, and shake her again with a little more force.

She still doesn't wake.

I glance around the room and notice her purse on the nightstand. My brow furrows as I notice a pill bottle sticking out of it. I grab the purse and pull it out, cursing the moment I do. Fentanyl.

What the fuck is she doing with this?

I throw the bag down and return my attention to my comatose wife. Pulling back her eyelids, I check her pupils, which are dilated as fuck. She's high on pills, which may explain why she was so disappointed when I didn't give her the aspirin on our wedding night.

I rush into the bathroom and open the drugs cabinet, finding the Naloxone and syringe. Quickly, I work to get it ready and return to her lifeless body on the bed. She may or may not have overdosed, but I have no intention of taking any risks.

I push the syringe into her outer thigh and inject her with it. Suddenly, she bolts upright and then pukes all over the side of the bed. I groan, as I'm a fucking clean freak when it comes to my home. All this woman has done since she got here is make a mess of it.

"What the fuck, Liv?" I ask, glaring at her.

She glances around, her eyes glassy as they dart between the packet of Fentanyl on the nightstand and the Naloxone and syringe on the bed. "Did you inject me?"

"Of course I fucking did. The moment I couldn't wake you up because you're too high on this shit." I grab the packet.

Her eyes grow more lucid as she shakes her head.

"Thanks a fucking lot," she says, jumping to her feet. She wobbles, but steadies herself. "I was away from it all until you barged in and brought me right fucking back."

"What are you talking about? Away from what?"

Her face pales as if only now remembering who she's talking about. "It's nothing. I..." She glances at the puke on the bedsheets. "I better clean this up—"

I grab her wrist and yank her against me. "Start talking. Or I'll make you."

She shakes her head. "It's nothing. I find it easier to sleep if I take the pills." Her gaze remains fixed on the floor, and I know she's lying to me. There's a deeper reason for her reliance on pills.

I grab her chin and force her to look at me. "How long have you been taking them?" She's only twenty years old, which is young to be hooked on pills.

"Since I was sixteen."

Fuck.

"I'll enroll you into rehab tomorrow," I say.

She shakes her head. "No, please. I'd do anything not to go to one of those fucking centers."

I raise a brow. "You're a junkie, Livia."

"Fuck you!" she shouts, pointing a shaking finger at me. "I'm not a junkie, I just..." There's a vulnerability in those pale green eyes that I haven't witnessed before.

What secrets does my princess hide behind her walls?

"I can't have an addict as a wife, Livia." I think

about what this could do to the family's reputation. Clearly, her mother is mentally ill. Is it possible Livia is too? "You need to do something about it." I cross my arms over my chest, waiting for her response.

She's silent for a while until she finally meets my gaze. There's an odd expression on her face, one I can't read. It seems my wife is almost impossible to read most of the time. Livia steps forward, eyes fixed on me. She stops once her firm breasts in a too tight shirt are pressed against my chest, her nipples hard.

I clench my jaw, trying to ignore the tug of desire between my thighs. "What do you propose? You can either go to a center or—"

Livia yanks me forward violently, her lips crashing into mine. She bites my lip and then sucks on it.

I groan, forgetting about sending her to a rehab center for a moment. My arms wrap around her back and I grab a fistful of her hair, pulling on it hard.

She moans into my mouth, biting and nibbling at my tongue as I push her toward the wall. Even though she's just thrown up, I can't find it in me to care. Her hands press against my chest as she tries to stop me, but she's not strong enough.

I grab her wrists and force them above her head on the wall, breaking away from her. Those green eyes are practically glowing with intent, but as I stare down at her, I realize that she's trying to distract me, trying to use my insatiable desire for her to make me forget.

"Stop that," I growl, glaring at her. "You'll go to a rehab center or at least a fucking meeting for addicts. There's no way I'm letting you weasel your way out of this."

Her eyes flash with rage. "Like hell I will."

I slam her wrists harder into the wall, using all my weight to pin her against it. "You can't manipulate me, Livia. You have a pill problem and you'll deal with it. I don't care what you want to do or don't." I can't understand people who give in to this kind of weakness, using substances to overcome problems never works. "I'll enroll you in the best rehab center near Chicago for a week. It'll be like a fucking holiday at a five star hotel, so quit your whining." I let go of her and she glares at me.

"I need to find myself a drink," I say, turning around.

She grabs my wrist and yanks me. "So it's okay for you to self medicate with fucking whiskey, but I can't take a few pills."

I turn to face her, regretting it the moment her fist slams into my jaw. "Fuck's sake," I growl, grabbing my jaw and clicking it back into place. "Alcohol is legal. The shit you're fucking taking may as well be heroin."

Her nostrils flare. "Like you give a shit what I take. All you want to do is punish me."

I turn around and walk away from her without a word, because the worst part of what she said is that I do give a shit about what she takes. Fentanyl is a dangerous drug and she could end up dead if she carries on using it the way she is. I won't lose my wife within weeks of marrying her.

Liva might see a rehab center as punishment, but in the end she'll thank me. I've seen the first hand results of drug abuse working within my father's corporation and it never ends well.

13

LIVIA

*M*axim stands by my side as we stare up at the rehab center he booked me into a forty-minute drive from the city.

"Seriously, this isn't necessary," I say, keeping my voice calm as up to now fighting him over it hasn't worked. "I don't even take pills all the time."

He raises a brow. "Hence why you asked me for aspirin the moment you entered my apartment."

I sigh, knowing that I'm in no place to face my demons with a bunch of strangers. They'll want me to talk about why I use, and there's no discussing that with anyone—not unless I want to get sectioned. "You don't understand. It's dangerous to force me into rehab when I'm not ready."

"Dangerous?" he questions, looking amused. "Why? Are you going to snap and shoot everyone inside?"

I swallow hard, gazing into my husband's pale blue eyes. Without him to fight, to harm, to fuck and then no pills either, I can't say what I'll do in that building. Tear someone's eyes out, most probably. "I'll do something I'll regret."

He shakes his head, losing his patience. "Livia, these people are the best in the business. They can help you, if you'll let them."

"There's no cure for what I have," I mutter to myself.

He grabs my wrist and yanks me to face him. "There's a cure for everything, Livia." His eyes look manic. "I need you to get through this. As my wife, you need to play the part." He releases me and runs a hand through his dark hair. "I can't have you screwing this up."

I glare at him, gritting my teeth together to stop myself from taking my rage out on him. "Fuck you," I say, walking toward the entrance without another word.

I hear his fast footsteps follow me, so I speed up my pace and head right through the door into the building.

He catches me once I'm two feet inside the building, yanking me against a thick column in the lobby. "Do you want me to welcome you to this center by fucking you right here in the lobby?"

My breath escapes my lungs as I stare into his serious face. "Definitely not." The receptionist didn't look up when we entered, but it would only be a matter of time before she heard us behind the column.

"Then stop being such a brat," he breathes.

I glare at him. "I'll stop being a brat when you stop being a controlling asshole," I spit.

He grabs my hips and forces me around, pressing me face first against the column. A shudder races down my spine as I feel the hard press of his cock against my ass. "You really are asking for it, printessa."

I swallow hard, shaking my head. "Maxim, this isn't the time or place." My heart races when I feel him hitching up the skirt of my dress.

"I'll decide when and where is the right time or place." He runs the palm of his hand over my ass cheeks, making me shiver in anticipation. The lobby of this place is large and sound echoes. He spanks my ass cheeks with firm yet quiet strikes, making me yelp. The only way to silence myself is to bite my lip so hard I break the skin, tasting the metallic tang of blood on my tongue.

"Maxim," I breathe in warning. "Let me go."

He rubs his hand over my panties, groaning as he does. "You're so wet right now."

My thighs shudder as I struggle to keep my knees from buckling.

"How about a parting gift, baby?" he asks, dropping to his knees behind me.

I almost die when I feel his tongue against the lacy fabric of my thong. "Maxim, stop it," I hiss.

Natually, he ignores me, pulling my panties down to

my knees and inhaling my scent like some kind of feral wolf. "You smell like sin," he groans.

I want to fight him, but the moment his tongue slides between my thighs, all reasoning melts away. I bite my lip to stop myself from moaning as his finger finds my clit, and he rubs, pushing me towards the edge faster than I've ever got there. Perhaps it's the fucked up situation, knowing that only fifteen yards away a woman is sitting behind a desk. It's wrong, it's fucked up, and that's what I like.

All I should feel right now is total rage for Maxim bringing me here at all. He doesn't understand what he could uncover by bringing me here. The darkness he could entice to the surface, leaving havoc in its wake. I want to hurt people, and that's what is fundamentally wrong with me. That's why I take the pills, to quieten the violence.

Maxim slides two fingers inside of me, making me bite my lip so hard I wonder if I'll need stitches. "You're such a good girl," he purrs, thrusting them in and out of my dripping wet pussy. "So wet and yet keeping so quiet." His voice is barely above a whisper.

I whimper, struggling to stop myself from moaning out loud as he fits another finger inside of me. Every muscle in my body tenses when I feel his tongue against my asshole. "What the fuck?" I hiss, as quiet as I can.

He groans, digging his fingernails into my ass cheeks hard, while his other fingers plunge in and out of me as he thrusts his tongue against such a filthy part of my body. It both arouses and disturbs me as he continues to send such a foreign sensation through me.

"I want you to come like the dirty little girl you are while I lick your ass right here in public," he breathes, his voice quiet and yet I fear too damn loud.

The pressure builds as he hits the spot that undoes me over and over, pushing me unwillingly toward the edge. I claw at the column in front of me, trying to control my reactions, but it's no good. Maxim thrusts once more and I can't stop the climax that hits me like nothing ever has. I moan, way louder than I should, biting my bloodied lip when I realize that sound came from me.

Maxim laps up every drop like a starving animal, licking me clean before sliding my panties back in place. His hard cock presses against my ass as he stands and molds his chest to my back. "Such a good girl," he purrs into my ear, sending an odd sense of pride through my chest at his praise, which makes no sense.

He spins me around and captures my lips, licking the blood from them as he does. "Now, let's get you checked in."

I yank at his collar and look him in the eye. "Don't leave me here, Maxim."

He raises a brow. "Sorry, printessa. You haven't left me with a choice." His hands slide to my hips and he squeezes. "Give me a good reason why, and I'll take you straight home."

I stare into those cold, emotionless eyes and know

there's no way in hell I'm baring my soul to him. He can't know how dark it is, how messed up I am. It would only give him power. No one knows the true me and I intend to keep it that way.

"Didn't think so." He yanks my wrist and pulls me toward the reception desk, where the receptionist looks up with bright red cheeks.

"How can I help you?" she asks, not looking either of us in the eye.

She knows what we were doing behind that column, which is humiliating.

"I'm here to check my wife in, Mrs. Livia Volkov," Maxim says, nodding toward me.

I don't think I'll ever get used to being called Mrs. Volkov. It sounds too weird.

The receptionist, whose name is Ally, types frantically at her computer. "Oh yes, one-week stay in our presidential suite, is that right?"

Maxim nods and hands over his credit card. "Yes, thanks."

She picks up her phone and dials a number. "Hi Jane, can you come down here to show Mrs. Volkov to the presidential suite, please?"

I lean toward Maxim. "Presidential suite. What is this, a hotel or a fucking rehab center?" I whisper.

He chuckles. "It's the finest rehab center money can buy, that's what it is." I shudder as he places a hand on the small of my back, tracing his thumb in circles over it.

It's an oddly intimate gesture, but one that unnerves me.

Ally puts the phone down. "If you take a seat, Jane, our resident support worker will be here in a moment to get Mrs. Volkov settled in."

Maxim nods and steers me toward the plush sofa in the waiting area.

I sink down and shuffle away from him, wringing my hands together. Somehow, I need to convince him to change his mind. I can't let him leave me here. "Isn't this a bad idea, because someone might find out and use it against you?"

He shakes his head. "I've been careful. No one will know."

I sigh heavily. "I can tell my father about this. Say you forced me in here."

He raises a brow. "And what will your father say when I tell him about the Fentanyl?" He taps his chin. "Since the stash I found had his name on the prescription label of the bottle."

Shit. He doesn't miss anything, which is irritating.

I avert my gaze, staring down at my hands. There's no way I'm going to be able to convince him to abandon his plan.

The clack of high heels echoes through the room as an older lady approaches. "Hello, I'm Jane." She smiles at me kindly. "You must be Mrs. Volkov."

"Livia, you can call me Livia."

She nods. "Will your husband be staying on for the tour?"

"N—"

"Yes, I will," Maxim cuts in before I can say no.

"Very well, follow me." She turns around and I jump up from the sofa, following her swiftly.

Maxim remains close to my side, but I'm thankful he keeps his hands to himself.

"The center has excellent facilities including an on site gym, spa, swimming pool and sauna," Jane explains, signaling down a corridor with a door to the leisure facilities. "As one of the most important steps to healing from addiction is to get exercise." Jane glances at me. "May I ask what addiction it is we're treating?"

I shake my head. "I'm not addi—"

"Painkillers," Maxim answers for me, silencing my plea. "Unfortunately, my wife is in denial that she has a problem." He doesn't look at me as he says that, holding Jane's gaze.

"I see. It's very common." She smiles at me kindly. "The other direction is the cafeteria, where we serve freshly cooked meals to order for breakfast, lunch, and dinner."

I nod in response.

"But I'm sure you'd like to see your room now?"

Maxim answers for me. "I think that would be best."

Jane pulls out a key and nods further up the corridor. "The rooms are down here."

We follow her out of the main corridor into what can only be described as a hotel style corridor carpeted in luxurious carpets with heavy wooden doors lining the left-hand side of the wall. "You're in our presidential suite, which is the largest." She comes to a stop at the end of the corridor in front of a door and opens it.

The room is like something from a five-star hotel, but if Maxim thinks that any of that is going to change how I feel about staying here, he's wrong. I don't care about fancy rooms and swanky gyms. All I care about is keeping the darkness at bay.

"I'll leave you two to say your goodbyes." She passes me the key. "Lunch is served in one hour."

"Thanks," I reply, taking the key and turning it over in my hand.

Once she's gone, Maxim takes a stroll around the room. "Not too bad, hey?" he asks, glancing at me.

"It doesn't matter if it's a fucking five-star hotel or a run-down motel. I don't want to be here."

He sighs and walks toward me. "I know, but it doesn't matter what you want. Addicts never want to kick an addiction."

I clench my fists by my side, ready to slam it into his too perfect face. "Seriously, Maxim. You'll regret this."

He raises a brow. "I've given you a chance to give me a viable reason why I shouldn't leave you here, and you haven't." He walks toward the open door and leans against the frame, a whisper of a smirk on his lips.

I glare at Maxim, hating him more than ever in that moment, as he's enjoying this.

"Don't look at me like that, printessa. You can't give me one reason I shouldn't leave you here, can you?"

I want to tell him, but that would give up my one weakness. If I told him the truth, he'd know every dark and twisted secret I bury deep within. Ever since my father made me torture people when I was younger, he awoken a beast that should never have ever existed inside of me.

Instead of dignifying his question with an answer, I glare at him.

He chuckles. "At least give your husband a goodbye kiss."

I'll give him a goodbye headbutt if he doesn't get the fuck out of my room. "I'd rather eat my own eyeballs."

He advances toward me. "Now, that, I don't believe for one second."

I tilt my head. "Well, you should, because if you come any closer, I'll hurt you."

"Oh that, I believe." He doesn't stop moving.

I stand from the bed and get ready to fight him.

However, he's too fast. One second he's a few feet away and the next he's got my wrists in his hand, pinned above me. "But I'm getting good at capturing you before you have a chance."

I slam my head forward, groaning as my forehead connects with his jaw.

"Now that, I didn't see coming," he growls, pressing his lips to mine in a forceful kiss. His tongue thrusts through my lips and he doesn't let my resistance stop him, which only turns me on more. I claw at his shoulders, trying to scratch the skin beneath his white dress shirt.

"Such a feisty woman, aren't you?" he breathes, breaking away to look into my eyes. "I'll miss fucking you for seven days, baby."

"Maxim, please don't leave me here." I hate the vulnerability in my voice.

"Are you begging me?" He genuinely looks surprised.

"No, I'm asking you not to do this as my husband."

He steps back and turns away, shaking his head. "As I said, you haven't given me one good reason not to. You have an addiction, and these people have a track record for helping people get over addictions." He shrugs as he glances back at me. "It's not personal, printessa. And you'll thank me when you're clean." He turns and walks out of the room, shutting the door behind him.

I won't thank him when this place unearths how dark my soul really is. Daughters of mafia bosses are supposed to be sweet and innocent. It's one thing my father fucked up during my upbringing. Allowing me to be privy to the twisted methods he used on enemies, as I became an addict to inflicting pain. At fifteen, he decided it was time for me to stop having a hand in the

Bianchi tortures, leaving me empty and broken. That's when I turned to pills.

There's no way I'll get my hands on any pills here, which means it's a matter of time until the staff uncover the truth. Once they do, I don't know what will happen. All I can hope is that blood doesn't run like a fucking river from this center before Maxim comes to collect me.

14

MAXIM

I sit in my office at the headquarters of Datatech Corporation, our legitimate holding group for the Bratva, staring blankly at the screen in front of me.

It's been six days since I left Livia at the rehab center. Each day, they've given me an update as promised. Unfortunately, she's been rather angry and antagonistic toward the staff. The staff believe she needs to remain in for far longer than a week, but I'm going out of my mind without her here.

I never thought I'd care whether she was with me, but it seems I got hooked on our rough and feral fucking. Ever since I sent her there, tasting her in the reception before leaving her, I've been insatiable, jerking off more than I did as a teenager.

There's no chance in hell I'm leaving Livia in there

for another month. I'll have her out tomorrow, and then she can attend group sessions for the anger and continue her sobriety. Not only because I want her back home, but because if she's gone that long, my family will ask questions. My father's birthday party is next week, and she's expected to attend.

Someone knocks on my door. "Come in," I call.

Artyom enters. "How's it going?" he asks.

I regard my uncle warily, as I don't trust him. "Fine. What can I do for you?"

He gestures to the chair opposite my desk. "May I sit?"

I'd rather he didn't, but I nod in response. We still haven't found out who leaked the news about my wedding to Livia, but I'd bet any money on my uncle being behind it. Although Timur is the best at what he does, Artyom is smart. He'll make sure nothing can link him back to the leak, which means we'll never find out for sure.

Artyom sits and crosses one leg over the other, leaning back. "Have you heard about your father's plan?"

I raise a brow. "Which plan are you talking about?"

"The one involving capturing one of the Morrone's relatives."

I hadn't heard anything about it, but I've been avoiding my father. Ever since I had to check Livia into rehab, I've wanted to make sure he had no reason to question me about her. If there's one person alive who knows when I'm lying, it's my father. "I'd heard something about it, but I don't know the details," I lie.

He leans forward, resting his elbows on his thighs and steepling his fingers. "Do you think it's wise when we're in the middle of war to aggravate tensions with an enemy who isn't even the one the war started with?"

I level my gaze at my uncle. "I think that my father's the wisest person I know." I cross my arms over my chest. "He wouldn't do anything that would jeopardize the Bratva, if that's what you're suggesting."

He shakes his head. "No, I just wanted your opinion on it."

"I think that hitting the Morrone family before they strike shows power." I run a hand through my hair, growing tired of my uncle's constant attempts to undermine his brother. "If Father thinks that the best option is to snatch one of their relatives, then I agree with him."

He leans back, nodding. "Fair enough."

When he makes no move to leave, I have to ask, "Is there anything else, Uncle?"

"How is married life treating you?" he asks.

I shrug. "Fine."

A smug smirk twists onto his lips. "Funny, I was told a woman fitting the description of your wife was seen at an exclusive rehab center in Geneva."

The blood rushes from my face as I stare at my

uncle, knowing that he couldn't have easily happened on that information. "Is that right?"

The bastard must have someone following me around. It's the only explanation. I haven't told a fucking soul about Livia being enrolled in rehab.

"Yes, apparently she's been there since last Sunday." He raps his fingers on the edge of my desk. "What exactly is she hooked on, Maxim?"

I grind my teeth. "I don't know what you're talking about, but whoever saw her must be mistaken."

He laughs. "Don't play me for a fool. I know she's there."

I stand, my fists clenched by my side. "Get out," I roar.

Artyom looks surprised by my sudden outburst, standing from his chair. "Calm down, I merely wanted to extend my concern for your wife and the state of her health."

I step around my desk, feeling adrenaline pump hard through my veins. "Get the fuck out before I throw you out." My nostrils flare as I clench my fists so hard I feel my bones crack.

He holds his hands up and nods. "Whatever you say, your majesty."

I growl at that, as he has always called me the little prince. It has pissed me off since I was a kid. Father says it's because he's angry I'm going to have first refusal for the throne over him and his sons when he's gone.

Artyom slithers out of my office like the snake he is, no doubt off to stir up trouble for me.

I have to get Livia out of there before he uses her weakness against me. One day early won't be the end of the world. I dig my cell phone out of my pocket and call the center.

"Hello, Geneva health and wellness center. How can I help?" the receptionist answers.

I clear my throat. "Hi, it's Mr. Volkov. I need to check my wife out today. Can you get her ready as I'll be there in—" I glance at my watch. "An hour and a half."

"One moment." I hear her typing on her keyboard. "It's not advised that we allow Mrs. Volkov to leave, especially not a day before the end of a short one-week stay."

"I don't care if it's advised or not. I paid a fuck load of money for her to go in there, and you're not stopping me from taking her out. Do you understand?" I practically growl at the phone.

There's a few moments of silence. "Yes, I understand. We'll have your wife ready, Mr. Volkov."

I cancel the call and ring my driver, Gregor.

"Sir, are you ready to leave?" he asks.

"Yes, I need to go to Geneva now. Can you pick me up outside?"

"Of course. I'll be parked out front in no more than two minutes."

"Perfect." I cancel the call and grab my briefcase from the side of my desk, rushing toward the elevator.

When it opens, my stomach dips. "Maxim, I didn't know you were here," Father says.

I shrug. "Had to do some work on the numbers for the Datahub merger."

"Are you leaving now?" he asks.

I nod. "Yes, I've got a dinner I've got to get to with my wife," I lie.

He steps out of the elevator. "Very well. I've got some things to catch you up on. Are you free for lunch tomorrow?"

I swallow hard, nodding. "Sure. Text me the details." I jump into the elevator before the door shuts, leaving my father without a goodbye.

The elevator crawls as it travels to the bottom floor from the thirtieth. It feels like I'm in there for twenty minutes, even though I know it's only a couple of minutes. Once it gets to the ground, I rush out as a few people crowd to get in.

The black town car is waiting for me. Gregor opens the door as I approach. "Afternoon, sir."

I nod at him. "Take me the fastest way you know to Geneva." I slide into the back.

Gregor senses the urgency in my voice as he's quick to shut my door and get us on the road. "Do you have an address?"

"Geneva health and wellness center. You should find it on the GPS."

Gregor uses the time stopped at a red to key it in, and then he drives in silence, leaving me to repeat the conversation with my uncle over and over in my mind.

Why the fuck does he care if my wife is in rehab?

I've known for a long time that Artyom can't be trusted, but if he was attempting to blackmail me with this information, I would fucking kill him. There's no way I'm being shaken down by my worthless, scheming uncle. However, if I tell my father, it means admitting to him that Livia indeed has a drug problem.

My father is more of a psycho than me. He wouldn't have put Livia in a rehab center, he would have chained her in his basement and beaten her black and blue until she promised to never touch the stuff again. I know how he works, and despite my desire to inflict pain, his methods would be too harsh.

The journey feels longer than an hour and a half. We may as well have been on the road all day, at least, that's how it feels. It's strange how eager I am to see my wife, touch her, taste her, fucking consume her. As the gates come into view for the exclusive wellness center, as they call it, although everyone knows that's code for a rehab center, I feel an easiness settle over me.

Gregor approaches the gates and rolls down the window. "Mr. Volkov is here," he says into the intercom.

The gates swing open and he navigates up the winding driveway toward the modern building, parking in front of it. "Stay here, Gregor. I won't be long."

"Of course, sir."

I get out and head inside, recalling the way Livia glared at me when I left her here. The hatred she had for me grew that day, and I relished it. The more she hates me, the more she fights. Instantly, I notice her sitting with her bags in the waiting area, her head hung low as she stares at the floor.

I swallow hard and approach the desk. "I'm here to check Livia out."

She nods. "Yes, she's over there, but she's not doing well." Her brow furrows. "The doctor wants to speak with you."

A doctor approaches, wearing a white coat. "Mr. Volkov, I assume?"

I nod in response.

"I'm concerned about Livia and her mental health." He glances down at a clipboard in his hand. "Although it's not a certain diagnosis, I've seen some telltale signs of OCD and anxiety while she's been here."

"Anxiety?" I question.

He nods. "Yes, it's rather concerning. I've only noticed mild signs, but I fear she keeps it at bay with the pills." His brow pulls together. "We had one rather groundbreaking session of hypnotherapy and it became clear to me she has very violent thoughts."

Violent thoughts.

I know exactly what that's like as I struggle to deal with rage daily, which manifests in some pretty fucked up thoughts. Although I wouldn't put it down to anxiety or fucking OCD. These doctors like to have a box to fit everyone into and it's bullshit.

Livia and I come from a violent world, so it's only natural that it's rubbed off on us. Perhaps we're more similar than I first believed. It would explain her desire to hurt me when we're intimate.

"Okay, well, I intend to take her to therapy, but I'm afraid she can't stay at the center any longer."

The doctor's jaw clenches, but he doesn't talk me out of it. Perhaps it's clear I've made up my mind. After all, the staff know who my family is. "Of course." He unclips the paper from his clipboard and passes it to me. "Please hand over my findings to her next therapist and perhaps in a few weeks she could return for a day session?" he suggests.

"Perhaps," I reply, but I've no intention of bringing her back here, not since I know my uncle has compromised this place.

I approach Livia, who is still staring at the floor as if she's broken. "Livia?"

She looks up at me, her green eyes look hazy and unfocused, so much so I wonder if they've got her on pills here.

"I'm here to take you home," I say.

Livia stands without saying a word, shouldering her bag.

"Are you okay?"

She shrugs in response.

I decide not to push her to speak here. I can talk to

her in the safety of my town car. "Come on," I say, gently steering her toward the exit.

Once we're outside, Gregor quickly takes her bag and opens the door for her. She slips inside without even a thank you. And as I stare after her, I wonder if I've broken my wife for good.

They were supposed to help her, not destroy her. I don't even recognize the girl who just got into my car.

15

LIVIA

*B**lood.*
It's all I can fucking think about. As I watch the lake that I spent six painful days living next to, all I can see is blood filling it. The blood I want to spill and rain terror down on the people who have caused me pain. Namely my father, but also the man sitting next to me.

He thought it was a good idea to get me off of those pills, but he does not know the monster he's unleashed.

"Livia," he says my name so gently, I'm not even sure it's my husband speaking.

"What?" I snap, not bothering to look at him.

"Are you okay?"

I laugh, and it sounds devilish to my own ears. "Okay?" I stare at him. The intensity of violence rolling under the surface of my skin is stronger than anything I've felt before. "What the fuck do you think?"

"I think I made a mistake putting you into rehab," he deadpans, no emotion in his voice.

"No shit, sherlock."

"What happened to you in there?" He places a hand on my thigh, gripping me too hard.

I tense, feeling like a viper ready to strike. "Get your hand off of me," I say, the warning audible in my voice.

His brow pulls together, but he doesn't remove his hand. "I'm worried about your mental health, Livia."

Mental health.

Ever since I was little, I always vowed I'd never be like my mother. Weak and depressive, even though she can't help it. "I don't have mental health problems." My eyes narrow. "I'm not my mom."

"You could have fooled me." He squeezes my thigh, reminding me he's still touching me. "I hardly even recognize you."

"I asked you to remove your hand," I repeat, glancing down at it on my leg.

"What exactly happened to you in there?"

That's when I snap. I hate people not respecting my wishes, and that's what Maxim is doing. I grab his hand suddenly and use all my strength to bend his fingers back. The crack of his bones breaking is beyond satisfying as he shrieks in pain.

"Fuck," Maxim growls, pulling his hand away. "You fucking psycho!" He holds his wrist as he stares at his broken fingers, face flushed in pain.

I shrug. "I asked you to take your hand off of me twice." I return my attention out of the window as the dark lake disappears in the distance. Breaking his fingers was the least he deserved for touching me when I told him to stop and for leaving me in that center.

"You're unhinged," Maxim says, using his good hand to press the intercom through to the driver.

"Sir?" the driver answers.

"Pull over and let me out of here," he says, pain lacing his tone.

"Right away."

I feel him swerve to the side as he pulls off the road onto the verge. Maxim glares at me, an odd expression on his face.

"What?" I ask.

He scoffs, shaking his head. "Is that seriously all you have to say?"

Suddenly, he lunges forward, wincing as he wraps his good hand around my throat so hard it's like he's trying to crush my windpipe. And yet, I can't find it in me to care or fight, staring into the blazing inferno in his eyes.

"Give me one reason I shouldn't squeeze the life out of you and leave you dead on the side of the road," he demands, nostrils flaring.

I don't have one. In some ways, the promise of a release from myself is refreshing. So I stare him in the eyes with no fear, accepting his wrath.

He growls as the driver opens his door, releasing my

throat. The driver looks concerned as he stares into the back of the town car, waiting for his boss to get out. He turns from me and slides to the edge, swinging his legs out the door. Slowly, he glances over his shoulder. "You'll wish you were never born when I punish you for this, Livia. Mark my words."

Bring it on.

He stands and I hear him say to the driver. "The crazy bitch broke my fingers. I'll need you to take me to the private hospital in Chicago and then run my wife home." He glances at me. "Lock the elevator and make sure she goes inside. I want you to stand watch outside of the front door until I return."

"Of course, sir." He bows as he speaks, which is amusing. The guy is old enough to be Maxim's father and yet he has to show him respect.

"I'll ride up front." Maxim slams the door of the car hard, making it rattle. He's angry that I stood up to him, but I don't care.

I stare down at my hands, wondering what I'm capable of. Are the sick thoughts in my mind truly who I am?

The longer I'm off the pills, the more out of control I feel. I fear Maxim might be right that I have mental health issues, which would be my biggest nightmare come true. All my life, I've vowed not to be like my mother, and perhaps that's exactly what I'll become.

I rest my head back on the leather headrest, shutting my eyes and releasing a shaking breath.

What the hell is wrong with me?

I broke my husband's fingers because he touched me. In my defense, I told him twice to get his hand off me and I'd warned him before, but it's clear that my desire to harm and maim people is a sickness. A sickness I need to cure, somehow.

The thing that scares me the most is that there may not be a cure for what I have.

All my life, I've been scared of becoming a headcase like my mother. As I stare at the dark privacy screen in front of me, the future I never wanted is quickly becoming closer to reality. The reason is the bastard behind that screen, the man I pledged to spend the rest of my life with until death do we part.

I should just kill him and be over with it. Then my problems would finally end, and I could return to Catanzaro to hide from the wrath of his father.

GREGOR IS an idiot if he thinks I didn't see the code he used to lock the elevator. Which means, while he stands watch dutifully outside for Maxim, I'm going to visit my mother.

It's been two weeks since I saw her, and I know that's too long. A part of me has been relieved not to have to deal with her unstable mood swings, but I know deep down my desire to visit her now is selfish. I want to find out if she, too, is plagued with the same violent thoughts I can't escape.

Could I have the same disorder as my mother?

It seems unlikely, considering I don't have those manic episodes followed by long periods of depression, and yet I fear that could be the way I'm heading. Without the pills to keep the demons at bay, who knows what could happen?

I grab my coat off the rack next to the front door and head toward the elevator, calling it. My Uber should be outside any minute. The keypad lights up red on the outside, expecting the code. I key in the code I saw Gregor put in earlier, nine, seven, eight, four and six. The panel turns green. My hands shake as I know the moment Maxim realizes I've escaped he won't just be angry, he might kill me. Or maybe I'll kill him first.

All I know is that I have to visit my mom. It's been too long since I last saw her and I need answers. I push the button on the elevator to take me to the parking lot level, where I intend to slip out unnoticed. As long as there aren't any guards in the parking lot, I should be fine.

The elevator crawls to the bottom and dings as it reaches the underground level, making my heart race. I clench my fists, waiting. A vision of Spartak standing there makes my stomach drop, but I let out a relieved breath when I see the parking lot is empty.

I head for the exit onto the street above, climbing the steps two at a time. My heart pounds as hard as my feet pound the concrete when I get to the top and push through the door. A quick glance in both directions up the street proves it's clear, and that's when I see a guy lingering by a blue ford focus. My Uber driver.

"Hey, Uber for Livia, right?" I ask.

He smiles and nods. "Yeah, get in."

I slide into the back of the car and rest my head back, letting the relief wash over me that I made it out of the house without getting caught. Maxim will lose his mind when he returns home, but I can't find it in myself to give a shit. He did this to me and now I need to find answers before it's too late.

The Uber driver takes a shortcut toward my family home, which I've barely spent a couple of days in since we moved just before the wedding. As he pulls up to the gates, I ask him to stop. "I can get out here, thanks."

"Are you sure?" he asks, eyeing the seemingly long driveway.

"Certain, thank you." I slide out of the car and stare at the gates, which are surprisingly not guarded.

I press the intercom and wait.

"Hello, who is it?" David, head of security, answers.

"It's Livia. I wanted to come and see mom. Is she home?"

There's a few moments of silence. "She is, but it's not a good day, Livia."

"When is?" I ask, shaking my head. "Can I come up, please?"

"Of course." The buzzer sounds and the electric

gates swing open, allowing me to walk up the twisting driveway.

David is sitting in a small security lodge at the top of the drive. "How have you been, Livia?"

I smile, but it feels forced. "As well as I can be." I turn my attention back to the gates. "I thought Father intended to station guards at the gate."

David nods. "He did, but not few of the men have arrived from Italy yet."

My brow furrows. "I thought they were supposed to arrive not long after my wedding."

"Unfortunately, your father is having a hard time convincing all of them to up and leave their homes." He runs a hand across the back of his neck. "Thirty have arrived, but he was expecting a hundred more than that."

I nod. "Well, I'm sure he'll convince them in the end." I give him a wave. "I'm going to head inside now."

He smiles. "Of course."

I walk toward the entrance of the grand home my father purchased. It's silly really since it's only him and Mom living in there, and my mom never leaves the confines of her bedroom, but it's all about status and image. The front door isn't locked and I push it open, finding the house eerily quiet. There aren't any staff to be seen as I head through the entrance hall and up the stairs, toward my mom's bedroom.

She hasn't shared a bedroom with my father since

we were kids, opting to save herself from the constant beatings. I come to a stop outside her door. A part of me wants to turn around and leave, as the thought of asking her the questions I have to ask makes me sick to my stomach.

Instead, I knock on the door and wait for a reply.

"Who is it?" she asks.

"It's me, mom, I've come to visit."

"Oh, come in," she calls.

I push open the door and find her at least out of bed, sitting on the sofa on the left side of her room with a book in her lap.

"It's so nice to see you, Livia. It feels like you've been gone forever."

I smile. "I know. I'm sorry I didn't come sooner."

She waves a hand at me dismissively. "Don't worry, come and have a seat."

I sit down next to her, fiddling with my hands in my lap. "How have you been?"

She shrugs. "Same old, really." There's a far off, sad look in her eyes. "I wish we never came here, Livia."

I'm surprised David said she was bad, as this is nowhere near as bad as I've seen her before. It makes me wonder if perhaps my father has been telling everyone she is.

I take her hand and squeeze. "Me too." A silence falls between us as I stare at my mom, wishing I didn't have to ask her about her illness. It's something we were always brought up to ignore and not talk about.

"Mom, can I ask you about your disorder?"

Her brow furrows. "Of course, love. It's only your father that bans us speaking about it."

I swallow hard. "I've been having some trouble, mentally."

"It's not a surprise after what that son of a bitch has put you through." There's a guilty expression in her eyes. "I'm sorry I was never capable of protecting you from him."

I shake my head. "It's not your fault, Mom." I release a breath and prepare myself for my next question. "With your disorder, do you have violent thoughts?"

Her brow furrows. "Violent in what sense, Livia? I never have thoughts of hurting people, if that's what you mean."

A flood of relief washes over me, but it's only short lived. As if my tendency toward violence doesn't mean I've also got bipolar disorder, what is wrong with me?

"I see," I murmur, brow furrowing.

"Do you have violent thoughts?" she asks.

"Sometimes," I breathe, hating how fearful I am of showing my true self. "It's been worse since I got married."

She pulls her cell phone out of her pocket in her gown and swipes before passing it to me. "He's the best therapist in Chicago." She sighs. "Go and see him if you want answers, love. Your father forbid me to go to my appointment I made next Tuesday, but I hadn't

canceled yet. You can take it if you want." Her brow
furrows. "I guess I was hoping that he'd change his
mind."

"He makes you worse and forbids you to get help.
Why don't you leave him?" I ask.

She laughs, sadness in the tone. "Your father would
never let me go, Livia and you know it."

I do, but I wish it weren't the case. "Why don't you
tell Father that we're going out shopping next Tuesday?" I suggest. "And then I can take you to the
appointment." I shake my head. "While we're there, I'll
make another one for myself."

"Really?" she asks.

"Yes, you need to go and see someone." I squeeze
her hand, noticing at that moment the book she had set
down. *The Bipolar Disorder Survival Guide.*

It angers me so much that she wants help, but my
father refuses to get her it. He refuses to accept that
mental health problems even exist, which is ridiculous.
You could force anyone to live with that monster for
long enough and they'd develop mental health
problems.

"Thank you, Livia." She smiles, and it's the first
genuine one I've seen since I arrived. "Why don't we
watch a movie together, like we used to?"

"Sure, sounds good." I grab a throw and pull it over
me, lifting my legs up under me. "What shall we
watch?"

"What about finding nemo?" she asks, knowing it

was my favorite when I was a kid. Sometimes, it's as if she doesn't realize I'm no longer twelve and a twenty-year-old married woman.

"Finding nemo it is," I say, settling in under the soft throw.

My mom smiles, selecting the movie on the TV. I'm beyond glad that I managed to escape my husband's clutches and get to see her today. Especially after what I did to him in the back of that car. I can't be sure what he'll do to me in retaliation, but I know it won't be good.

For now, I'm going to focus on the fact that I'm home and safe with my mom. Even if I know it won't last forever. This is the only place I'd go in the city and once Maxim realizes I'm gone, he'll come charging in here and drag me back home, that I'm sure of.

16

MAXIM

The doctor gave me a splint for my two broken fingers to help with healing, since Livia broke them. Luckily, she broke them on my left hand, which means I can still handle a gun, but it's going to make me less capable.

I had to tell my father that someone tried to mug us in the street and I broke my hand punching his face in. There's no way I'm ever letting anyone know that Livia is responsible. Gregor has sworn to me on his life he'll never tell a soul about what she did.

However, none of that matters. The problem is that my wife is clearly more unhinged than I am. This shit can't go unpunished. The rehab center may have uncovered her demons, but she's about to meet the king of hell and she'll bow, even if I have to break every part of her until she cracks.

I've seen some telltale signs of OCD and anxiety while she's been here.

I can't get that doctor's diagnosis out of my mind.

Clearly, the doctors at the facility were probably right in their deduction that she has some kind of mental health issues, but it's an undesirable weakness for the mother of my future children. It's a matter I'll have to cover up, no matter what. If it becomes common knowledge, enemies can use it against me.

I grind my teeth as I sit in the back of my father's town car, which he sent over to get me after I explained Gregor was looking after Livia. Hopefully, she won't have given him any trouble. I removed every pill from the house the moment I checked Livia into that place. She'll find no painkillers or any other form of drugs in the apartment.

Yury, my father's driver, pulls the town car into the underground parking lot beneath the town house. I don't want my injury to become public knowledge yet, so it's easier to go unseen from the basement.

He turns off the engine and gets out, opening the door for me.

I slip out and give him a nod. "Thanks, Yury." My brow furrows as I regard my father's driver. "Not a word to anyone about this, alright?"

"Of course, I won't breathe a word."

I clap him on the shoulder with my good hand and turn toward the elevator, ready to face my wife. The biggest thorn in my backside since I was fucking born.

If she thinks she can break my fingers and get away with it, she's mistaken. The elevator ride feels like an age as I thump my foot on the floor, waiting for it to arrive at the top. Finally, the bell chimes and the door slides open, straight into the front room.

The apartment is quiet. That's the first thing I notice when I enter. No sign of Livia in the open plan living area. Instead of searching for her, I head for the front door and open it.

Gregor looks surprised when he sees me. "All sorted now?" he asks.

I nod in response. "Doctor gave me a splint for my fingers." My brow furrows. "Any trouble with her since you left me?"

Gregor shakes his head. "No, she went inside without protest and I've heard nothing since."

"Okay, thanks. You can head home now."

Gregor gives me a nod. "Of course. Let me know when you need me next."

"Will do," I say, shutting the door on him.

I don't expect to leave this apartment for a few days at least, as that's how long it'll take me to exact my punishment on my wife. She'll beg for mercy once I'm through with her. The open-plan kitchen and living room are empty, so I move through toward the bedroom, assuming she's in there. I'm surprised to find the door wide open and no sign of my wife in the room or the adjoining bathroom.

My brow furrows as I turn my attention to the other

parts of the apartment, investigating the office and library, followed by the two guest bedrooms. All of them are empty. Livia has escaped, but fuck knows how. That's when it hits me. I asked Gregor multiple times before he left me to lock the elevator, but when I returned, it was unlocked.

I clench my fists and march toward the front door, ready to follow him out and pummel him into a pulp. "Gregor," I shout his name down the flights of steps, knowing he's probably already gone. When I don't hear a response, I pull my cell phone out and dial his number.

He picks up on the second dial tone, the distant sound of an engine in the background. "Is everything alright, sir?"

"No," I growl, pacing in and out of my front door. "Livia isn't in the apartment. I told you to lock the fucking elevator, and it's only just occurred to me that it was unlocked when I arrived."

There's a moment of silence. "I did lock the elevator, sir. I assure you."

I glare at the wall, hating it when people don't own up to their mistakes. "If that's true, how the fuck did she get out?" I ask, clenching my phone so hard it's a wonder it doesn't crack. "And why was it unlocked when I arrived?"

"Is it possible she could have known the code?" Gregor suggests.

I inhale a long breath of oxygen, shaking my head even though he can't see me. "Not unless you were stupid enough to key the code in front of her."

Gregor turns very silent on the other end of the phone. "Shit. She was in the elevator still, I think, when I locked it."

Fuck's sake. It's as if I can't rely on anyone. "Great." I cancel the call and walk into the apartment, slamming the door behind me. The CCTV from the elevator would corroborate his story, so I head into the locked security room off the kitchen. The screens show every entrance and exit of the building. I pull up the elevator footage from around the time Gregor and Livia would have arrived back, finding that Gregor does indeed lock it, but Livia watches him as he does.

Idiot.

I fast forward thirty minutes and see Livia dressed in a new pair of khaki pants and a beige sweater, unlocking the elevator and heading out of the apartment. "Fuck," I growl, shoving my hand through my hair.

The last thing I need is my wife on the run. I cast my mind back to the day after our wedding.

I think I'll visit my mom today.

Livia has been desperate to visit her mom since the day she arrived here, so that's where she'll be. I walk out of the security room, locking the door and head for the elevator.

Once I get my hands, or hand in my case since she fucking broke my fingers, on my wife, she'll wish she never stood up to me. I'll break every ounce of resolve she still clings to and test how tough my printessa really is.

I WALK UP the stairs of the Bianchi mansion, following the directions the security guard gave me.

Apparently, Livia arrived here over an hour ago and went straight to see her mother. For a woman who constantly perplexes me, she's oddly predictable. I push open the door without bothering to knock and I'm met with a rather unexpected scene.

Livia is curled up on the sofa with her mom, watching a movie, finding nemo, of all fucking movies. Her mom is next to her, wrapped in a thick, fluffy blanket.

I clear my throat, drawing Livia's attention over to me first.

Her eyes widen, and she pales a little. "What are you doing here?" she asks, startling her mom.

"Oh," Greta Bianchi says, jumping to her feet. "We weren't expecting company." She gives her daughter an uncertain glance. "Do you need to be somewhere, Livia?"

Livia opens her mouth to reply, but I cut in first. "Yes, she does. We have an important event to attend."

She scowls at me. "That's not true."

I cross my arms over my chest, ignoring the throbbing pain radiating through my hand. "It is." I give her mother an apologetic look. "I apologize for coming here like this, but it was a last-minute event."

Livia glares at me. "We're in the middle of a movie. I'll be home afterwards."

I shake my head. "Now, Livia."

Her mom pales at my tone, setting a gentle hand on her daughter's arm. "Perhaps we can finish the film another day, love." It's clear from her reaction that she's no stranger to a husband's wrath and is trying to protect her daughter by forcing her to give in. No one can protect Livia from the consequences of her actions earlier today.

She sighs heavily, realizing that she can't make a scene in front of her mom. "Fine." She points at me. "I'm coming back here next week to finish the movie."

I smirk at her, as she's going to be in no condition to visit her mom next week, but give a small nod in response. It's best not to make a scene in front of her mother, who I know isn't mentally stable.

Her mom's brows furrow as she notices my hand. "What happened to your hand, Maxim?" she asks, walking toward me.

I glance between Livia and her, knowing that even her mom can't know the truth. "I got into a bad fight with a mugger who tried to steal from me," I lie.

Livia's smirk is as irritating as the fact she broke my fingers, but I'll wipe it off her face soon enough.

"Oh, that's terrible! I hope it heals quickly."

I shrug. "Doctor reckons two weeks until the splint can come off, but another couple of weeks for my fingers to heal completely."

She nods. "Well, make sure you don't get in anymore fights."

Livia places her hand on her mom's shoulder and pulls her into a hug. "I'm sorry I couldn't have stayed longer, but I'll see you next week."

Her mom hugs her back and I notice her whisper something as she does.

When my wife pulls back, there are unshed tears in her eyes as she smiles at her mom, shaking her head. "I'm going to be fine," she says before turning her attention to me. "Let's go then."

I gesture to the door. "After you, printessa."

I notice the flash of irritation in her eyes at the use of her nickname, particularly in front of her mother.

"See you soon, love," Greta calls after us.

Livia gives her a wave and walks out the door, stomping on ahead of me.

I hasten my pace to keep close to her, breathing down her neck. The tension in her shoulders is evident as she moves down the stairs, because she knows what's waiting for her. A fuck load of pain. No one makes me hurt like that and gets away with it. I'm now practically useless in a fight for a month because of her, which isn't ideal when you're the heir of a powerful criminal organization during a fucking war.

I'll make her pay, I'll make her bleed.

If she thought I was a monster before, she'll wonder what nightmare she woke up to once I get her back to our apartment.

17

LIVIA

*M*axim's silence is fear provoking. It's crazy how silence from a man like him can set me on edge more than any words that come from his mouth.

I must have really fucked up his fingers, as he's got a splint binding two of them together. He sits in the car, keeping his distance from me as if he learned his lesson from earlier. As I observe him, it's hard not to notice the tension in his shoulders and back and how he sits unnaturally still. The only movement is the shallow rise and fall of his chest as he breathes.

I curl my fists into balls, hating that I fear what's coming next. Maxim isn't known for being a merciful man and I broke his fingers. Even if I think my actions were justified, I know he won't stand for them. He wants a meek, pliable wife who he can bend to his will, but he married a woman who can't submit or won't. A woman who struggles to contain her own violence daily.

The driver, who isn't the same man I duped earlier, pulls off the road and into the basement. I swallow hard, wondering if my actions led to the death of Maxim's regular driver, Gregor. I wouldn't put it past Maxim to take his rage out on his man.

"Where is Gregor?" I ask, not daring to look at Maxim.

Maxim stiffens next to me. "I'd already sent him home before I realized you'd run away."

A flood of relief washes over me, learning he's not dead because of what I did. I couldn't stand the guilt if he were. The driver cuts off the engine, making my heart race as I know the only thing waiting for me in that apartment is pain and suffering.

Maxim waits for the driver to open his door and slips out, not giving me the signal to follow. Instead, he stands and waits, expecting me to get out. I do, deciding not to provoke a man like him when he's like this. Once I'm stood next to him, he thanks the driver, whose name is Yury. He's considerably older than Maxim's driver, Gregor. He has to be in his sixties, I would say, with silver hair and a matching silver beard.

Maxim nods to me to follow him into the elevator. My legs are like jelly beneath me as I follow the monster into his den, knowing that nothing I say or do can save me now. Speaking with my mom helped, but I don't know how to contain the rage and violence brewing like a storm inside of me. I step into the elevator and stand a good distance from my husband as the doors shut, locking me inside with him.

He doesn't glance at me, staring forward in the most unnerving manner. If he were shouting and angry, I know I'd feel more at ease, as it's what I expect. This cold and calm demeanor is freaking me out. I'm ready for him to strike at any moment.

I tap my foot on the floor, hating how long the elevator takes to get to the top. The building isn't even that tall. Finally, it dings, signaling our arrival at the flat. It opens and Maxim steps out, but I hesitate, wanting nothing more than to ride it back down, run out of here and never look back. I shouldn't have gone home. I should have gone straight to the airport and got on a plane back to Italy, where he can't find me.

"Don't make me drag you out, princessa," Maxim says.

I swallow hard and step out of the elevator. Cowards run, and I'm not a coward. I wait, staring at his tense back.

"You broke my fingers." He turns around and meets my gaze. "As if you don't give a shit about who I am or what I'm capable of," he says, nostrils flaring as he remains frozen to the spot, staring at me.

"I asked you to remove your hand from me twice and you didn't." I shrug, trying to ignore the tug of warning in my gut about provoking him. "I think I was justified in breaking your fingers."

He growls, and it's a sound so feral I wonder if it came from an animal rather than him. "You'll regret it." He comes for me fast, and I do the only thing I know to do, lift my fists up, ready for a fight.

"Come near me and it won't just be your fingers that are broken."

He smirks, tilting his head slightly once he's one foot away. "If you try to hurt me, it won't work. I'm on very strong painkillers."

The word painkillers feels like a taunt, as he knows about my addiction. "Fuck you," I spit.

He laughs and shakes his head, advancing forward.

I punch him in the jaw, but he doesn't seem fazed. Instead, he grabs my wrist with his good hand and twists it behind my back, making me shriek.

"Let go of me!" I shout.

Maxim chuckles. "If you think this is bad, you have seen nothing yet, printessa." He keeps my arm twisted behind my back and pushes me toward the bedroom. "You broke two of my fingers. Did you think there wouldn't be consequences?"

I'd hoped I'd broken more, but unfortunately he still has limited use of his left hand with the thumb and two fingers I didn't break. "I wish I'd killed you instead."

He freezes at that, body turning stiffer than a board against my back. "You wouldn't dare."

I swallow hard, as I'm walking a dangerous line revealing the depths of my depravity to this man. A man who wants to hurt me for what I did to him. "You don't know me," I say.

He pushes me forcefully onto my back on the bed and masterfully, using one hand, claps the restraints fixed on the bedposts around my wrists.

I struggle against him, trying to overpower him, but he's too strong, too large. Before I know it, I'm trapped with nowhere to go as I stare at evil incarnate, wondering what I did to end up here, hitched to this son of a bitch.

He leaps off the bed and disappears into the bathroom.

I grind my teeth, staring up at the ceiling. If I could turn back the clock, I would have run before my father could have put me on the yacht over here. I'd still be happy, living a semi-normal life back in Catanzaro. Instead, I'm imprisoned by my own husband.

When Maxim returns, he's holding a small, serrated knife that sends my heart rate soaring but also sends a pulse of need coursing between my legs. "What are you going to do with that?"

His ice-cold eyes remain completely blank as he stares at me. "You get off on inflicting pain, so let's find out how much pain you can take."

I shudder as he moves toward me, trying desperately to get out of the restraints. The metal cuts into my skin, making me bleed, but I don't care. I need to get away from this man. "Don't you fucking dare!" I shout.

He stops a foot from the bed and throws his head

back, laughing. "Don't I dare? You're the one who broke my fingers for putting my hand on your goddamn thigh." He shakes his head. That dark rage I'd been looking for in the elevator rising to the surface. "You were the one who told me you wished you'd killed me. Wife or not, no one gets away with what you did to me today."

My body shakes as he gets onto the bed, looming over me. He uses the knife to slice my sweater in two—my favorite fucking sweater. "What the fuck?"

He tilts his head, but continues to cut my clothes from my body. "If you think me cutting some clothes off you is fucked up, wait until I explore how high my little printessa's pain threshold really is." He presses the cold metal of the knife against my skin, sending shivers down my spine.

A dark, depraved voice in my head is goading him on, chanting for him to cut my flesh. I want to see myself bleed. I want to watch while this man who's as dark and fucked up in the head as I am, do his worst. Fuck the pain, I want release. "Do it," I spit.

He smirks and makes a soft tutting sound. "Patience, Liv," he murmurs.

I ignore the use of the name I hate so much, the name that reminds me of my father's abusive behavior. Instead, I focus on the shields around my mind. Maxim may think he can break me, but I won't let him. Deep down, I think I knew this would happen. Maybe it's exactly what I wanted, to unmask the true man I married and see every ugly, twisted part of him bared to me.

He gets to my panties and gently drags the knife through the fabric, cutting them from me but not grazing my skin. The man is masterful with a knife, which makes me wonder how many women he's done this to before. A sensation like a punch in the gut hits me as I watch my husband as it rolls over me in waves, heating me from the inside out. It feels a lot like rage, but that's when I realize the sensation is jealousy. Unexplainable jealously over all the women that came before me. All the women that had my depraved, evil husband.

He cuts off my bra, flinging the ruined fabric onto the floor. Maxim groans, eyes showing an ounce of emotion—desire. Even after I broke two of his fingers, he still wants me. "Such a beautiful woman, aren't you, Livia?" he muses, running the serrated edge of the knife over my skin so gently it makes me shiver. "I think you want me to cut you," he breathes, running the knife gently around my nipples in a way that makes it impossible not to moan in pleasure. As he drags the knife gently, he leaves pink marks in its wake. Small scrapes in my skin, but he's not gone deep enough to cut yet.

"Bullshit," I spit, denying that I want this, even though deep down I do. I want him to hurt me.

He brings the tip of the knife to his lip and taps it there. "Why is your pussy so wet, then?"

I shudder as I try to squeeze my thighs together,

forgetting he's restrained my ankles too. I'm spread open for him and I have no way of hiding how fucked in the head I really am. "That doesn't mean shit."

He moves the knife and slides the tip gently through my soaking wet folds, making me gush more. It makes him chuckle. "I think that you're a dirty little slut who can't wait to feel my knife cut open your skin." He holds my gaze and moves the knife to my stomach, trailing those pink scratches into it. "I think you want to watch yourself bleed."

I search Maxim's eyes, wondering if I'm that easy to see through. How can a man like him look into the darkest depth of my soul like that? "Is that what you want?" I breathe, my chest heaving frantically in anticipation.

He groans, cock straining against his pants. "I want to cut you, Livia. I want to watch as the blood drips from your wounds and then lick it all off." He slides the metal over my breasts, increasing the pressure. "And then I want to fuck you while you bleed from the marks I inflicted. I want you to scream in pain and pleasure while I punish you for what you did."

Most people would fear the acts Maxim is describing, and yet the sickness inside of me craves it. "Do it then," I spit, feeling unashamedly desperate to feel the metal slice through my skin.

He shakes his head and uses the tip of his knife to lift my chin; the pressure drawing blood as he does. "Do you really think you deserve any of that after what you did?"

I whimper, like a fucking junkie being denied crack. "Please, Maxim," I beg, hating the desperation in my voice.

"No," He says coldly. "You don't get to enjoy your punishment." He turns his back to me and drops the knife on a nearby chair. "You don't get to beg me for anything." I watch as he disappears into the bathroom, slamming the door and leaving me utterly broken as I stare at it. The promise of pain was so close I could taste it, and then he ripped it away.

A tear escapes my eye and trickles down my cheek, as I feel more helpless than ever. My punishment is going to be far more torturous than I ever expected for all the wrong reasons. My husband knows what makes me tick, and he's exploiting it, making me pay for standing up to him.

18

MAXIM

"What the fuck did you do?" I ask, pacing up and down the length of the warehouse, shaking my head.

My father has gone rogue.

I glance back up at the young Italian girl strung up by her wrists in the center of the abandoned warehouse. "And why the fuck didn't you consult anyone first?"

My father crosses his arms over his chest, standing tall as he walks toward me. "Who do you think you're talking to, Maxim?"

I narrow my eyes. "This is Remy Morrone's niece." I point out, shaking so hard I can hardly believe how angry I am. "We had enough on our plate trying to fight the Irish, but you open fire on the fucking Italians too?"

My father snaps, slamming his fist hard into my jaw. "Remember your place," he growls, eyes flashing with that fierce rage I grew to fear as a child. "I don't have to consult anyone before doing anything." His eyes snap to the innocent girl strung up in his basement. "They needed to be sent a warning about trying to bring in reinforcements from other cities."

"How is this going to get them to back off?" I ask, knowing I need to take a more diplomatic approach rather than attack his decision head on.

"Because I'll snatch one of their family members on a weekly basis until they agree to a truce." His jaw clenches as he keeps his gaze fixed on the girl. "We've no reason to go to war with them, but I won't stand by while they become stronger right under our noses."

I don't point out that he's being a fucking hypocrite, considering that's what he's doing with Vito. Instead, I turn my attention to the girl. She's knocked out and hasn't woken up yet to the nightmare that has become her reality. My father is sick, even by my standards. He'll do unspeakable things to her, that I'm sure of.

"Does this girl even have any part to play in any of this?" I ask.

His nostrils flare. "She's Remy's niece. That's the part she plays."

"You can't choose your family," I murmur under my breath.

"What was that?" he snaps.

I shake my head. "Nothing, you do what you want, Father. Why did you ask me here? I thought we were having lunch."

"A change of plan. I want to show you something instead." He paces away from the girl toward the back office. "I want to discuss a different matter."

I follow him reluctantly, glancing back once more at the woman. She can't be a lot older than me, maybe twenty-six years old, but she's going to be lucky to walk out of here alive after my father's through with her. "Where are we going?" I ask.

"Quit asking questions and follow me." He walks past the office and out into the main yard, leading me toward the dock.

A large vessel is docked there, which my father approaches. Someone I don't recognize disembarks and I watch as my father goes to greet him.

I approach warily, sensing my father's about to drop another bomb on me.

"Come and see our new cargo," he says, smirking.

I narrow my eyes and approach the back, where the guy climbs up the steps toward a shipping container.

We follow, but I have a bad feeling before I even see this *new cargo*.

He unlocks the back door and slides it open, and I step forward to see it full of young women, looking beyond frightened, gagged and bound.

"What the fuck?" I ask, glaring at my father, who has clearly lost his mind.

He nods at the guy who slams the door shut and locks it. "Leave us."

I clench my fists by my side. "We don't deal in flesh."

Father crosses his arms over his chest and although he's an inch shorter than me, he still makes me feel small. "Now we do. The Morrone family make a killing in trafficking and we need to get in on the action."

"Why do that when we make more money with drugs and it's not so messy? Those girls have families that will look for them."

He shrugs. "Drugs are lucrative, but if we want to expand, then this is the way to do it."

I sigh heavily. "I thought we agreed we'd expand into arms, since Timur was an arms dealer before he joined the Bratva." I stand taller, glaring at the man who lately is off his head with the decisions he's making. "Who has any experience in our outfit with trafficking?"

"Artyom," he says.

I wince at the mention of my uncle, knowing that if he's behind this, then it's definitely a bad idea. "I don't trust him, even if he's your brother. Never have and never will."

Father chuckles. "Me neither. Why else do you think I have Osip's men surveilling him around the clock?"

I raise a brow. "Really?"

He nods. "Yes, I'm not stupid enough to think he doesn't want the crown. He's been after it since we were teenagers."

I nod reluctantly. "Fine, but I don't like this." I

shake my head. "We're not slavers and never have been."

"Don't worry, we're only dealing in high end girls. They'll want for nothing. You can hardly say they'll be slaves."

My father lacks morals on a fundamental level, but stooping this low is beneath me. I'm all for making money and I don't care who I have to hurt to keep the organisation safe, but selling innocent women goes a step too far. If he keeps on this path, I'll be unable to stand by it. "I don't like it."

"Don't be a fucking sissy, Maxim." His jaw clenches. "I taught you to have thicker skin than to piss yourself over a few women being sold."

A tingle races down my spine as he means the abuse he subjected me to as a child—apparently that should have given me thicker skin. It did, but it also ignited a rage I sometimes struggle to control inside of me and a deep hatred for the man who raised me. "This isn't the Volkov way." I cross my arms over my chest. "Since when do we go around copying our enemies?"

My father scrubs a hand across the back of his neck. "Since their power has increased, unchecked, while war wasn't on the cards. The Irish may have started this war, but we both know they're not the true threat to us. There are only two real players in the war and it's us and the Italians."

I raise a brow, as my father is underestimating the Callaghan's power in this city as well as the Estrada

Cartel, who are remaining impartial for now. For a couple of years, as he slowly eased me into the business, I've learned that my father isn't the most level-headed when making decisions. He's impulsive and reckless more often than not, which makes standing by his decisions difficult.

"I've got to go," I say, turning my back on him.

His hand shoots out and lands on my shoulder, yanking me to face him, hard. "Remember your place, boy," he growls, fists clenched by his side. "You don't turn your back on me unless I dismiss you."

I clench my jaw, staring into his familiar eyes—eyes that remind me of my own. "I apologize, but I'm late for a meeting with Timur to discuss Andrei's reaction to us cutting him off."

Father's brow furrows. "What reaction?"

I slide my hand into my pocket and pull out a letter from him, passing it to my father. "He's not happy."

My father is silent as he reads, his face turning redder as he does. "That fucking piece of shit," he growls as he finishes, thrusting the letter into my chest. "Why didn't you tell me about this?"

"Because I don't tell you every little thing that happens, Father." I slide the paper back into my pocket. The main reason I didn't come to him with this is because he's not diplomatic enough.

Andrei has basically issued threats on our territory if we don't reconsider our decision to cut New York off. His advancements on territory have slowly come grinding to a halt after his failed attack on the Gurin Bratva's pakhan in Boston. No one trusts the guy anymore, and this letter is merely a desperate ploy to force us to change our mind.

"I'm the pakhan of this Bratva, and if something as significant as a threat from the Petrov Bratva lands on your desk, you come to me first, do you understand?" He asks, poking his finger into my chest.

I nod. "Yes, I merely thought Timur was best at dealing with this. After all, it's only words. He wouldn't dare attack us here in Chicago unless he has a death wish."

My father's nostrils flare, and he shakes his head. "You don't know Andrei and what he's capable of." He spins around. "Report to Timur and get his opinion on how to handle it. I want a meeting setup for tomorrow morning to discuss this."

"Sure," I say, glancing at my watch. "I'm going to be late—"

"Go," he says, waving his hand dismissively. "I'll see you tonight at the party."

My stomach dips as I almost forgot about his party tonight, and I forgot it's his birthday today. "Of course, S dnyom rozhdeniya." I wish him a happy birthday in Russian and turn away, walking back through the warehouse and passing the young woman, who is still unconscious.

I try not to look at her as I walk away from the madness that my father is concocting. He's going too far, stealing innocent women from their homes to turn them into sex workers. It's sick—sicker than even I can handle. I always wondered how the Morrone family justify it, but I guess they've been into selling people for years, so it's second nature to them.

It's not the Volkov way, and yet I'm powerless to stop it. What use is it being the prince of the kingdom, if I have no power over what our family does?

Timur agrees I should have kept Andrei's threat from my father, but unfortunately, it's too late. He's going to set up the meeting for tomorrow morning, and we'll discuss it then. It turns out I wasn't the only one he kept the new Volkov trafficking ring from either, as Timur did not know of it.

I loosen my tie as the elevator rises to my apartment. Six days have passed since my wife broke my fingers. Six days of torturing her and denying her when she begs me.

I know what she wants, for me to hurt her and fuck her. I've resisted for these past six days because she needed to be taught a lesson after breaking my fingers. There are always going to be consequences to her actions with me. However, I know my willpower is waining. I've had to take matters into my own hands too many times to count in the last six days.

The elevator door opens and I step into the apartment, which is quiet and empty since I lock Livia in our bedroom whenever I'm not home since she returned from the retreat. She can't be trusted alone in the apartment.

I head toward the bedroom, knowing that tonight I'll finally give us both the release we crave. There's no sound on the other side as she's been sleeping a lot in the day, so I grab out the key and slide it into the lock. I push the door open, surprised when I see the room is empty.

"Livia," I call out.

"In here," she replies, her voice carrying from the adjoining bathroom.

For a second, I wondered if my printessa had escaped. Relief floods me hearing her sweet voice and I step toward the bathroom, pushing open the door. Panic hits me at the scene in front of me.

Livia is lying in the bath full of blood-stained water. It looks worse than it is as blood and water always make for a horrific sight, as I notice the non-lethal cuts etched into the skin on her arms, purposely cut vertically.

I rush toward her, my heart thudding at a hundred miles an hour in my chest. "What the fuck are you doing?" I growl, feeling my entire body tensing as I glare at the wounds she inflicted, wounds I should have given her.

She smiles at me, looking a little manic in that moment. "You wouldn't do it, so I got desperate."

I reach down and lift her out of the bath, ignoring

the ache at the pressure on my two broken fingers and the bloody water that stains my thousand dollar shirt.

She laughs, sounding almost high on drugs. "What are you doing?"

My nostrils flare as something that feels like guilt twists my gut, making me feel sick. I pushed her too far. A woman who experts warned me was showing signs of mental health issues in that rehab center.

What the fuck was I thinking?

I swallow hard and hold her against my chest, not caring about the blood soaking into my shirt.

"I'm sorry," I breathe, an apology that I'm not sure she even hears. I can hardly believe I am apologizing to her, as I never apologize. Slowly, I carry her back into the bedroom, setting her down in the center of the bed. "Wait here."

"Where am I going to go? I'm a fucking prisoner," she spits.

I swallow hard, rushing into the kitchen in search of the first-aid kit. This is my fault, and that's what I can't get over. Sex was never complicated before I got married. It was a transaction that gave me no liability to the damage done, even though some women didn't take me seriously about how brutal I could be. I had a few complaints of sexual assault, one who tried to take me to court, but I gave all of them fair warning about what they were getting into.

I return to the bedroom, where Livia is sitting up.

Her eyes find mine, and they appear completely lucid. "What the fuck are you doing?"

"I'm going to patch you up." I hold up the first aid kit.

"Don't be a fucking pussy, they're hardly scratches." She jumps off the bed, buck naked, folding her bloodied arms over her chest. "Why don't you lick the blood off like you teased you would repeatedly?"

My mouth salivates at the suggestion, but it only calls to question what the fuck is wrong with me? I drove my wife to self-harm, and she's standing there goading me to make good on my promise and bask in the sickness of it all. I should get her help, not fuel both of our twisted desires, and yet I'm powerless to resist the temptation.

"Is that what you want?" I ask, stepping toward her. "You want me to lick the blood off of you?" I feel my cock harden at the mere thought. "You want me to chuck you on the bed and fuck you, getting your blood all over both of us and the bed?" Although the wounds aren't bad, the water from the bath makes it look like she's covered in it.

She groans, eyes flickering shut as she clenches her thighs together. "I want you to stop teasing me," she breathes.

"My wife is as twisted as I am," I murmur, reaching out and sliding my fingers into her damp hair, yanking her toward me with it. "Such a twisted, complex little thing," I breathe.

Her eyes dart open, the pale green almost glowing now. "Stop teasing and do it."

I kiss her lips, enjoying the softness against my own. It's been too fucking long since I indulged in her.

She moans, clawing at me as if she's been needing this to survive—needing me. I drown in her desperation, allowing her to scratch me, bite me, hurt me as much as she wants.

I rest my injured hand on her hip, keeping my other hand firmly in her hair and yanking her head back. "Lie down."

Those beautiful eyes flash, but she doesn't refuse my order and lowers herself onto the sheets. I follow her onto the bed and lift her left arm first, gently dragging my tongue down the cuts she's etched into it with the razor blade, enjoying the metallic tang. "Do you like me acting like a feral animal, baby?" I ask, watching as her breathing speeds up with each lap of my tongue.

She nods, her throat bobbing.

I groan as I lift her right arm and do the same, cleaning the wounds on her skin. I should have been the one to mark her. Even though she's right, the cuts are shallow and unlikely to leave permanent scars. I kiss a path up her stomach, licking and nipping at her soft skin. "I've missed this," I breathe, hating to admit it.

Livia is like my pain killer. A drug I can't quit, no matter how badly she wants to hurt me. It's as if, for the times while we're intimate, she heals some of the sickness, or makes it bearable at least.

She doesn't speak, pushing her hips toward me in a silent plea.

I can't take my time with her, but I don't think that's what she wants. Quickly, I remove my clothes and chuck them off the bed, setting my arms on either side of her head as I can't prop myself up with my left hand.

She moans as my cock nudges at her entrance. "Please," she breathes, clawing at my neck viciously.

I groan, as it's the first time she's begged me for my cock. The stubborn woman who walked through those doors on our wedding night is no longer recognizable as she stares up at me, lips swollen, blood coating her skin and a flush in her cheeks that drives me wild. She's desperate and needy and so fucking sexy.

I slide my hips forward, thrusting into her soaking wet cunt. In that moment, everything else fades away and it's the two of us, submitting to our mutual, twisted desires and submitting to the hatred we feel for the world.

Livia digs her fingernails hard into my back, clawing them down my shoulder blades so hard I'm sure she'll leave scratches. "Fuck me," she breathes into my ear, moaning as I roll my hips with harsher, faster movements. "I want you to break me apart."

I groan, unable to believe the violence that Livia harbors inside her. A deep and dark need to hurt and maim, which can only be born out of an abusive past. It irritates me that a part of me wants to know more about my wife, to connect with her on another level. "Such a good girl," I purr, as I dig my nails of one hand into her hips and flip us over, so she's straddling me. "Ride my cock, printessa." I rarely ever have sex in this position, but it feels right.

She drags her nails down my chest, leaving pink marks as she rolls her hips hard and fast. Her body moving fluidly above me as if she was made for this. Her beautiful breasts jiggle with every vicious roll of her hips.

"You look so fucking sexy like this," I breathe, grabbing one of her breasts in my good hand and squeezing.

Her head falls back as she moans, picking up the tempo as she fucks herself on me.

I run my hand further up from her breasts and wrap my fingers around her slender throat, choking her.

A soft whimper escapes her lips as her eyes fly open, connecting with mine. A blaze of bright green fire staring at me, daring me to push her further, choke her harder. If there's one thing I've learned about my wife in the last few weeks, it's that she loves pushing her limits.

I flex my fingers around her slender neck, squeezing a little harder as she continues to rise and fall on my cock, moving frantically above me as she chases her orgasm.

"Fuck, you look so good riding my cock, baby," I

say, squeezing a little tighter but knowing that I'm not going too far.

Livia's eyes flicker shut and her mouth falls open on a silent scream. She shudders above me, her arousal dripping over my cock and balls as she comes. It's all it takes to make me explode. My cock being squeezed by her tight cunt forces every drop of seed from my balls to spill deep inside of her. It's the most intense orgasm I've ever felt.

I thrust my hips into her, fucking her through the orgasm as I continue to keep my hand around her neck. We're sick fuckers, I realize at that moment, looking at the mix of her blood and bathwater smeared over her breasts and my chest. And yet, I can't find it in me to give a shit.

19

LIVIA

I gasp for air, unsure whether it's because of the intense orgasm my husband coaxed from me or because he choked the air from my lungs. As more time passes, I think I'm becoming addicted to this twisted, intimate game we're playing. He's forced me to kick one addiction, but it's only been replaced by another.

I collapse next to him, placing my hand where his hand was, trying to sort through my muddled thoughts.

We're both clearly fucked up, as my blood is on his chest and face, since it spread everywhere mixed with the bathwater. I don't understand when I became this twisted in the head, but it seems Maxim brings out the worst in me.

"Let's get washed up," he says, grabbing my hand and yanking me out of bed.

I'm too exhausted to fight him, so I let him drag me

into the bathroom, where he turns on the waterfall shower. He pushes me beneath the water, his hands moving gently over my wounds as he washes away the blood from my skin.

I shudder, feeling vulnerable as he washes me gently, almost tenderly. It's easier when he's vicious and brutal, but this makes my stomach flutter in ways I don't want it to.

"Do I need to remove the razors from the bathroom in future?" he asks.

I shake my head. "Not if you let me out of this room and stop locking me up like an animal." I've never had thoughts of self-harm, but he made me desperate. It's crazy what you can be driven to when you're desperate.

He nods and continues to clean me, grabbing the soap and squirting some on his palm before lathering it all over my body. "I'll allow you out on one condition," he breathes into my ear.

I hate the way my heart flutters in my chest. "What condition?"

His touch sends fireworks blistering over my skin as he moves lower toward my center, which I try to ignore. "Never cut yourself again," he murmurs into my ear.

My nostrils flare as I glance over my shoulder at him. "Why? Because you want to be the one to do it?"

"Exactly," he says, washing off the rest of the soap. "You're mine, after all."

"I don't belong to anybody," I reply, but my

response is more feeble than normal. Deep down, I think I know he's slowly staking a claim on me and I can't stop it, no matter how hard I try to resist.

He's quick to clean himself, and I don't offer to help. After all, I have to remind myself of the monster he is. The man who forced me into rehab and forced the demons to the surface. A man who doesn't understand and never could understand how dark my soul is.

"Come on," he says, shutting off the shower and yanking me out. Maxim grabs a thick, plush towel and wraps it around me, allowing me to dry myself.

Once dry, I walk back into the bedroom and head toward the closet.

"Wait," he says.

I freeze on command, irritated that my body responds to his order at all.

"Let me bandage your arms."

I swallow hard. "I told you—"

"Now, Livia. Sit on the bed."

I clench my fists, but go to sit on the edge of the bed.

Maxim sits down next to me, his ice-blue eyes giving away nothing as he grabs the first aid kit. He bandages the cuts on my arms gently, and I feel an odd pang in my chest as I watch him work. This man who tortured me for the past six days, pushing me toward the edge without a care in the world, is being gentle and it freaks me out.

I don't know what he expected me to do, but I was

going fucking crazy locked in here. I needed the pain he promised to give me and then denied me every time, so I took matters into my own hands.

"There," he says, finishing tying the bandage. "Luckily, I think you have a few long-sleeve dresses in the closet."

My brow furrows. "What for?" I ask.

"My father's birthday party is tonight and we're expected to attend."

My stomach dips at the thought of attending a social gathering. "I'd rather not."

Maxim sighs. "Let's not do this, Livia."

"Do what?" I ask.

"Fight about this." He squeezes my hand, bringing it to his lips and kissing the back of it. "I have to attend my father's birthday party, and I can't attend without you."

I twist my fingers together in my lap, hating the idea of mingling with his friends and family. "Will my father be there?"

Maxim shrugs. "Possibly. I'm not sure if my father invited him."

The last thing I want is to see that son of a bitch. I'd rather go through the rest of my life and never see him again after what he subjected me to. He's derailed my world by shipping me to a country I can't stand and forcing me into a marriage with a man who is as sick in the head as I am. "I don't want to see him."

Maxim packs away the first aid kit, brow furrowing. "What did he do to you?"

I tense at the question, warning prickling at the back of my neck. "What do you mean?"

My husband gives me an irritated glare. "You hate your father. That much is clear, so what did he do to inspire such hatred?"

I swallow hard. "I'd rather not talk about it."

Maxim shrugs. "Perhaps it would help to get it off your chest."

It may well help, but there's no way I'm revealing myself to this man—a man who wants power over me. "No, thanks." I stand and walk toward the closet. "I best find a dress, then." I walk into the walk-in closet and start looking through the dresses which Maxim had purchased for me in my size. There are only two with long sleeves. A simple black maxi length gown and a pink fabric gown with a v-neck line.

I swallow hard, preferring the pink one, but knowing the black will draw less attention to myself, and that's all I want. So I reach for the black one, only for Maxim to grab my hips and jerk me backward. "The pink one, printessa."

I shake my head. "No, it doesn't suit me."

He presses his lips against my shoulder and bites down hard. "It suits you more than the black."

"The pink draws attention and is showy. I want to blend into the shadows," I reply.

He bites my earlobe. "Put on the pink one," he orders.

I tense against him, knowing that submitting to him will only set a precedent. "No."

His tongue darts down the center of my back, sending shivers through me. "Still playing hard to get, even though you begged for my cock?" he asks.

I shake my head. "No, it's called having some fucking control over my own life. I like the black, so that's what I'm wearing."

"Is it?" Maxim asks, tracing his tongue back up the length of my spine. "You're my wife, Livia. Heiress to the Volkov Bratva and you won't blend into the shadows, no matter what you wear. Put on the pink." He squeezes my hip before leaving me alone, naked, and staring at the two dresses.

I grind my teeth together, knowing that he's right. Many members of his family I'm yet to meet, which means I'll be paraded around and introduced to everyone. Even though I like the pink more, the part of me that wants to melt away and not be seen longs for the black. It's like I'm fighting myself and him in this decision.

Fuck it.

I grab the pink one and step into it, not bothering to put on underwear. Then I look at myself in the mirror, shuddering as I look into my own eyes. I hardly recognize myself, but perhaps that's because for almost two weeks now I've been off the painkillers. The violent thoughts I've spent years trying to bury have become more regular and yet I don't feel out of control, as I feared I would.

I feel empowered by my thoughts, finally free to be myself. There's an odd sense of power that comes with freedom. Even if my husband has spent the past two weeks keeping me locked away, he's released the true Livia Volkov. The question is, will he live to regret it, or perhaps not live to regret it?

I fear the violence we toy with will only escalate, which means one of us may end up a casualty. If I have anything to do with it, it won't be my death ending our marriage vows.

I walk out of the closet and bedroom toward the living room, wearing the pink dress.

Maxim's smirk is enough to make me want to walk over to him and smack it right off of his face. "I knew that was the one you preferred," he says.

My brow furrows. "What do you mean?"

"I'm not stupid enough to believe you put that dress on because I ordered you to, Livia." He runs a hand through his neatly styled hair, his eyes glinting with a mischief. "You wanted to wear the pink one. You just needed a nudge in the right direction."

A shiver travels down my spine, as it's as though he can see right through me—right through the bullshit I try to hide behind. "Whatever," I say, grabbing the gold clutch I picked out and placing my cellphone in it.

Maxim sneaks up on me, wrapping his arms around

my back and pushing me into the elevator. "You look so beautiful that I have half a mind not to attend this party and spend the entire night fucking you," he murmurs, as he selects the basement level on the call buttons.

"I think your father would be less than impressed if you didn't turn up to his birthday party."

He licks my earlobe, sending a shiver down my spine. "But what would you think?" he asks.

I swallow hard, knowing I'd prefer to spend the night tangled up in my husband rather than forced to smile and be polite to people I don't know. "I'd say I'd rather fuck you than socialize any day." I feel him smirk against my skin.

"Are you admitting that you want me?"

"I'm admitting that fucking you is more agreeable than going to a party full of people I don't know." I spin around, gazing into his ice-blue eyes. "If you think that means I want you, then that's your problem."

He laughs, and it's the most genuine laugh I've heard from him. "I know you want me, printessa." He bites my collarbone, making my back arch. "I can practically smell your arousal." He moves his hand up my thigh and groans when he slips his finger through my soaking wet entrance. "And you didn't even wear panties. How thoughtful of you?" He kisses me chastely, nipping my lip as he pulls away. "Perhaps if you're a good girl, I'll eat this pretty little pussy in the back of the car and make you come all over my face. How about that?"

I moan. The mental picture of him getting me off in the back of the car turns me on more than it should have. Before I can say anything, the elevator door opens.

"It's a deal, baby," he breathes, pushing me out of the elevator toward his town car, which has the engine running already. Maxim opens the back door for me and I get in, twisting my fingers together in my lap.

He slides in besides me, pinning me with his intense gaze. "I need you to promise one thing, though."

"What?" I ask.

"Promise you won't break my fingers."

I smirk at that and nod in response. "I promise."

He shifts and kneels between my legs as the car moves, pushing my dress up to my hips as he holds my gaze. "Such a greedy thing, aren't you?" he asks, groaning as he moves his attention to my soaking wet pussy. "So wet and ready, even though I made you come on my cock."

"What do you expect after six days of torture?" I tilt my head. "I'd say you need to make me come at least five more times to make up for it."

He smirks and presses his tongue against my clit, flicking it with the tip. "Greedy," he murmurs.

As much as I hate to admit it, he's right, I am greedy. It's as if no matter how many times we have each other, it's never enough. There's nothing on this earth that can douse the fire inside of me or kill the demons that long to escape.

I sit up and claw my fingers through my husband's perfectly styled hair, dragging my nails along his scalp viciously. The leather beneath my ass squeaks as I push my hips forward, grinding against his mouth shamelessly.

I whimper as his tongue moves from my pussy to my inner thighs, irritating me beyond measure. "Stop playing with me," I rasp.

The mischief in his eyes makes them sparkle. "Or what? And don't say you'll break my fingers."

I bite my bottom lip. "I can hurt you in different ways." I claw harder into his scalp, digging my nails into his skin.

His eyes dilate as he groans, moving his mouth back to my pussy and flicking his tongue against my clit. This man knows how to make my blood boil in my veins with each touch.

"Look into my eyes while I eat this sweet pussy, printessa," he orders.

I meet his gaze, hips pushing forward in need of more from him, and as if he can read my body like a book, he slides a finger inside of me, quenching that ache that he ignited deep within me. My nipples harden almost painfully against the soft fabric of my dress. He fucks me with one finger slowly, building that unbearable tension deep within me.

I bite my lip, trying to quieten the moans that long to escape, knowing that although there's a privacy screen, it's not soundproof. Heat blazes across my skin as the bundle of tension coils tighter inside of me with every flick of his tongue and thrust of his finger.

"Fuck," I breathe, knowing that any moment I'm going to freefall from the edge. I grind my hips faster, chasing my orgasm as his finger slides in and out of me brutally.

"That's it, ride my finger and come on my face," he teases.

I shut my eyes as a flood of ecstasy hits me like a hard, untameable wave pulling me beneath the surface. I forget about keeping my voice down because of the driver, crying out my husband's name as he looks up at me with wet lips, licking my arousal off of them. And then he slides casually next to me and smirks. "When are you going to admit that you love it when I do that?"

"Never," I say, almost out of habit.

He shakes his head, placing his right hand gently on my thigh and glancing out of the window. My stomach dips as I stare at his hand on my thigh, knowing that the day I broke his fingers was an all-time low.

I fear the part of me that wants to create chaos and burn everyone and everything around me to the ground, but somehow Maxim eases the chaos, which in itself scares me more than anything.

20

MAXIM

*L*ivia looks stunning in the pink dress, which I know she didn't wear because I ordered her to. I saw her expression in the mirror when she looked between the two, torn over the one she wanted to wear and the one that made her more inconspicuous.

I struggle to keep my eyes off of her as I stand at the bar, waiting for our drinks. We shut Podolka down for the night to host my father's birthday party, but it's heaving with Bratva members, family and friends.

Artyom approaches Livia, sending a prickle of awareness across the back of my neck.

I glare at the bartender. "Can you speed this up?"

He hurries, his hands shaking, no doubt because he knows who I am. "Sorry, sir." He places the two drinks down on the bar and I grab them, wincing as I use my thumb and good fingers to clutch onto Livia's glass of wine. These broken fingers are a pain in my ass, most of the time because I forget about them.

I rush through the crowd toward my wife, hoping Artyom hasn't done too much damage. He's the only man that knows the truth about my wife's condition, or at least has an inkling about it.

Livia's laugh echoes toward me, sending a flood of relief through me. "Thank you," she says.

"Uncle," I say, approaching Livia from behind and setting the glass of wine in her hand. "I see you've already met my wife?"

He smiles, and it's not pleasant. "Yes, she's exquisite, Maxim. I'm sure you must be pleased."

I set my injured hand on Livia's back, edging closer to her. "Yes, very," I say, keeping all emotion from my voice, as I wouldn't say I'm pleased in the slightest by my father's cocked up choice. I may be attracted to her, but she's more hassle than I ever expected.

"Do you have any children?" she asks, smiling at my uncle. It's crazy to see the difference between Livia at home resisting me and this woman who is acting like the elegant wife of the Volkov heir.

Artyom signals to Valeri. "Yes, here is my eldest son now. Valeri, meet Livia Volkov." He smirks at me. "Maxim's new wife."

Valeri takes her hand and kisses the back of it, sending tension coiling through me at the smarmy look on his face. "It's lovely to meet you."

Livia smiles, reclaiming her hand. "It's lovely to meet you, too."

I clear my throat. "Adrik not made an appearance yet?" I ask.

Valeri shakes his head. "He'll be late, as always."

Artyom looks irritated by the mention of his youngest son. "That boy is older than you, Maxim, but he acts like a jilted child."

"Who is Adrik?" Livia enquires, drawing everyone's attention to her. The bratva often expect their women to look pretty and shut up, rather than take part in the conversation, however there's no chance in hell that's happening with my wife.

"My younger son. There's one year between him and Maxim." Artyom's smile is tight. "He's not very responsible."

My father approaches us, looking as calculating as always as he eyes his brother suspiciously. "What are we all talking about?"

Artyom smiles and spins around to hug his brother. "S dnyom rozhdeniya!" he exclaims, and Valeri is quick to repeat the sentiment.

"Thank you." My father's attention lands on Livia, his eyes sweeping down her dress in a way that makes me want to throttle him. "Nice to see you, as always, Livia." She's his fucking daughter-in-law, and he's looking at her like she's a stripper he's allowed to ogle. He's not, though, because Livia belongs to me, whether he's pakhan or not. I can't understand why it bothers me so much, as he looked at her the same way the first time we met her and at the wedding, but now it feels different.

Her fists clench by her side and her nostrils flare, but she doesn't say a word.

I rub my hand in soothing circles on her lower back, trying to ease that rage that's bubbling inside of her. "Don't let him get to you," I whisper into her ear.

She looks surprised at my comment. Her big green eyes widen as she looks at me. "What makes you think I would?"

I smirk. "The way you clenched your fists by your side like you wanted to punch him in the face."

"Maxim, I have some business we need to talk about," Father says, giving me a sharp glance that tells me I'm in trouble. No doubt Timur has confronted him about the trafficking.

I lean toward Livia. "I won't be long. Excuse yourself and go to the bathroom and then wait by the bar for me," I instruct, not wishing to leave my wife alone with my uncle and cousin.

She looks reluctant, but gives me a nod. "I'm going to go to the ladies' room," she says, turning and walking away.

I return my gaze to my father. "Lead the way."

He grunts and leads me through the club toward the back office. The music playing in the main club fades away as we enter the rundown back office. "What is it?"

He spins around. "You told Timur about the women."

I nod in response. "Yes, you didn't tell me to keep it a secret." I run a hand through my hair. "In fact, I assumed Timur knew about it."

He growls, shaking his head. "No one knows about it, Maxim. We can't risk this leaking to the Morrone family before we make a move."

I raise a brow. "Are you saying you don't trust your Sovietnik?"

"No, I'm saying I don't trust anyone." He paces the office floor. "We still don't know who leaked the news about you wedding to the entire fucking world, and we're in the middle of a war." He glares at me. "You keep making the wrong choices, so how am I supposed to trust you to take over?"

I scoff at that. "That's rich, considering your recent choices."

"What the fuck is that supposed to mean?" he asks, walking toward me.

"I don't agree with you snatching Remy's niece and I don't agree with you buying women," I say, standing as tall as I can.

"Is that right?" He stops a foot away from me. "And why is that other than the fact you're a pussy who can't accept what needs to be done?"

I clench my jaw, knowing I'm so fucking close to punching him in the face, on his birthday of all days. "Because Remy Morrone wasn't focused on us, and now he is. We've increased the pressure on both sides, rather than dealing with the Irish and then turning our attention to the Italians." I crack my neck, holding my father's gaze. "The trafficking isn't our scene and never has been. We deal drugs and we've dabbled in arms, but not people. It's a complication we don't need, especially while trying to survive this war."

He holds my gaze for a few beats before his shoulders sag. "Timur says the same thing." His eyes narrow. "I'll sell these girls because I've bought them, but we'll make sure it's anonymous so that Remy doesn't catch wind of it, and then I'll drop it."

An odd sense of relief sweeps over me, hearing my father actually listen to me for once.

"However, Remy's niece is already done." He shrugs. "There's no turning the clock back on that one, but I know how to twist it to our advantage and use her as leverage."

I nod. "I know it's already done, but I wish you would consult with me more before acting." I cross my arms over my chest. "I know you're the pakhan, but the bratva is a brotherhood. A collective."

"I agree." He crosses his arms over his chest. "I'll try to include you more."

It's strange for my father to back down. "Is that everything we needed to discuss?"

He nods. "Yes, enjoy the party with your wife."

I clench my jaw and turn to leave the office, heading into club. The bar is busy, but I don't see Livia there as I instructed her to be. Fuck's sake. I notice my uncle and approach him. "Have you seen my wife?"

There's a flicker of amusement in his eyes as he shakes his head. "Not since she went to the bathroom."

A sense of unease rushes over me as I head toward the ladies' bathroom, knowing something isn't right. If that son of a bitch sent people after my wife, I'll throttle him to death. I don't care if he shares our name.

"Fuck you!" I hear from the other side of the door, instantly recognizing Livia's voice.

"You don't have very nice manners for a slut."

I freeze when I hear that voice—Daniel, one of my father's brigadiers. The man is renowned for being forceful with other men's women, but I didn't think he had the guts to try to hit on mine.

I charge through the door, fists clenched and teeth bared. Those unmatchable predatory instincts kick in the moment I see Daniel with my wife backed against the wall. He has one hand on her throat and the other inching up the skirt of her dress.

"A dirty little slut who doesn't even wear panties," he says, clearly not noticing he's no longer alone. The fucker put his hand on her cunt. I'll fucking kill him.

"Daniel," I growl his name, knowing that killing him here and now wouldn't be accepted.

He freezes, his entire body turning rigid. Quickly, he lets go of my wife and turns to face me, holding up his hands. "Maxim, what a pleasant surprise. I was merely admiring your new wife."

Adrenaline pulses through my bloodstream as I step forward, feeling that thrum of power buzzing through my veins. I want to kill him, but I'll have to wait. No one in the bratva dies without my father's say so, unfortunately. "You have some fucking nerve," I say, shaking my head. "Livia is mine and only mine," I growl.

Daniel pales, stepping further away from Livia, who is watching me with a mix of curiosity and fear.

"You'll pay for this," I say, moving closer.

He chuckles, but it's full of nervous energy. "Come now, Maxim. I'm sure we can talk about this."

I lunge forward and slam my right fist into his face. The impact knocks him down, but my fists aches already from the hit.

I beckon Livia forward. "I want you to reach into my pocket and pull out the cuffs," I say.

She does, pulling out a pair of metal shackles I'd intended to use on her in the car later. Her brow hitches up, but she doesn't question me. "Fix them around his wrist and then bottom of the sink." Livia nods and does as I say, restraining the bastard who thought it was okay to touch what is mine.

"Good girl, now let's go and find my father and tell him what happened."

Daniel's eyes widen. "Maxim, please, we can work this out!"

I yank her out of the door, feeling on edge. "How far did he get?" I rasp when we're out of the bathroom, desperate to know how badly I need to torture him.

"Not very far." Livia smooths down her messy hair. "I gave him a fight, but he finally overpowered me and then he touched me, but it didn't go beyond that, thank God."

Father is standing with my uncle, who notices me and gives me a smug smile. It wouldn't surprise me if he was behind Daniel's attempt to rape my wife, or if he didn't at least encourage him toward it. "Father, I'm sorry to interrupt, but I need to discuss an important matter with you."

He glances between me and Livia, before nodding. Once we're out of earshot, he asks. "What the fuck is this all about?"

"Daniel sexually assaulted my wife, and I walked in on him in time to stop it going further." I look toward the bathroom. "I've restrained him in the ladies' bathroom, as I want permission to kill him for this."

Livia gasps. "Isn't that a bit drasti—"

I give her hip a warning squeeze. "The man disrespected me by touching what's mine and I won't stand by while it goes unpunished."

My father grins at the thought of a bratva member torture so soon after the last one. "No, it can't go unpunished." His brow furrows. "The question is, who will take Daniel's place?"

"Does that fucking matter?"

He shakes his head. "No, I'll have some men string him up in the basement. We can leave him there for a day or two before getting down to it, as long as you can wait that long." He gives me a pointed look.

"Of course. I'm taking Livia home."

My father gives me a clap on the shoulder. "See you at tomorrow's meeting."

I nod and steer my wife toward the club's exit, knowing that I won't be able to rest easy until Daniel's heart is no longer beating. Livia is mine and I'll die before I let anyone touch her and get away with it.

I GLANCE either way down the street, making sure no one followed me. After all, I've come straight here after a shit show of a meeting with my father. No one could agree over what to do with the girls he bought or what to do with Remy's niece. It was chaos, and I sense that's what Artyom wanted, to stir up chaos during a fucking war and divide us. As it turns out snatching Imalia was also his idea.

I shake my head, trying to focus on the task at hand. Once I'm satisfied it's clear, I head into the small cafe nearby the Callaghan residence. I smile when I see Viki already sat near the back, tapping her fingers nervously on the table.

It's strange, we've never been that close as children and yet since she married Rourke, I've felt more connected to her than before. She always seemed so meek and accepting of my father's bullshit until she stood up to him and that's when a new found admiration was born for my baby sister.

"Hey Viki," I say, sitting down opposite her.

She smiles. "Hey, how have you been?"

I run a hand across the back of my neck, shaking my head. "Not sure where to start, to be honest."

"I heard about the wedding." There's a sadness in her eyes. "I'm sorry I wasn't there."

I swallow hard. "I wanted you to be, Viki, but our father wouldn't allow it."

She nods. "Don't worry, I knew you wouldn't have purposely excluded me."

The waitress walks over. "What can I get you both?"

I allow Viki to order first. "I'll get a Mocha please with cream and one of those famous chocolate muffins."

The waitress smiles and nods. "And for you?"

"Coffee black with one sugar, and I'll try one of the muffins too."

She jots it down. "Coming right up."

"Did you make sure you weren't followed?" Viki asks.

"Yes, uncle has been having me followed. As well as Father." I sigh heavily. "You'd think as his son he'd trust me enough not to have me followed." I glance up. "But we all know why Artyom has me tailed."

Her expression turns sour at the mention of my uncle. "I've always hated that man."

"Father has him watched too, though. I guess it goes both ways."

"Really? I always thought he trusted him completely."

The waitress returns with our drinks and muffins, setting them down in front of us.

Viki and I say thank you in chorus and she leaves us alone.

"So did I, but apparently not." I take a sip of the coffee. "Anyway, enough about the bratva. How have you been?" I ask.

She bites her bottom lip, warning me she's unsure of what she is about to say. "Can you keep a secret from Father?"

"Of course, he doesn't know I'm meeting you."

She sets her hand on her tummy. "I'm twelve weeks pregnant," she says.

My eyes widen and I almost spit out my coffee. "Wow, congratulations, I guess?" I ask.

She smiles and nods. "Yes, we're both excited. Although it's a bit nerve-wracking in the middle of a war."

I can't imagine bringing a child into this toxic, messed up world, and yet that's exactly what I'm supposed to do with Livia. "It can't be easy." I take a bite of my muffin, surprised how good it is. "Wow, that's a good muffin."

Viki laughs. "That's why they're famous." Her brow furrows. "So what's your wife like?"

I'd hoped to keep the conversation off of Livia, but it was a stupid expectation. What is my wife like? Fucking crazy is one way to put it. "She's difficult," I say, trying to be as vague as possible.

"Come on, what's she really like?" Viki pushes.

I sigh, shaking my head. "A serious pain in my ass, but she's strong and beautiful, so I guess it could have been worse."

Viki raises a brow. "Beautiful, hey?"

"She's not bad." I clear my throat. "Can we talk about something else?"

"Looks like my big brother has fallen in love," she teases.

"No chance," I say, knowing that I don't even have the capacity for love. I'm dead inside and broken beyond repair. "I don't love her." Even as I say that, it leaves a bad taste in my mouth.

Do I love her?

No, it's not possible. We have some primal level attraction to one another and our desire to both inflict and take pain binds us together, but it's not love. Love isn't toxic and bitter. I witnessed love when I saw the way my mom looked at my father before she got sick. Livia never looks at me that way.

"Whatever," Viki says, sipping her mocha. "I hate that I can't meet her." She pouts.

"Maybe next time I'll bring her along if you like?" I suggest.

Her face lights up. "Yes, please! I've always wanted a sister."

I swallow hard, knowing I was probably one of the most rotten siblings in the world. No wonder she wanted a sister. I was a fucking asshole to her. I'm surprised she can even stand sitting opposite me, but I'm thankful she can. "Deal, I'll bring her when we next have time to meet up," I say, finishing the rest of my muffin.

I can't understand why butterflies beat around in my gut at the thought of introducing her to my wife. Perhaps because I fear what Viki will see when she meets her, as I suspect Livia is just like me. Will she notice the darkness my wife harbors?

21

LIVIA

I'm about to head out of the apartment to visit my mom when the elevator opens. My stomach dips when I see Maxim, even though he's no longer confining me to the apartment. He said I had to inform him if I was leaving, which I had no intention of doing.

It goes against the very essence of who I am, answering to this man.

His eyes rake down my dress as he leans against the elevator door. "Where do you think you're going?"

I clench my jaw. "I was going out to visit my mom."

He raises a brow. "What did we talk about, Livia?"

My nostrils flare as I glare at him. "I'm not your pet. You can't order me about."

He shakes his head, tutting. "Is it that hard to inform me of where you're going?" Those ice-blue eyes are devoid of all emotion as he steps out of the elevator.

"We're at war and as your husband, I need to know where you go at all times for your safety."

"Bullshit," I say, biting the inside of my cheek. "You need to know because it gives you power over me."

He grabs my hips and yanks me against him, the warmth of his body infecting me instantly, along with the musky, masculine scent of him. It's heady and intoxicating. "You have no idea what you're talking about," he says, moving his lips to within an inch of mine. "Chicago isn't Catanzaro, Livia." His nostrils flare. "There are enemies around every corner."

I tilt my head. "And would it be such a loss if someone were to off me?" I ask, searching his eyes. "After all, you were never happy about this arrangement, either."

He growls, a flash of rage igniting in his eyes. "No one can touch you but me, whether to pleasure or to harm." He slides a hand around my throat, choking me gently. "That's why I'm here, actually. I wanted to pay your attempted rapist and visit, and thought you might like to watch."

I narrow my eyes, wondering if this is a test. Maxim already knows that I'm not averse to violence and when we first met, I told him I enjoy torturing men like him with a knife, but I fear showing him that side, baring myself to him fully.

"Maybe you'd like to show me how much you enjoy using a knife during torture," he murmurs, lips inches from mine, his breath falling against them. "It's my favorite instrument too, printessa."

My knees shake and my thighs dampen at the gravelly tone of his voice, feeling utterly sickened by my body's reaction to talking about the two of us torturing a man who thought he could take what he wanted from me. It's clear we're both as bad as each other. "Okay," I murmur.

He kisses me, his tongue sliding between my lips and forcing its way into my mouth.

I rock my hips against him, searching for friction as I lace my fingers in his hair, drawing him closer. Maxim definitely brings out the worst in me, but the thing is, I like it. I want to drown in my sickness. Let myself be free to be who I really am, deep down behind all my walls I've spent years erecting. When my father introduced me to the brutal side of this world, he unleashed a monster that doesn't want to be caged.

"I love how turned on you get at the thought of torture," he breathes, his voice raspy and uncontrolled. "Come on." He yanks my hips and drags me toward the elevator, still nipping and kissing me as he does. "This is going to be fun, baby."

I shudder against him, embracing the chaos that swirls into life like an errant storm inside of me. "I do love carving up men that think they can take what they want." I give him a pointed look.

He chuckles. "Is that a warning?"

I shrug. "Perhaps."

The elevator moves to the basement level, where I assume we'll be able to access the room where they've locked up my attacker, Daniel. Apparently, he was a brigadier for the bratva, essentially a high level officer who oversaw a group of soldiers, but now he's going to die a slow and painful death for touching me.

Maxim leads me toward the back of the basement, past all the parked cars, where a heavy steel door sits.

My stomach churns as I follow my husband, wondering what I'll find back there.

He opens the door with a key and pushes it forward, leading into a dark corridor with doors on either side. "This is the Volkov torture chambers where we bring traitors."

I tilt my head. "Is Daniel really a traitor, though?"

He growls, grabbing my hand and pulling me against him. "The worst fucking kind for touching a superior member's woman, even after you told him no, even after you fought him." The intensity in his gaze takes me aback as his eyes are blazing with fiery rage, all because a man tried to have his way with me. In the end, I would have fought him off, that I'm sure of.

"You underestimate how hard I would have fought him." My eyes narrow. "If you'd been a few seconds later, I'd noticed the knife in his pocket and had every intention of grabbing it and slicing his throat open."

The rage eases, and the edge of his lips turns up into a smirk. "Of course you would have, my feisty printessa." He kisses me. "You'll have that chance once we've had some fun with him."

I grab his hand, squeezing. "Lead the way."

There's almost a manic look in his eyes, as if he's enjoying my compliance in this far too much. I ignore it, allowing him to lead me a hundred yards to a door on the right. He slips the key into the lock and opens it, pushing it open.

Daniel is sitting, practically naked, other than his boxer briefs, on a chair in the center of the room. His skin is already bruised black and blue and he's chained to the chair with metal restraints.

Maxim shrugs off his jacket and hangs it up, pulling off his tie too and unbuttoning his shirt half-way. Only then does he turn his attention to the man in the center of the room. He walks toward him and once he's a few feet away, claps his hands loudly, startling Daniel awake.

A sweet and innocent mafia princess would be shocked to see this—a man being treated no better than cattle led to the slaughter—but I'm not innocent. My father made sure of that.

"Daniel, Daniel, Daniel," Maxim says, walking slowly around him in a circle, like a shark circling its prey. "What are we going to do to you?"

The man's eyes are wide as he tries to say something behind the gag shoved in his mouth. His eyes move to me and he almost looks like he's pleading with me.

Unfortunately for him, I have as little sympathy for him as Maxim does.

"Carve him up," I suggest, stepping closer.

My husband's smirk is devilish as he nods toward a table ladened with knives and torture instruments. "Select your instrument, printessa."

I walk over to the table, gently running my fingers over the hilt of a large, ornate serrated knife that caught my attention before I even got to the table. I pick it up and weigh it in my hand. "This one."

"Good choice." He beckons me over and I walk toward him, my heart pounding harder as adrenaline races through my veins. "I'll let you have the first go at this bastard."

I turn my attention to the man who is shuddering now, eyes wide and face so pale it's hard to believe he's not already dead. The darkness I've tried so long to bury rises to the surface as I glance down at the knife, twisting it in my hand. "Where should I cut him first?" I say, doing a circle around him like Maxim did. "I don't want to bleed him out too fast and hit a major artery."

Maxim's smirk widens. "Certainly not, printessa."

I stop in front of him and tap the flat of the blade against my chin, contemplating. "I love maximum pain and minimum damage." I pull at his fingers, forcing them straight and stab the end of the knife into his middle one, making him squeal.

"Nice choice," my husband says, praising me.

I don't stop there, forcing his other fingers straight

and stabbing the end of the sharp knife in to each one, until sweat beads on the man's forehead and he drools around the gag. Adrenaline pulses through my veins as I look into his dilated pupils, seeing the fear and pain in them. I thrive off of it, feeling that darkness take a further hold on me. For some reason, Rizzo's face enters my mind. I'd hate for him to see me like this. What would he say if he knew how fucked up his older sister really is?

I push it from my mind and pull the knife out of his finger. "I wonder how much pain this rapist can take?" I ask, glancing at Maxim, who's looking almost demonic right now with how much he's enjoying this.

"I don't know, but I think I found my new addiction."

I tilt my head. "And what's that?"

"Watching my wife torture other people, it's sexy as hell." He grabs his crotch, drawing my eyes to the thick bulge there. Heat bristles over my skin, turning me into a molten puddle inside as I clench my thighs together. It's sick, but we both love this, both get off on causing pain to each other or others.

"Good, because I expect you to get me off once we're finished," I say, circling the man again.

Maxim groans, eyes flickering shut as he tugs on his cock a couple of times. "With pleasure, baby."

I turn my attention back to the man who tried to rape me at the party, feeling hatred flood my guts as he tries to plead with me with muffled grunts, eyes begging.

Quickly, I thrust my knife against his throat and press, only just breaking the skin so one drop of blood trickles down his chest. "What's that?" I ask, tilting my head. "Are you begging me to stop like I countlessly told you to stop last night?" I ask, searching his dark, fear-filled eyes. "Why would I stop when you didn't give me the same courtesy?"

I move the knife lower and cut a shallow groove over his collarbone, making him squeal in agony. The sight of blood eases some of the tension built inside of me as I step back. A vision of my father in the same position floods my mind. For as long as I can remember, that's all I've wanted. To watch my father die a torturous and painful death. I've wanted to make him feel the pain he put me and Rizzo through during our childhood, all those countless beatings he gave us.

I feel my grip on my tenuous control slip as I carve the bastard up in front of me faster, frantically cutting him everywhere and anywhere, as if I'm no longer in my own body. I'm watching from afar, watching as blood spills and turns the image in front of me into a beautiful canvas of pain and chaos.

It's only once Maxim's deep, dominant voice echoes through the room that I'm pulled back to reality. "Livia, that's enough. If you don't stop, I won't get a chance to have some fun before he's bled out." I swallow hard, taking a step back as I look at what I've done to him. Blood covers almost every inch of his body and his head lulls to one side as he struggles to keep conscious, muttering something behind the gag.

Maxim's strong arm slides around me and he takes the knife from my hand, whispering into my ear, "You did good, baby."

His praise assuages the guilt I feel at not having control. "Now let me have a go, before I fuck you against that wall with his blood over both of us," he breathes.

I nod in response, watching as my husband moves toward the man. He slaps his face, forcing him back to reality as he grips his chin and looks him dead in the eye. "You made a grave fucking mistake going anywhere near my wife, Daniel," he snarls, pushing the knife between the man's legs. "I should cut your dick off for this and feed it to the wolves."

My stomach churns as I watch him, wondering if that's what he intends to do.

"But I'd rather not touch it. It's not fucking worth it anyway, as only men with tiny dicks rape other men's women." He slides the knife slowly through the center of his chest, cutting through a tattoo that Maxim has as well. I can only assume that it's a crest of the Volkov Bratva. "We're going to bask in your death, Daniel." He lets go of his chin and his head lulls to the side. "Come here, Livia."

I walk to his side. "Let's end him together, moya lyubov."

He grabs my hand, which is slick with blood, and

wraps it around the knife, keeping his hand over mine. And then he brings the knife to the man's throat. "Let's end him."

I feel grounded as he tightens his grasp on my hand and we both drag it through the man's neck, slicing his throat open. He gurgles on his own blood and it spurts everywhere as he does. His eyes are wide as slowly the life drains away, and I feel nothing but satisfaction. Satisfaction that he can't try to rape a woman again. Satisfaction that his scourge no longer walks this earth.

"You're such a good girl," Maxim purrs into my ear, sending shivers down my spine.

He drops my hand, and I drop the knife, spinning to face him.

Before he can speak, I launch myself into his arms, kissing him as if my life depends on it. The gratitude I feel is overwhelming. I never thought I'd be able to show my deepest and darkest side to anyone and they'd embrace it, and yet Maxim embraces it. He's just like me and with him by my side, I don't feel so out of control.

His bloodied hands tear at my dress as he yanks it down my body and discards it on the floor, groaning as he looks at me. "You're utterly perfect."

I swallow hard, struggling to believe he can really think that, knowing my darkest secrets. "You aren't too bad yourself," I say, taking in the vision of him in his half-unbuttoned shirt stained with blood.

He chuckles and unbuttons his shirt the rest of the

way, revealing his scarred and tattooed skin I've grown to love. It's a sign of what he's been through, even though we've never discussed it. I get the sense our childhoods were rather similar. The shirt flutters to the floor and then he unzips his pants, freeing his hard cock, so it's jutting out of the blood smeared dress pants he's wearing. And then he comes for me, arms wrapping around my waist as he hoists me off the floor.

I grunt as my back hits the wall and Maxim cages me against it, biting and licking my collarbone.

"You were fucking beautiful at work," he murmurs, kissing lower until his mouth covers my hard, aching nipple.

I arch my back, moaning.

"I was as hard as a rock watching you," he breathes, sliding his fingers into my panties and tearing them in two.

I gasp as I feel the head of his cock at my entrance. Maxim isn't teasing me now. He's as desperate for this as I am.

"I've never wanted to fuck anyone as badly as I wanted to fuck you in that moment," he growls, thrusting forward and burying himself to the hilt inside of me. At the same time, he bites down hard on my shoulder, bruising the flesh with his teeth as he does. We're both splattered in blood, fucking mere feet away from a man we killed, and yet I've never been more aroused.

My nipples ache as he drives into me over and over,

thrusting me against the brick wall so hard I know I'll bruise, and yet I want to. I've known for a while that I often have to experience pain to get aroused before I married Maxim. If I played with myself alone, I'd always have to use nipple clamps or other implements to inflict pain, otherwise I wouldn't come.

Every sensation is heightened because of the adrenaline coursing through my veins, as his huge length stretches me open. The jagged brick grazes my back as he fucks me against it roughly. I dig my nails so hard into his back I know I'll break his skin, but he grunts into my mouth, sliding his tongue in and out of my mouth as if he's fucking me with it.

The longer we're married, the more intense our need for each other grows. It doesn't matter that we hate each other, or hated each other, as that is twisting into something different. A mutual addiction that we can't escape, no matter how hard we try.

"Maxim," I cry his name, struggling to breathe as he drives into me brutally.

His beautiful blue eyes are full of unexplainable emotion as he holds my gaze, slamming into me with all his strength. "Come for me," he grunts, digging the fingers of his good hand into my hips and supporting me with the other. It must hurt, but he doesn't seem to care. "I want to feel that beautiful cunt milk my cock." He brings his injured hand around, using his good fingers to pinch my clit.

It's all it takes to unravel me, along with his dominant command. "Fuck!" I scream, my pussy tensing around the thick length of him as I writhe in his arms, groaning and whimpering as the intensity of the orgasm is almost too much to endure. Maxim's hips jerk forward erratically twice more before he roars against my skin, flooding my insides with his seed.

He drops me to my feet and spins me around to face the wall, but keeps a steadying hand on my hips as my knees almost give out. We remain like that. His chest is flat against my back, as my body shudders with erratic breaths.

For the first time in my life, someone has seen the real me and instead of being disgusted, he embraced it. Could it be that this fucked up arranged marriage was always meant to be?

Perhaps Maxim is the cure I've been looking for, or if not the cure, the answer.

22

MAXIM

*L*ivia's brow furrows as she pulls out her cell phone. I'm surprised it even has reception down here. She answers it on hands free.

"Livia, please come quick," her mother's panicked voice echoes around the room. "I need you."

"Mom, what's wrong?" Livia asks, but the line crackles, and Greta's next words are impossible to make out. And then the line goes dead. "Fuck!" Livia shouts, pacing toward the exit of the torture chamber where we tortured a man to death and then fucked like a couple of psychos. "I've got to get over there now."

I race after her, grabbing her wrist before she is out of the room. "Stop, printessa." I yank her against me, molding my body to her back. "It sounds like a trap."

She strains against me, trying to get out of my grasp. "Let go of me!"

"Calm down and take a deep breath and then I'll let go," I instruct.

Livia's chest heaves as she draws in a deep breath of oxygen, and then I release her. "First, you need to go out into the street and try to ring her back." I grab her hand and lead her out of the basement. "It was probably your reception down here."

I'm surprised when she doesn't protest, allowing me to pull her toward the exit and out onto the street in front of our home. Once there, she dials her mother's number and puts it on speaker again. The dial tone sounds twice before it cuts to messaging.

"Shit," Livia says, looking more worried than I've ever seen her. "What if he's finally gone too far?"

"Who?" I ask.

Her jaw clenches as if she didn't mean to say that out loud. "My father." She shakes her head. "I need to go over there and check on her." Livia types away on her phone. "I'm booking an Uber."

I grab the phone out of her hand, placing it in my jacket pocket. "What the fuck for?"

Livia's beautiful pale green eyes turn furious. "Give me my phone back."

"We have six vehicles in the basement and two drivers in the fucking building, and you want to book an Uber?"

She shrugs. "It's easy and convenient."

"Well, I'm driving us."

Her brow furrows. "Why would you come with me? Don't you have work to be getting on with?"

My nostrils flare. "I'm not letting my wife walk into a potential trap alone." I swallow hard, knowing that what we did together strengthened this bond we share. It's becoming almost impossible to ignore the way I feel about my wife. She's so like me, it's insane. "Come on," I say, tugging her back inside and descending into the parking lot below ground.

I stop in front of my car, which is covered with a dust sheet to protect it, since I drive it less often than I'd like.

Livia watches me, looking intrigued as I grab the sheet and yank it off to reveal the Aston Martin DB5 beneath. Her brow raises. "That's not what I expected," she murmurs.

"No?" I tilt my head, genuinely curious about what she expected. "What were you expecting?"

She bites her bottom lip. "A muscle car or something."

I'm a little offended by that, as it's too cliche. A young, rich guy always has to have some powerful mustang or chevy. "Are you saying that the Aston is too refined for me?"

My wife clearly senses my irritation but grabs the passenger's side handle. "Perhaps," she says, sliding inside of my car. "I like it, though."

I smile as I get into the driver's seat, turning over the engine.

Livia twists her fingers in her lap, something I've noticed she does when she's nervous. "Do you really think it's a trap?" she asks, not looking at me.

"Possibly." My brow furrows as I place my phone on the hands-free stand on the dash and give Livia back hers. "You can't be too careful while at war," I say, pulling out of the basement and onto the street as I call my father.

She tugs at her blood splattered clothes. "God, my mom is going to freak when she sees me like this." Her eyes move to my dress shirt, which isn't much better, but I can cover it with my jacket. "Who are you calling?" Livia asks.

"My father. I want to know if he's heard from Vito lately."

Her nose scrunches up at the mention of her father.

"What is it?" Father answers rather sharply.

I drum my fingers on the steering wheel. "When did you last speak to Vito?"

There's a pause. "Yesterday, before he left to tend to business out of town, why?"

I swallow hard, knowing that means Livia's mom can't be calling about Vito. "So he's not in town?"

"That's what I just said, Maxim."

I grit my teeth, finding my father's lack of patience insufferable. "I'm on my way to their house now with Livia. Her mom rang her in a panic, asking for her to come over right away."

"Fuck," he says, blowing out a long breath. "I'll send a unit over. It could be a trap. Don't go in until they arrive."

I glance at Livia, whose eyes are wide as she stares at the phone. "Is my mom in danger?"

"Most likely," Father answers, completely tactlessly.

Thankfully, I don't think Livia is one for dramatics. She slumps back into her chair, pinching the bridge of her nose.

"I'll update you shortly," I say, canceling the call.

I can't understand why there's this odd, tugging desire to comfort my wife and tell her everything will be fine. Even though I don't know that. "We'll get her to safety, printessa," I say instead.

Livia bites her bottom lip, shaking her head. "Someone wanted to get to me. Why?"

There's no doubt who's behind this, Remy Morrone. It's an attempt at retaliation for my father snatching his niece. "I think it's my father's doing."

"What's that supposed to mean?" Her fists ball in her lap as she glares at me.

I shrug. "A hunch, but Father snatched a relative of Remy Morrone yesterday." I tighten my grasp on the steering wheel. "It's probably a retaliation."

"Shit," Livia says, rocking back and forth in her chair. "He will kill her."

I move my hand over hers and squeeze. "Not if me or the bratva have anything to do with it. He won't have a chance." I stare at my wife, seeing her in a new light after what we did together. There was no way in hell I ever believed I'd meet a woman who could witness the depths of my depravity and not run away as fast as possible. Livia embraced it and showed me just how depraved she is too, and I know in that moment I've never felt more connected to another human being on this planet. "I promise I'll do everything in my power to save her."

I mean that with everything I am. The last thing I want is to see her hurt. I remember something my father said to me when he told me I was to marry Livia.

If you ever found a woman like your mother, you'd be a very lucky man.

My mother was brave and fearless, although I'm sure she wasn't as dark and damaged as Livia. I believe I truly have found a woman as strong and brave and beautiful as her.

"What are you staring at?" Livia asks, cheeks flushing pink. "Shouldn't you focus on the road?"

I smirk and tear my eyes off of her. "I was admiring my stunning wife."

Her throat bobs as she swallows, and she opens her mouth, only to shut it again. A tense silence floods between us as I sense she wants to ask me something.

"Spit it out, baby," I encourage.

"How can you see how fucked up I am and still call me stunning?" she asks, her voice quieter than I've ever heard it.

My brow furrows. "How could I not? You and I are more similar than you might believe, moya lyubov." It's the second time today now I've called her that, but it feels right. *My love.* She's so dear to me, and although I'm not sure I have the capability for love, I've never felt this way about anyone before.

"What does that mean?"

I meet her inquisitive gaze, drawing in a breath. "It means my love."

Her eyes widen and her cheeks turn a darker shade of pink as she nods and stares out of the window, abruptly ending the conversation.

The rest of the journey to her home is full of tension as I navigate the busy streets of Chicago. It feels like it takes too fucking long to get to her house, which is guarded as it usually is, so all appears in order. I let Livia speak with the guard, who she recognizes.

"There are men coming as backup," I add, as she's about to say goodbye. "Can you assure they're let in?"

The guard's eyes narrow. "On whose authority?"

I run a hand across the back of my neck. "Spartak Volkov, your boss's biggest ally."

"I can back that up. They're on their way to support us if there's anything amiss at the house."

The guard crosses his arms over his chest. "There won't be anything amiss, as no one has gone past these gates."

Livia's brow furrows. "What about the entrance through the woods?"

He stands straighter. "What entrance?"

She releases an irritated sigh. "There's a dirt track with access on the other side of the property where anyone could drive straight in. Isn't it guarded?"

"I didn't even know of it, Livia." He adjusts the gun he's holding in his hands and looks at me. "I'll let your men in when they arrive."

We drive through the gates toward the Bianchi mansion when Livia tugs on my sleeve. "Those cars don't belong to this household," she mutters, pointing toward a few SUVs parked near the woods.

"No, they don't." I recognize them instantly as only the Italians drive Alpha Romeo SUVs. "The Morrone family has your mother inside."

Livia's eyes widen, and she reaches for the doorhandle.

I grab her wrist and yank it away. "No, we need to wait for backup. It's too dangerous to go in alone."

She glares at me. "There's no chance in hell I'm hiding out here while the fucking Morrone family holds my mom captive."

I sigh heavily, releasing her arm. "We'll be walking into a trap. Your mother will be safe until you arrive, at least."

"These people killed my grandparents. I'm not taking the chance."

I get out of the car and so does Livia. "Let's do this then." I pull open the trunk and throw her a bullet-proof vest. "Put that on."

She quickly shrugs it on and fastens it as I put one on, too, under my suit jacket.

I grab a rifle and give it to her. "Do you know how to use a gun?"

"Yes." She grabs it and checks the safety is on before checking it's loaded. "Come on."

I smile as I grab my rifle, slinging it over my shoulder. Typing fast, I warn my father that the Morrone family are here and we're going in before jogging after her.

She's fearless, beautiful and everything I could have hoped for in a partner. My belief she would be my captive and slave has been quickly squashed, as she's my equal in every sense of the word.

Although I'm not sure I'm ready to admit it to her yet, she's feisty enough as it is. If I tell her she's my queen, my equal, she might tear me apart and claim the throne for herself.

23

LIVIA

*M*y heart bangs against my ribcage in uneven thuds as I creep through the front door of my parents' home. I breathe as quietly as I can, fearful that one wrong sound could spell disaster for my mother.

Maxim moves behind me fluidly, and I can't deny that I'm thankful he's here. If I'd had to come and deal with this alone, I would have probably walked straight into a trap unarmed. Spartak is the reason they're here attacking my mom.

I may have warmed up to my husband in some ways, but his father I still hate with a passion. There's nothing good in him, even if many would argue the same for Maxim. As I get to know him better, I sense he's just wounded and broken. There's no mending some damage, as I know all too well.

"Livia," he whispers my name. "Stay close to me."

I roll my eyes, but drop back so I'm shoulder to shoulder with him.

"Where do you think they'll keep your mom?" he asks.

"She never leaves her room, so I guess we try there first?"

Maxim nods and heads toward the stairs, taking them one at a time with his gun pointed ahead of him. I swallow hard as I make sure my safety is off, shouldering the rifle as I follow him. I have used a gun before, but I've never shot a person. My father used to force me and Rizzo to shoot at a gun range near Catanzaro for years. At least it will come in handy today. If it's a Morrone or my mom, I won't hesitate to kill.

Once we get to the top of the stairs, Maxim glances at me.

I nod to the corridor to the right and he takes it, walking to the end where my mom's room is. The sound of hushed voices comes from the other side of the door and Maxim comes to a halt, glancing at me.

"Follow my lead," he mouths.

I nod, knowing there's no way I'm going taking the lead, not when my mom's life is at stake. Rizzo would know what to do and, more than ever, I wish he was here. Instead, my pathetic excuse of a father is God knows where leaving my mom alone and prone to attack.

Maxim places his hand on the doorhandle and mouths. "Gun ready."

I swallow hard, adjusting my arms as I keep it in front of me, nodding.

He pushes the door open and shouts. "Don't move. Hands in the air or we shoot."

Three men surround my mom, who is tied to a chair with a gag in her mouth. Our sudden entrance takes them aback as two of the men drop their guns, thrusting their hands in the air. The third man, however, doesn't, aiming his gun at Maxim and smirking cockily.

"Luca," Maxim growls. "Drop the gun." He keeps his gun trained on the man who clearly is the leader, while I focus mine on the other men, moving between them slowly.

"Well, well. I expected Livia, but not you, Maxim." He moves forward, but Maxim cocks his gun, forcing him to come to a halt.

"I said don't fucking move."

He keeps his gun trained on my husband. "Well, it looks like we're at an impasse, doesn't it? Who can shoot quicker?" The man, Luca, glances at me. "Your mom will die for this, Livia, mark my words."

The threat snaps something inside of me as I cock my gun, aiming it at his head.

"Livia, gun on the others," Maxim warns.

I swallow hard, listening and moving it back to the two men who look ready to run for their lives.

"It's simple really, Maxim. Your organization has

taken something precious, my cousin." He points the gun at him. "We want her back."

"I don't know what the fuck you're talking about, but we don't have your cousin." It's a lie, but he's convincing.

Luca tilts his head. "Maybe Daddy hasn't told you about his plot to end the war, snatching our family members."

I notice the way Maxim's muscles strain at that, as if he hit a nerve. "Bullshit. So what? You thought you could snatch my wife and trade her."

His smirk widens. "That was the plan, but since you're here, maybe I'll take you instead."

Maxim laughs such a cold, vicious laugh it sends shivers down my spine. "I'd like to see you try to take me, Luca." He shakes his head. "You'd end up with your throat carved out before you could put a hand on me."

Luca's jaw tenses as he sizes up his opponent. They're both very similar in size and build, but I feel the young Italian is probably not as tough as Maxim. I know my husband and what he can take. He's ruthless and calculating and the strongest person I know.

Every muscle in my body tenses as I hear someone at the door as it pushes open. A man with a gun appears and when he sees Maxim pointing his gun at his boss, he doesn't hesitate.

It feels like my heart comes to a standstill as the bullet ricochets toward Maxim, who heard the man enter and is staring right at the bullet. He moves out of the way so fast I can hardly believe his reflexes are human, but that's when all the blood drains from my face.

The bullet grazes my mom's arm instead, and she cries out in pain as the blood soaks her white blouse.

"Mom!" I shout, concern blazing through me.

I don't think of consequences in that moment as I swing my gun toward the intruder who shot my mom. I shoot him right through the head, not batting an eyelid as his blood splatters over my already bloodied clothes.

Luca's face twists in fury as he watches his man drop to the floor. "You fucking whore," he growls, rushing toward me.

I point the gun at him, but even I'm not stupid enough to believe I'll get away with shooting a Morrone family member. Even in Italy, it's a golden rule no matter what the offspring of organization leaders aren't to be touched.

Maxim launches himself at him instead, tackling his legs and slamming him into the ground. "No one disrespects my wife!" he shouts, slamming his fist into his jaw so hard a crack echoes through the room.

A lump forms in my throat, watching a man I hated at some point come to my defense.

Luca appears to take him by surprise, breaking free and slamming his own fist into the right side of his face.

"Is that all you've got?" he goads, thrusting his fist hard into Luca's stomach repeatedly.

Luca twists his hip and gets one foot onto Maxim's stomach, kicking him off of him. "Fuck you," he growls, eyes flashing with rage as he moves for Maxim again.

This time he punches him in the chest, but it won't hurt since he has a bulletproof vest under his jacket. I smile as he grabs Luca's hand and pulls apart his fingers, using the same move I used on him to crack his fingers.

Luca squeals like a girl, eyes dilating in pain as he clings onto his hand and shuffles away from me. "You son of a bitch."

One of Luca's men comes to his side, whispering something in his ear.

Luca's eyes darken. "So you bought backup?"

I swallow hard, glancing out of the window nearby to see three SUVs racing up the driveway toward the house.

"Perhaps." Maxim tilts his head. "What are you going to do now, Morrone?"

He runs his good hand across the back of his neck. "We need a peaceful sit down." He slips his hand in his pocket, which forces both of us to tense, pointing our guns at him. "Relax." He pulls a piece of paper out of his jacket, glancing at us through narrowed eyes. "There's a small family event we're holding tomorrow evening and as we're at an impasse, let's agree to sit down neutrally and discuss how we can work through this."

"You have authority from your father to agree with this?" Maxim asks, his voice dripping with skepticism.

He nods. "I do. It was our intention to snatch your wife and send you the invite." His attention lands on me. "It's clear we underestimated how smart your wife is to bring you along, but the offer to speak about a truce still stands." He signals to the paper. "May I?"

Maxim nods, and Luca steps toward him, stopping a few feet and extending the piece of paper.

"Tomorrow night, eight o'clock. Shall I expect to see you there?"

"Perhaps." Maxim glances down at the invite. "The pakhan will make the final decision."

Luca bows his head and signals to his guys. "Well, as lovely as this meeting has been." He works his jaw as he glances down at his bruised and broken fingers. "We had best be going."

I step forward. "If you need to go out unseen, there's a back staircase if you carry straight down the hallway on your right." Although these fuckers broke into my home and one of his men shot my mom, I know the importance of diplomacy in matters like this. He didn't get what he wanted when he came here, and that's all that matters.

Luca nods and heads for the door, flanked by his two men. He says something in Italian to them but I don't catch it. They bend down and pick up the man I shot dead. The first person I've ever shot and yet I feel no remorse over it. He shot my mom, so he deserved to die. In fact, he should have died a slow and painful death, even if the gunshot wound she has sustained is only a flesh wound.

The moment he leaves the room, I drop my gun and rush toward my mom, who has lost quite a lot of blood. "We need to get her to the hospital." I cup her pale face in my hands. "It's going to be okay, mom."

Maxim flexes his muscles and walks toward us. "I can drop you both there, but my father is going to need to be briefed on this."

"Fine," I say, nodding.

He helps my mom out of the chair and steadies her. "Can you walk, Mrs. Bianchi?"

My mom nods. "Yes, of course."

I swallow hard as Maxim helps her out of the room and toward the stairs, following behind them. If he hadn't been with me when I got her call, I would have headed alone straight into a trap. As I watch him tentatively help my mother, it's hard not to feel anything but admiration for a man I so desperately despised weeks ago.

A flood of footsteps rush into the home along with men speaking Russian.

"Ustupat," Maxim says. "They aren't here any longer."

The men all relax, looking relieved. "What happened?"

"All will be revealed." He glances at me. "Can you help your mom?"

I nod and support her as he walks over to a medium height man with a shaved head and angry scar running through his left cheek. "Timur," he says, clapping him on the shoulder. "I need you to call a full bratva meeting in two hours. I'll get my father in the mean time and explain what happened here. Can you arrange it?"

Timur nods. "Of course, leave it to me."

"See you in two hours. Text me the location."

Maxim returns to us, supporting my mom. "Let's get her in the car and to the hospital," he says.

My mom remains quiet, looking a little disorientated as all these men stand in the entrance of her home. "What's happening, Livia?"

"We're taking you to the hospital."

I know full well that's not what she meant. She wants to know why those men held her at gun point and why there's a load of Russian's wielding guns in her home, but I can't get into that with her right now.

Her disorder has removed her from reality and she no longer understands what our family is involved in. The criminal activities that fuel my father's greed and lifestyle. All I need is to get her to the hospital, rather than upsetting her further.

24

MAXIM

I pace the length of my father's study, waiting for him to enter.

Apparently, he's been down in the basement, torturing someone.

For the first time, I actually felt genuine fear. Not for my safety, but for my wife's. I have something to lose now that I've got to know the woman behind all that rage and hatred.

Finally, the door opens and my father strides in, looking a little disheveled. "What is it, Maxim?"

"Luca Morrone was at the Bianchi mansion. He intended to snatch Livia in retaliation for you taking Imalia."

The mention of Imalia makes his eyes flash. "That bastard."

I shake my head. "You started it. What did you expect?"

"I assume you dispatched him successfully?"

"If you mean I let him go with an agreement to consider a proposal from his father, then yes."

Father's nose turns up in disgust. "What kind of proposal?"

I pass him the invite, which asks us to join Remy and his family for a high-stakes poker game. While I know my father hates the idea of sitting down and discussing anything with the Morrone family, I know he can't resist a game of poker.

"Idiots." He slams the paper down. "They'll lose millions."

"So we'll attend?" I confirm.

"Of course." He turns to face me. "I don't back down from a challenge, as you know."

My brow furrows. "Could it be a trap?"

"No, he wouldn't dare try to attack us at a negotiation." He sounds so certain, but I don't know how he can be. The winner is always the one willing to take the biggest risks, but I doubt even Remy is that stupid. "I'll have an insurance policy, anyway. If he harms any of our men in attendance, I'll have men on standby to carve up his niece and send her to him in pieces."

I swallow hard, remembering how hopeless and innocent that girl looked strung up at the docks, unconscious. "Is she still at the docks?"

His brow furrows. "No, she's in our basement. Who else did you think I was torturing?"

I shrug. "I never know with you."

"What's that supposed to mean?" Father growls, nostrils flaring. "You've had a chip on your shoulder for weeks, Maxim, so why don't you tell me what your problem is?"

I clench my fists by my side, digging my nail into my palm. "You know what my fucking problem is." I glare at him, as he knows why I can't stand to be around him anymore. There's no going back from what he did to Viki, and it means I'll never trust him, not in the way I used to.

He sighs, pinching the bridge of his nose. "Because of Viki?" he asks, his voice calm.

"Yes, because of Viki," I snap, wanting nothing more than to punch him repeatedly until he understands how fucked up it was to shoot his daughter.

When he opens his eyes, I'm almost bowled over by the sheer emotion in them. "It was a dick move, Maxim. I know that now."

"Do you?" I ask, pointing at him. "You haven't apologized to her. Hell, you tried to fucking kidnap her from the hospital after shooting her."

His jaw works. "We're at war and I felt it meant I had to make hard decisions." He crosses his arms over his chest and leans back against his mahogany desk. "It was a wrong decision and I'll carry the guilt with me for the rest of my life."

"How am I supposed to trust you when I know that family means nothing to you?" I ask what I've wanted to ask him ever since it happened, perhaps before then.

"It doesn't mean nothing to me." He slides his fingers through his messy hair. "It means everything to me."

"Bullshit. Ever since mom died, you've—"

"Careful, Maxim," he warns, a flash of rage igniting in those blue-gray eyes.

Every time I speak about my mom, he has the same reaction and I'm sick of it. "Careful of what? Calling you out on this shit after years of acting the victim." I cross my arms over my chest and glare at him. "I lost her too, you know? So did Viki, and there was nothing we could do about it. It's not like our enemies murdered her, so why let the rage eat you?"

Instead of an angry response, which I fully expect, he slumps into the chair behind his desk and rubs his temples. "It's hard to understand what the death of someone you cherish does to you, Maxim, unless you've experienced it."

"Are you saying I didn't experience it when I lost her?"

He shakes his head. "No, not at all. I'm saying that when you lose the person you vowed to spend your life with, it's a different loss." When he glances at me, all I see is raw emotion behind those blue-gray eyes. "I loved your mother, but you're right. It's been almost eight years since she died, and it's time I let go of my anger over her death."

I swallow hard, hating that even as he admits this to me, I still can't trust him. My lack of trust in the man who raised me wasn't born when he shot Viki, even though I said it was. I never trusted him, I feared him, but now even my fear is overwhelmed by the strong hatred I have for him.

He maimed my body repeatedly as a lesson to teach me how to be tough and withstand pain, but what he did to mentally scarred me in ways he'll never understand. A father isn't supposed to abuse his children, even if he is a powerful, ruthless pakhan.

"Timur is arranging a meeting with the entire bratva. We need to work out a plan for tomorrow night," I say, swiftly changing the subject.

Father nods, standing and walking to the dresser in the corner to pour himself a drink. As always, he doesn't ask me if I want one. Instead, he sips on his vodka and pinches the bridge of his nose. "What a fucking shit show!"

"We'll sort it out. Morrone was bound to retaliate for his niece being taken." I run my hand across the back of my neck. "What's the plan for tomorrow night?"

My father's eyes narrow. "What do you think we should do?"

I'm surprised he's asking for my opinion, but don't question it. "I think four of us should attend. You, me, Osip and Timur."

"Artyom won't like that," he says, smirking slightly. "I agree, though."

I nod. "I'll also have Livia as my date, as a fuck you to the fact they couldn't take her."

His smile widens. "I like it."

"Artyom, Valeri and Adrik can be on surveillance of the club from a van parked outside, with direct contact with two of the brigadier's groups stationed nearby, in case it all goes to shit."

Father knocks back the rest of his vodka. "Sounds good. What time is the meeting?"

I glance at my watch. "One hour from now." I pull my cell phone out of my pocket, finding a text from Timur. "At our warehouse by the docks."

"Okay, get cleaned up." He gives me a pointed look, glancing at my blood-stained shirt. "I noticed Daniel didn't last long. Where was my invite?"

"Sorry, but I felt it was something my wife and I should handle alone."

Father's brow raises, but he nods. "Meet in the basement in twenty minutes."

I nod and leave my father's study, heading upstairs to the bedroom to get out of my bloody clothes. It's a risk taking Livia into the lion's den with me tomorrow night, but I know she can handle it. She's stronger than anyone believes, and I want her by my side.

It's been months since we had the entire bratva in one room for a sit down. And yet Timur has pulled it off within two hours as the high-ranking members sit around a makeshift boardroom table in the middle of our warehouse at the docks, and the soldiers stand, watching.

Father stands. "Today, the Morrone family attempted to attack us head on, but we foiled their plans to snatch Maxim's wife."

A few men cheer.

My father ushers them to be quiet. "However, I've agreed to hear what they have to say tomorrow evening. I want Maxim, Timur and Osip by my side—"

Artyom stands, clearing his throat. "As your brother, I would have hoped—"

"Sit down," my father growls.

He pales and drops into his chair. "I have roles for each of you." He gives his brother a pointed look. "Now, I don't want to be interrupted again."

"Artyom, Valeri and Adrik, if he can be bothered to show up." My father glares at Adrik, who thumbs through his phone, not paying attention. "I want you three to head up a monitoring operation outside of the club. You'll listen outside and make sure that the situation doesn't go south. If it does, you get Roman and Vitaly's groups in to recover us and take out as many bastard Italians as they can."

Despite the high importance of my uncle's role, he looks pissed that he's not being taken into the viper's den.

"Artur, you'll be at my home ready with a live feed,

along with your men." My father's smirk doesn't have its usual kick as he motions almost reluctantly to a picture of the poor innocent girl he snatched. "You'll be with Imalia Alegro, Remy's niece, as an insurance policy. If everything goes wrong and I'm no longer here to instruct you, you will kill her and carve her into pieces, sending her to Remy."

"Sir," Artur replies, as his group nod in unison.

And then my father turns his attention to Anton, the replacement brigadier, since Livia and I tortured to death Daniel. "You will be stationed here at the docks, ready to hit a shipment Remy is expecting at midnight."

"A shipment of what?" I ask, feeling a prickle of unease.

His jaw works. "Guns."

People chatter at that, but my father holds his hands up to quieten them. "Yes, we're expanding from drugs into arms and it's about time. They're having reinforcements sent from up the coast, and we need all the extra firepower we can get during the war." He glances at Timur. "We're also negotiating with the Estrada Cartel for supply of weapons, since they're a neutral party in the war."

I'm thankful his answer wasn't women, as that's what the Morrone family are renowned for dealing in, not guns. It's odd that he's done a U-turn on the intention to branch out into trafficking, but perhaps Timur made him see sense. It's the messiest trade in organized crime and one that we don't need to think about during a war.

"Are there questions about your roles tomorrow evening?" he asks.

Everyone is silent, clear about the parts they will play, even though Artyom is stewing over the fact he's not being brought into the casino with us. Valeri doesn't look bothered though, and neither does Adrik, who is flicking through his phone with disinterest in the meeting.

"Good, meeting dismissed."

Everyone stands, except for my uncle, who glares at Father.

"Is there a problem, Artyom?" he asks, looking disinterested as he shrugs his jacket on. We both knew that there would be some resistance from his brother.

"Only the fact you have me on surveillance rather than on the front lines." He points at my father. "You need family by your side."

Father doesn't look at him. "You're by my side. Surveillance is key to our survival and I wouldn't trust anyone but family with the job." With that, he turns and walks away, leaving Artyom gawking after him.

I hide my smirk as I follow him out of the warehouse, knowing that tomorrow night is going to be dangerous but more fun than I've had in a while, especially with my princess by my side.

25

LIVIA

I tap my feet on the cheap linoleum floor in the waiting room, struggling to contain my anxiety as I wait to be called to see my mom.

She's only been in there for twenty minutes, but it feels like forever. The doctor insisted he see her alone first to patch up the wound and check her vitals. A part of me wishes Maxim could have stayed, as I know he would keep me calm, but the Morrone family attempted to kidnap me and he needs to sort it out.

The invite is to an exclusive high-stakes poker game tomorrow night. Maxim left me here and intends to convince his father to attend the game to see what they have to say. Spartak is the one who started this by stealing away Imalia Alegro, Remy Morrone's sister's child.

My phone rings, and it's Rizzo.

I called him in the car, but I assume he was in class.

"Hey," I say, answering the phone.

"What's up?" he asks, instantly sensing that something isn't right.

I take in a deep breath. "Before you panic, just listen, okay?"

"Livia, tell me what the fuck is going on."

"It's a long story, but mom got shot. It's only a flesh wound and they're—"

"Fuck this, I'm coming home," he growls.

"No, you don't need to leave school. Seriously, it was just a flesh wound to the left arm."

He sighs heavily on the other side. "There's nothing you can say that'll stop me. I'll be there in twenty-four hours." He cancels the call, and I stare at my phone in my hand, knowing he's right. There's nothing I can say that will stop him from coming home, but I expected him to ask more questions.

The doctor, who was tending to Mom, comes out of the swing doors.

I jump to my feet and rush over to him. "Is she okay?"

His brow furrows as he stares down at the clipboard in his hand. "Please come with me so we can discuss my findings in private," he says, sending alarm bells ringing in my head.

"Is she okay?"

He nods to the door and ushers me through, but doesn't take me into my mother's room. Instead, he takes me into an empty room and shuts the door. "I need to ask you a few questions about your mother's living conditions."

"Living conditions?" I echo, unsure what he means.

"Yes, who does she live with?"

I sit down on a hard plastic chair in the room. "She lives with my father and some of their staff. Why?"

"Am I right in assuming that she has no medical conditions other than bipolar disorder?"

I nod in response, as I filled out her form and she's had no other health issues.

"I'm asking these questions because we found quite a high dose of levodopa in your mother's bloodstream." He taps the end of his pen against the clipboard. "She insists she's never heard of the drug."

"Neither have I," I admit.

The doctor bites his bottom lip as if hesitant to say the next words. "Levodopa is used to treat severe Parkinson's disease and has a tendency to cause mania in patients."

It feels like my entire world spins as I process what he's saying. "Are you saying—"

"Yes, I'm saying your mother's bipolar disorder may well be the effects of this drug. The question is, who's slipping it to her?" He glances down at the clipboard again. "Her liver is okay, but it's clear it has suffered from the constant use of this drug. We estimate your mother may have been on it for upwards of ten years."

"Ten years?" I ask, shaking my head. "If that's true, the only person who has lived in our household for that long is my father." I clench my fists, realizing that if he's been slipping her the drug, he's the one who has been making her ill this entire time. It sounds about right, though. As they diagnosed my mom with bipolar not long after I turned ten years old.

The doctor gives me a sad smile. "It's best to speak to your mother and father and work it out, but if you feel in danger at any point, you can call the police to handle it."

I clench my jaw, knowing that there's no chance the police will be involved. The desire I've had to murder my father is ten times more intense as I nod my head calmly, trying to hide the inferno that's been lit inside of me. "Of course. Can I see her now?"

The doctor smiles and nods. "Yes, follow me." He leads me through the corridor and we come to a stop outside my mom's door. "I know you stated she was shot at a mugging, but have you filed a police report?"

I shake my head. "Not yet. My main priority was to get her to the hospital."

The doctor nods. "We'll have to alert the authorities, and they'll have some questions for her."

I swallow hard, knowing my mom could easily say the wrong thing to the police. "Is it really necessary right now? She's in a very fragile place. I promise we'll go to the police once she's feeling better."

The doctor's jaw clenches a little as he searches my eyes. "It's against hospital policy."

I sigh heavily. "I fear it will send her spiraling until those drugs are out of her system."

"I'll see what I can do," he says, giving me a nod. "But I can't make any promises."

"Thank you," I say, turning my attention back to my mom, who's lying on the bed, her eyes clamped shut. I push open the door and she opens them, smiling when she sees me.

"Hello, love."

"Hey, Mom. How are you feeling?"

She shrugs. "I've been better. Did they tell you about the levodopa in my system?"

I nod, tears stinging my eyes. "Yes, it means Father has been drugging you this whole time."

"I should have known something was wrong." She shakes her head. "It was all so convenient that they diagnosed me not long after I told your father that I was going to leave him." Tears stream down her cheeks. "He was so desperate to keep me under his thumb that he drugged me and made me believe I wasn't capable of looking after myself or my children." Her brow furrows. "He threatened to take you both from me because I was mentally ill."

I approach the bed and squeeze my mom's hand. "He won't hurt you anymore."

"Livia, that's very naïve. Your father is a bad man and he'll do anything it takes to stop me from leaving him." She squeezes my hand back. "I fear I'm trapped forever."

"No, Maxim will help, I'm sure of it."

She raises a brow. "The husband I was sure you hated will help?"

"He's not as bad as I first thought." My cheeks flame as I realize he's morphed from the devil in my life to my savior. The first person I think about in a predicament like this is him. "I know he'll help. Maybe we can get you moved back to Catanzaro and find you a place of your own?"

My mom's face lights up. "I would love that, cara mia, but it sounds a bit unrealistic."

"I promise I'll make it happen."

Her smile drops, and she shakes her head. "What about you and Rizzo? I can't leave you both."

"I'm fine. Maxim will take care of me and Rizzo can make up his own mind when he finishes his senior year." I shrug. "Perhaps he'll move back with you."

She sighs and rests her head back on the pillow. "None of it needs deciding now, but I can't return to the house, not with your father."

"I'm sure Maxim wouldn't mind you staying with us until we sort it out. We have a couple spare rooms." I don't actually know whether that's true. He'll probably be pissed off that he can't fuck me on the kitchen counter while my mom's staying there, but I don't care. She's family and she comes first.

"Thank you. Your father is out of town for a few more days, so I can pack some things."

I nod. "Don't worry, I'll sort all of that out for you."

I bite my bottom lip. "Rizzo is on his way home. I had to tell him about the gunshot, but I spoke to him before the doctor told me about the drugs."

"He shouldn't be skipping school." Her face scrunches up. "But I guess he needs to know, so we'll tell him together when he arrives." There's a brief silence as my mom looks down at her hands clasped together. "Does your father know what happened?"

"I haven't told him, but I assume it's only a matter of time until he hears from his men."

Her lips purse together. "Perhaps it's best I get my things quickly, before he heads home early."

I shake my head. "Rest, mom. Don't worry about anything, Rizzo and I will sort all of that out. You won't need to see him again."

She does as I say, resting her head back. "I do feel rather tired from all this." She shuts her eyes and sighs heavily. "I can't tell you how much of a relief it is to know that my mental problems aren't my fault. It's like a weight has been lifted."

I swallow hard, hating that all these years I've been living with my mother and father, unaware that the bastard was poisoning her. It all makes perfect sense now, why he never wants to get her help, worried they'll uncover the truth. It makes me so angry and, more than ever, I want to kill my father.

Rizzo bursts into my mom's hospital room as we're getting her ready to leave.

"Wow, how did you get here so fast?" I ask, blinking to make sure it's actually him standing there.

He shakes his head. "A friend lent me a private jet, which is so much quicker than taking the road."

"Rizzo, you didn't need to rush over here. I'm fine." My mom signals to her arm. "It's a little graze."

"Yeah, from a bullet," Rizzo deadpans.

My mom smiles and walks up to him, cupping his cheeks in her hands. "Thank you for coming, though."

He smiles and wraps his arms around her, pulling her into a gentle hug. "So the doctors have discharged you?"

"Not exactly," I say, approaching cautiously. "I discharged her as she's coming to live with me and Maxim."

"Like hell she is," Rizzo says, eyes flashing with rage. "I don't trust that—"

My mom stops him, squeezing his hand. "Listen to why I'm staying with them, Rizzo."

I swallow hard as he turns his piercing blue eyes on me. "The doctors ran some general tests on mom and found evidence of levodopa in her system."

"What the fuck is that?" he asks.

"A drug used to treat Parkinson's disease, which is also renowned for causing mania in patients."

Rizzo's jaw clenches as he steps forward. "Are you saying—"

"Yes," Mom cuts in. "Your father has been drugging me and making me ill, we believe. The doctors say it's probably not reversible. Once you have bipolar even if it's caused by drugs, it can't be undone."

The rage in Rizzo's eyes is more vicious than I've ever seen. "I'll kill him," he growls, clenching his fists.

I step forward and place my hand on his arm, trying to calm his rage. "We're all angry about what he did, but unfortunately he is Spartak's partner, which offers him protection."

Rizzo's nostrils flare as he draws in a deep breath. "He doesn't deserve protection. Convince your father-in-law to push him to one side, as you and Maxim are in line to take over."

My mom clears her throat. "I don't want any violence over this, Rizzo. You won't harm your father."

His muscles bunch under his tight shirt. "How can you protect him?"

She shakes her head. "I'm not protecting him, I'm protecting my children. Killing your father will haunt you, and I don't want that for either of you. Both of you swear to me now that you won't lay a hand on that man."

We fall silent, and both exchange glances as neither of us wants to agree to that. I know Rizzo wants to kill him as badly as I do, and has for years.

He groans, shaking his head. "I don't fucking like it, but I swear I won't, Mom."

Her attention falls on me and I tilt my head. "What? Do you think I would kill him?"

Her eyes narrow, as if she knows exactly the demons I battle daily. "Livia, promise me."

I swallow hard and nod. "I promise."

She looks satisfied as she releases a long sigh. "Good, I don't want my children going down such a dark path."

Too fucking late. I'm already well and truly down the dark path and all the way in hell. There's no redemption for me, but I won't break my promise to her.

MAXIM

J walk into my apartment, only to come to a halt at the sight before me. Livia is cooking in my kitchen while her mom and brother sit at my kitchen island.

I clear my throat, drawing Livia's attention to me. "I didn't know we were going to have guests."

Livia's expression hardens at the tone of my voice. "Sorry, I didn't have time to warn you."

"A simple text would have sufficed."

"I couldn't explain everything in a text." She nods to Rizzo. "Can you keep an eye on this for me?"

He gives me an irritated glare before setting his cell phone down and moving to the other side of the kitchen island.

Without a word, Livia leads the way toward our bedroom. My stomach churns when I see a few suit-cases piled up in the corridor.

What the fuck is going on?

Once we're behind closed doors, I repeat my thoughts out loud. "What the fuck is going on, printessa?"

She pinches the bridge of her nose. "Well, the doctors ran some routine blood tests and found out that my father has been poisoning my mother for years." She shrugs, sitting down on the edge of the bed. "It's why she was diagnosed with Bipolar Disorder, although that side-effect is probably irreversible."

"Why the hell would he do that?"

"Because my mom threatened to leave him about ten years ago, and a few months later, she was diagnosed. He wanted to make her feel like she couldn't leave, even if she wanted to." Her throat works as she swallows. "I've said that mom and Rizzo can stay here for now, but Rizzo is heading back to school in two days, anyway."

I run a hand through my hair, not too keen on the idea of sharing my apartment with my mother-in-law. "Isn't there somewhere else she can stay?"

Livia stands and folds her arms over her chest. "Is that seriously all you're going to say right now?"

I move toward her. "It's going to be rather difficult keeping down the noise of our sex life for God knows how long. I'm only thinking of your mother's discomfort."

"You're a fucking pig. I just told you my father has been poisoning her for years and that's all you say?" She paces the floor, looking utterly manic. "I need to help her. She's my family."

I hold my hands up in surrender. "Okay, but I hope you enjoy being gagged, baby."

She huffs, looking exasperated. "Unbelievable."

I laugh, finding her adorable when she's like this. "What's the long-term plan, then?"

"If it was up to me, I'd string my father up in your basement and do my worst. That would be my only plan."

I raise a brow, partial to the idea, even though my father may have objections. "And why aren't you going to do that?"

"One reason, I assume your father wouldn't approve?" she asks, searching my eyes.

I shrug one shoulder. "Who knows? He loves torture more than me. Any excuse."

"The other reason is my mom forced me and Rizzo to swear we wouldn't hurt him."

"Why the fuck would she force you to swear that after what he's done to her?" I clench my jaw, feeling angry on my wife's behalf.

"Because she says that it'll haunt us if we kill our father." She shrugs and paces toward me, looking me square in the eye. "It's not just what he's done to her. He has been abusive for years to the three of us."

"I suspected as much," I murmur.

"You did?" she asks, tilting her head.

"Yes, the hatred you harbor for him was obvious, so

I assumed." A pain constricts around my throat as I look into my wife's beautiful green eyes. "I know what it's like."

"The scars?" she asks.

I nod, unable to elaborate further. "You may have vowed not to harm that piece of shit, but you just have to say the word, and I'll do it for you." I bare my teeth, hating the thought of Livia suffering under his fist. "I'll tear his eyes out and hand them to you on a platter.

Tears gather in her eyes as she stares at me with what I can only describe as admiration and awe. "That's the sweetest thing anyone has ever offered to do for me."

I chuckle, shaking my head. "Most people would say you're certifiably insane for saying tearing someone's eyeballs out could ever be sweet." I slide my arms around her waist and pull her against me. "But we're both just damaged, aren't we, moya lyubov?" I murmur against her lips.

"Yes, we are," she says just before I kiss her lips softly.

She claws at my hair, but doesn't dig her nails in. The aggression in her kiss is no longer apparent as she moans against my mouth, rocking her body against me in search of friction.

I grab her hips forcefully and push her away. "I don't think that's wise with your brother in the kitchen, printessa. Control yourself."

She bites her bottom lip in the most cock-stirring

way, driving me wild. "Fine, you're right. The food will be ready any minute." She walks past me and toward the door. "I hope you're hungry."

I groan, knowing that our encounter made me hungry for one thing only—my wife. "Don't be a tease," I say, as I follow her back to the kitchen. When I walked in here, I'd intended to give her the news that we'd both be attending tomorrow night's poker event with the Morrone family, but that can wait. Tonight, I'll try my best to be on good behavior for Livia's family, because I know how much they mean to her.

Rizzo looks up as we enter. "What you going to do, Maxim? Kick us out on the street?"

I ignore the dig. "Of course not. Livia's family is my family, too." I lean against the countertop, watching as Livia takes control of the cooking again. "You're both welcome here whenever you like."

I notice my wife's face light up, but she keeps focusing on the pot of pasta sauce she's stirring.

"That's very kind of you, Maxim," Greta says, smiling at me.

It's crazy the difference in her even only a short time after being off the drugs her husband was pumping her full of. Perhaps it's just the fact she knows now what is causing the sickness, but I sense her children will see a big difference now she's away from his abuse.

"Foods ready," Livia announces, grabbing the bowls and plating up a portion each. "Spaghetti carbonara."

We each take our bowls and sit down at my dining

table, which I'm not sure I've ever had company around until today. Livia sets a portion of garlic bread in the center and we all eat in silence. I've never been good at small talk and feel a little uncomfortable about being forced to sit with people I don't know.

Thankfully, it seems the Bianchi family doesn't talk much while eating either. As the companionable silence continues, I feel myself relax, enjoying my wife's amazing pasta.

"You look stunning," I say, as I lean on the door frame into our bedroom, watching as my wife puts her diamond earrings in.

She smiles at me in the mirror. "I can't believe we're actually doing this."

"Nervous?" I ask.

She shakes her head. "I'm excited."

Rizzo appears behind me, shaking his head. "Are you sure you want to do this, sis?"

I clench my jaw. Livia agreed to attend as my date without me needing to convince her, not that I believe I could convince her to do anything she doesn't want to, anyway.

"Certain, quit worrying, little bro."

Rizzo glares at me. "You better keep her safe."

"Always," I say.

He nods and then walks away, leaving us alone. I

step into the room and shut the door behind me, leaning against it.

"Why are you looking at me like that?" She twirls a loose strand of hair around her finger, proving she knows exactly why I'm looking at her the way I am.

"Don't play dumb with me, printessa."

She pouts and I can't deny that this new, flirty side to my wife is a real turn on. Even though I love her getting rough with me, I also love seeing her willing and compliant. "I don't know what you're talking about."

I growl softly and walk toward her, stopping a foot from her and unzipping my pants to free my hard cock.

She gasps as it bobs in her face, practically touching her lips.

"Stop pouting and wrap those pretty lips around me," I order.

Fire ignites in her pale green eyes as she meets my gaze. "Make me," she says, challenge in her tone.

I groan and thread my fingers through her carefully styled hair, thrusting my cock against her lips until they give way and allow me inside.

She gags the instant I hit the back of her throat, but I give her no reprieve, thrusting in and out of her throat like a madman. Tears prickle her eyes as she glares up at me, breathing through her nose as I fuck her throat.

I notice her hand slip down between her thighs as she plays with herself, which only spurs me on.

"Good girl, play with your cunt while you choke on my cock," I groan.

Livia moans around my shaft, breathing through her nose as saliva drips down to my balls and all over her face. It's a fucking beautiful sight. One of the most beautiful things I've ever seen.

She slips two fingers inside of herself, fucking her pretty pussy while I ram every inch of my dick down her throat. I try not to mess up her hair, but it's kind of hard to control myself as I use her hair to thrust even deeper and harder. She gags, warning me if I'm not careful she might throw up all over my dick, so I ease off and pull my cock reluctantly from her mouth.

"Stand up, baby," I order.

Livia does as I say, holding my gaze with those fiery emerald green eyes.

"Tell me what you want."

Her nostrils flare as she holds my gaze, looking irritated by my delay tactics. I want her to beg me for it, but I know she's not going to. "Stop messing about, Maxim."

I lean forward and kiss her lips, nipping and sucking at them. "You know what I want, baby."

She moans, lacing her fingers in my hair and drawing me in closer. "Then take it," she breathes against my lips, barely a whisper.

That snaps my resolve as I grab her hips and force her back to me, bending her over and hiking the skirt of her dress all the way up. My dirty little printessa didn't even have panties on and the sight of her glistening cunt nestled between her thick thighs makes me harder than granite.

"You're such a good girl, so wet and ready for her husband." I slide my finger through her entrance and bring it to my lips, sucking her arousal off of them. "I think I need a taste."

I kneel behind her and slide my tongue through her, groaning at the taste. She's so fucking sweet it makes me ache with need. Slowly, I trail my tongue all the way back to her asshole and she tenses, trying to escape me.

I dig my fingernails into her hips and claw her against me, moving away to mutter, "Let me lick that beautiful little hole of yours. I promise it'll feel good."

Her pussy gushes at my words, but she doesn't speak. I take it as an agreement as I thrust my tongue back against the sensitive ring of muscles, groaning as she arches her back. As I lavish attention on her ass, I thrust two fingers into her wetness and finger fuck her, making her moan loudly, forgetting her family is somewhere nearby in this apartment.

Gently, I pinch her clit and she squeals, her body tensing as I continue to her lick her ass. "Maxim," she cries my name, her whole body tensing as she comes undone.

"That's it, baby, come while I lick that tight little asshole," I groan, feeling my cock leak onto the floor. "I'd love to stretch it around my cock and feel you come while I'm balls deep in your ass."

She tenses at that, despite the orgasm still ripping through her. "No fucking chance," she spits.

I chuckle and pull her tighter against me, continuing to lick her there. "I love a challenge." Spreading my legs out so I'm sitting firmly on the floor, I yank her down over me and force her onto my cock in one swift movement.

She cries out, body bucking in reaction to the sudden violent invasion. "Fuck," she breathes, trying to ride my cock.

I hold her firm to me, so she can't move. "I'm in charge, printessa." I reach around with my good hand, despite my fingers almost being healed, and grab her throat, making her whimper. "Don't worry, I won't fuck that tight little asshole until you tell me you're ready," I breathe, my cock aching in protest. "I'll play with your ass and show you how good anal play can be, but I won't stick my cock in there, not until you beg me to give it to you."

Livia moans, arching her hips and leaning into my hand as if begging me to choke her harder.

I oblige, tightening my grasp as I rut into her from below, grunting as her cunt tightens around me like a fucking vice. "So damn good, printessa." I flex my fingers around her soft, delicate throat, pushing a little further. "Come for me while I choke you," I snarl.

Livia whimpers as I push even harder, feeling her tight muscles squeeze me so hard I know I can't last another second. One more thrust and my body tenses as my release hits me like a torrent, flooding me with ecstasy as I rut into my wife, draining my balls deep inside of her.

I release her throat, but keep it gently cupping her neck.

Livia's head bobs to the side slightly as I let her go, grabbing her hips and pulling her off of me. "Fuck," she murmurs, bringing a hand up to her hair.

"What's wrong?" I ask.

"I spent ages doing my hair," she says, glancing over her shoulder at me. "And now it's ruined."

"It was worth it, though. Wasn't it?"

She smirks but doesn't answer me, climbing off the floor and adjusting her dress.

I stand and walk to the dresser to grab her a pair of panties, returning to her side. "Put these on. I want you to feel my cum dripping out of you into them."

Livia's lips purse as she snatches the panties, sliding them on. "Fine, now let me sort my hair out since you fucked it up."

I chuckle and walk away, glancing at my watch as I make it to the door. "You've got ten minutes, printessa, and not a minute more."

As I leave my wife getting ready, I can't help but feel nervous about what we're about to do. I'm taking the most precious thing in my life into the most dangerous situation I've encountered in a long time. I hope it's not a decision I'll regret.

27

LIVIA

*A*ll eyes are on us as we move through the casino toward the back.

I swallow hard, knowing I wasn't quite expecting this frosty a welcome. Yes, the Morrone family and Volkov family are at war, but they invited us here. Luca, the man who invaded my home, notices us and comes to greet us.

"I'm glad you made it," he says, smiling and offering his hand to Maxim.

Maxim regards it skeptically, before shaking it. "It's only polite we hear you out."

Spartak steps up by his side and glares at Luca. "Where is your father, Luca?"

Luca glances toward the back of the casino, where many people are gathered around a table. "He's at the table, getting ready for the game to start. I'll take you to him."

Maxim squeezes my hip as Luca leads us toward the back of the casino, further into the lion's den. Adrenaline courses through my veins as I keep my body pinned close to his side, knowing that I'm out of my depth. My father always ran any events he took us to. In Italy, there isn't the same dynamic in one city, with multiple opposing syndicates operating side by side.

Luca stops and clears his throat behind a man, who I can only assume is Remy Morrone.

The man glances over his shoulder, unique hazel eyes flashing when he sees us behind him. He stands, towering over all the men in proximity, including his son.

I swallow hard, but try not to look too intimidated. He's classically handsome for an older man, with a square jaw and neatly cut hair which is styled impeccably so that no hair is out of place, in contrast to Spartak's messy and rough appearance, but they have to be about the same age. Tattoos are visible just over the collar of his white dress shit, which is buttoned all the way up and paired with a black tie.

Spartak appears unfazed by Remy's ridiculous height. He has to be close to seven feet tall as he glares down at us. "I'm surprised you came," he says, his voice obviously American with a lilt of Italian. He's lived in America for over twenty years, so it's expected.

Spartak shrugs. "The only way to end the war is to agree to a truce." He crosses his arms over his chest. "I assume you have a proposal, so I'm here to listen."

Remy nods. "And gamble, I hope?"

"Of course," Spartak says, a wicked smirk splitting his face in two. "I can't wait to bleed you dry."

His nostrils flare at my father-in-law's choice of words. "I wouldn't be so cocky if I were you." He sits back down and nods to the two empty seats at the table. "You and your son may join. Half a million buy in."

Fuck. That's a hell of a lot of cash to gamble with.

Maxim leans toward me and whispers, "Stay close and sit behind me."

"Make them pay," I breathe back.

I sit down on the closest seat to Maxim's chair, wishing it were closer. Luca sits next to me, to my annoyance, but Timur, Spartak's sovietnik, sits on my other side, reassuring me.

"So, Livia. How's married life treating you?" Luca asks, smirking as he watches Maxim's expression harden when he looks back to see him talking to me.

"Fine, thanks."

A server that is walking around with champagne stops in front of us. "A drink?"

I smile and reach for one, but Timur grabs my hand and shakes his head. "No drinks for us, thank you."

Luca chuckles and takes the glass I was about to take, tipping the contents back in one and then placing it back on the server's tray. "If you think we're going to poison you, then you've no idea what our style is." His dark brown eyes sparkle with mischief as he glances over at Timur.

"Fine, take one," he says, clearly satisfied that it's not laced with poison.

I grab another glass, and so does Luca, as I sit back and sniff the drink. It smells fine, so I take a sip but can't help the sense of unease at being forced to sit by a Morrone. As a child, my father taught us to hate the Morrone family for what they did to his parents, and yet I don't see how my father is any different from them.

He's a criminal who kills and maims for his own benefit, just like the Morrone family.

The dealer deals the eight players their cards and everyone turns quiet as they watch the high-stakes game begin.

Luca leans toward me. "Have you ever attended a poker game before?"

I shake my head. "No, my father isn't into gambling."

His brow furrows. "Strange, considering he owns so many casinos."

"It doesn't mean he gambles at them." I clench my jaw, wishing he'd leave me alone.

"Do you know the rules?" He asks, continuing the conversation.

"Yes, whoever has the highest hand at the end wins. It's pretty simple." I knock back the rest of my champagne and turn away from him, muttering to Timur. "Do I have to sit next to this asshole?"

Timur laughs out loud and then leans toward me to

whisper back, "Unfortunately, it would be impolite if you were to move away." There's a glimmer of amusement in his eyes, as if he's getting kicks from my discomfort.

"Thanks a lot," I say, crossing my arms over my chest as I focus on my husband.

His back is tense as he shuffles his cards in his hands and the dealer places three cards face up on the table. Where I'm sitting, it's impossible to see what those cards are.

Spartak looks to be in his element, casually smirking at his opponents and paying no attention to the cards in his hand.

Remy looks on edge as he shuffles his cards back to front, glancing now and then at the three on the table. I don't know who the other five players are, so I lean toward Luca. "Who else is playing?"

He smirks at me. "My two brothers, Massimo and Leo, he signals to the two young men who look strikingly similar to both Luca and his father. The two opposite are my cousins, Matteo and Rico."

I nod in response. "And the last man?"

His eyes widen, and he laughs. "You don't know who my father's consigliere is?"

I shake my head. "You forget I'm not from here."

"That's Lorenzo Di-Arturo, my father's right-hand man."

I swallow hard, realizing this really is a family affair other than Maxim and Spartak. There's a tension in the air as Remy places his first bid, upping the blind bet by fifty thousand.

Spartak calls, but Maxim folds, chucking his cards into the center of the table. Rico and Lorenzo both fold, but the others see Remy's bid. I sense there's a real family rivalry in the way his two older brothers look at their father, wanting to beat him more than anything. Desperation is etched into their expressions.

The dealer deals the turn, placing a fourth card in the center.

A few mutters break out around the table from the spectators, and I lean toward Timur. "Can you even see the cards from here?"

He shakes his head. "No, it's a shit place to sit."

I sigh heavily and get the attention of another server who is serving drinks and canapes. "Thank you," I say, as I grab a glass of champagne and a mini bruschetta.

Luca follows suit, grabbing one of each, too. "Good choice. The bruschetta is to die for."

Timur stiffens at his choice of words, grabbing my hand as I'm about to take a bite. "Eat yours first," he orders.

Luca rolls his eyes. "How many times do I have to tell you that poisoning isn't out style, bonehead?" He shoves it into his mouth, chews and then swallows and opens his mouth for Timur to see rather unelegantly.

"I think you put me off my bruschetta," I mutter.

Luca laughs and sips his champagne, leaning back in his chair.

Spartak raises the bid on this hand, adding another fifty thousand to the pot. Remy is quick to call, but Massimo bows out on this round, leaving Matteo and Leo left in with Spartak and Remy.

The dealer deals the river, and I notice the way Matteo's posture changes. I sense he has a bad hand from the irritated look on his face.

Spartak looks as cool as ever, glancing once at his cards before rapping his fingers rhythmically on the table.

Leo raises the blind bet to one-hundred thousand dollars, and I see the flash in Spartak's eyes the moment he does. He's ecstatic, which suggests he either has an amazing hand or he's fucking crazy. I'm not sure which it is yet.

Remy and Spartak call, but as I expected, Matteo folds, bowing out of this game.

"Right, reveal your cards," the dealer calls.

Leo goes first, throwing down a flush, all five cards belonging to hearts. "Flush," he says, looking pleased with himself.

Remy's lip twitches slightly into a smirk as he throws down his hand, revealing a full house, which beats his son's hand. "Sorry, son, but that's not the winning hand." I notice Remy reach for the chips.

Spartak clears his throat, shaking his head. "Neither is yours, Morrone." He throws down his cards, revealing the highest possible hand, a straight flush.

Remy growls softly, backing away from the chips. "Beginner's luck," he mutters.

Spartak smirks. "Believe me, I'm no beginner at poker." He claims his chips, stacking them up in piles. "I told you that I'd bleed you dry."

The dealer deals the next hand and the games go on in a similar fashion, resulting in Spartak building his chips up so fucking high. Maxim wins a few hands, but he's only about even when someone rings a bell.

Remy clears his throat. "Looks like it's a recess, gentlemen." His attention moves to Spartak. "How about we go somewhere private and have a chat, man to man?"

Maxim stands. "Not without me," he says.

"Fine, four of us can talk. You and your father, and Massimo and I." He nods toward the back where a guard opens a door. "We'll speak in one of the VIP suites."

I stand and approach Maxim, who wraps an arm around my waist and yanks me against him. "Are you sure about this?"

He nods. "There's no way out of this war without negotiating." He presses a quick kiss to my lips. "Stay with Timur and Osip and get them to cash our chips in case we need a quick getaway."

I nod and squeeze him tightly once more. "Be careful."

He shakes his head. "I'm always careful." With that,

he marches after his father, leaving me with his two men.

I approach Timur. "Maxim asked you to cash his and his father's chips, just in case."

Timur nods and Osip asks the dealer to remove Maxim and Spartak from the game, taking the chips.

I swallow hard, glancing at the shut door at the back of the casino. When I met Maxim, I never would have believed I'd be worried about his welfare. In fact, I thought I'd be the one who ended up murdering him or die trying.

One month into marriage and he's become the most important part of my world. My broken knight in shining armor. It would ruin me to lose him.

28

MAXIM

*R*emy glares at my father, the tension heightening. "Why did you come if you have no intention of releasing my niece?" He shakes his head, looking exasperated. "Surely you knew any agreement would hinge on her safe return."

Father's jaw tightens. "I'm not sure she wants to be returned."

My brow furrows as I wonder what the fuck my father is talking about. He snatched her the moment she made it to Chicago and held her captive in a torture basement. Of course she wants to be returned.

"Bullshit," Massimo says, clenching his fists on the table. "Imalia would want to be home with her family. Why can't you free her as part of a truce?"

There's an odd look in my father's eyes, but I can't work out what his problem is. This was always going to be the minimum ask when we came here, and while I know I can't question him in front of the Morrone family, I need to speak to him alone.

"Gentlemen, can you give me and my father a moment?" I say, standing.

My father gives me an irritated glare, but stands. "Yes, we'll only be a minute."

I lead him out of earshot of the family and turn to face him. "What the fuck are you doing? Why won't you release Imalia as part of the deal?"

His jaw works. "Because she's mine." The ferocity in his voice takes me by surprise.

"What?"

"I said, she's mine," he growls.

"For fuck's sake, you can't be serious." I run a hand across the back of my neck. "Get over it and let her go."

He grabs hold of the lapel of my jacket and thrusts me against a wall. "Would you let Livia go?"

"She's my wife. I don't need to let her go." I grab my father's hands and prize them off me, shoving him back. "You kidnapped a young girl and now can't get over your wet dreams enough to put the war and the brotherhood before your sick and twisted fantasy."

"Watch your mouth, boy," he snarls, looking positively feral.

"If you knew you wouldn't let her go, why the fuck are we here?"

He shrugs, a manic look in his eyes. "To play poker."

I run a hand through my hair. "Have you lost your mind? We're in Remy's fucking casino and you expect he'll let us walk out after flat out refusing the one fucking thing they want?" I pace the floor, unable to believe how out of touch he's become. "Agree to give her up or you'll escalate this fucking war."

My father walks over to me with danger sparking in his irises—danger I've only seen when he's about to torture or murder. "You don't give me orders, Maxim. Stand down before I put you down." With that, he walks back to the table and takes his seat, leaving me reeling.

Why the fuck did we come here tonight?

It made sense to come if we had any intention of negotiating terms, but it's clear that wasn't my father's plan. He's spent too long out of touch with reality and finally it's going to result in chaos.

The main reason I'm so angry is because he allowed me to bring Livia here, fully aware that we were walking into a hostile environment with no intention of giving them the one thing that would be non-negotiable. Their family member, who he snatched from Chicago International Airport.

I return to the table and take my seat, clearing my throat. "Sorry about that."

Luca claps his hands. "Any movement on the matter?"

I exchange heated glances with my father, but he's the one to speak. "Possibly. I'm willing to give her back in one week if your organization meets certain conditions."

Remy straightens. "What conditions?"

I sit up straighter, unsure what nonsense my father is about to come up with.

"A ceasefire between our organizations for seven days and an agreement on the Volkov Bratva dealing arms in the city."

Remy scoffs, shaking his head. "You expect us to agree to you muscling in on one of our most lucrative businesses?"

Massimo laughs. "What if we asked for an agreement to sell cocaine?"

"That's our entire business model. Guns are a small portion of your revenue," Father replies.

"It doesn't matter. The territory for guns is non-negotiable," Remy says, cutting off the negotiations.

My father stands and nods. "I guess this negotiation is over, then."

Remy growls, slamming his hands down on the table. "What about my niece?"

"I told you my price, you refused." Spartak shrugs. "If you change your mind, come and find me."

Timur and Osip have already cashed out our chips after my father made a fucking killing. They're waiting for us as we walk through the exit of the meeting room, but I'm expecting some resistance. I check my watch, grinding my teeth when I see it's just after midnight, which means Anton's group should have completed the seizure of Remy's gun shipment.

Remy's phone rings as we walk out, forcing me to hasten my steps.

"We need to get out of here, fast," I mutter to my father.

He glances at me and then at his watch, nodding in understanding. "Yes, we do."

Livia stands by Timur's side and her eyes light up when she sees me walking out of the room, alive.

I approach her and wrap an arm around her back, steering her toward the exit of the casino.

"How did it go?" She asks.

I shake my head. "Not good, and it's just after midnight."

Her brow furrows. "What does that mean?"

"It means that one of our teams have just stolen a fuck load of guns from Remy."

"Volkov," Remy growls from behind us, making my heart skip a beat.

Father glances at me and mouths the word, "Run."

"Livia, we've got to run." I grab her hand in mine and we take off. All four of us rushing as fast as we can toward the heavily guarded exit of the casino.

"How are we going to get past the guards?" Livia asks.

I squeeze her hand and force her to run faster, even though she's in heels. "Don't worry."

The guards notice us once we're about a few yards

away and pull out guns, making the crowd around them scatter.

"Fuck," I say, reaching for my gun and aiming it at one of them. I don't shoot to kill, hitting him in the leg and bringing him down.

Father is fast too, shooting another in both kneecaps. Osip misses his shot and the guard he misses shoots back, catching him in the shoulder.

"Fuck," he growls, blood splattering into the air as he continues to run.

Timur shoots the guard Osip missed, but it's a killer blow, right through his head. It leaves the exit open as we jump over the guards, rushing through the exit, only to be confronted with four more armed guards.

"Shit," Livia mutters, grabbing my hand again.

I lift our hands in the air in surrender, but suddenly the guards are shot from behind.

Livia's brow furrows. "You didn't tell me we had backup."

I smirk. "I couldn't be sure they'd actually back us up."

We rush toward them, where Adrik waits with the door to the van open. Father reaches it first, slipping inside, followed by Timur and an injured Osip. I try to run faster, but the heels slow Livia down. "Next time, wear flats," I say.

She bares her teeth at me. "Sorry, I didn't know we'd be running out of there for our lives."

"It was always a possibility."

The bang of a gunshot startles me and Livia's eyes widen, making me sure they shot her.

"Maxim," she cries, eyes welling with tears as she stares at my shoulder.

I look down to see blood coating my jacket. "Shit," I say.

Father returns, shooting at my attacker to get us into the back of the van. "Where are you hit?"

"They shot him in the shoulder," Livia says, tears streaming down her cheeks.

It's hard to believe that this vixen hated me less than a month ago, but somewhere along the line, it changed. She's worried about me. "I'll be fine, Livia."

Timur creates a tourniquet to stem the blood flow as Adrik drives the van away from the scene. Artyom leans down to look at the wound, as his father medically trained him when he was younger as a skill to bring to the bratva. "It looks like the bullet might have hit an artery, as there's a lot of blood. We need to get him to a hospital fast."

Livia's panicked expression hurts me more than the gunshot wound. "Will he be okay?"

My father grabs Artyom's shoulder. "You know we can't take him to a hospital," he hisses.

"It's either that, or he bleeds out in an hour tops," my uncle answers.

"Fuck," he replies, shaking his head. "Fine, we'll have to drop Maxim at the hospital with Livia."

He gives Livia a stern look. "You tell them that someone mugged you in the street, no other specifics."

She raises a brow. "Great, they're going to think I have some kind of mugging magnet or something."

"Why?" Father demands.

"Because that's the same story I gave them to my mom when she got shot at home."

"Shit," he growls, running a hand through his hair. "Fine, you tell them it was a drive-by instead. You don't know why they targeted you."

Livia nods. "Okay."

I feel my vision blur a little as I rest back against the side of the van, feeling nauseous. Fuck. Maybe my uncle is right, and it's a bad hit, as someone has shot me before, but I've never felt like this.

"Are you okay?" Livia asks, setting a hand against my forehead.

"I feel dizzy," I say, as everything swims in front of me.

Artyom nods. "That's the blood loss." He glances at Livia. "Try to keep him conscious."

I swallow hard, knowing I've not seen my uncle look so serious, perhaps ever. My injury isn't just a flesh wound, the bullet has clearly hit an artery.

Livia shifts closer to me, grabbing my good hand and squeezing. "Stay with me, Maxim."

Her eyes are glistening with unshed tears as she looks into mine and I feel her fear. She fears losing me, which is laughable considering how much she hated me when we met.

"You'll be okay, even if I don't pull through."

She shakes her head, jaw clenching. "Don't talk like that." Cupping my face in her hands, she looks me in the eye. "I love you, Maxim, and I can't lose you."

My throat tightens as I stare into her eyes and whisper, "I love you, too, moya lyubov." I don't want anyone else to hear, as my father would tell me not to express my feelings in public. After all, if you have something or someone to lose, you give your enemy a target.

Tears stream down her face as we sit in silence, staring into each other's eyes. I have to make it through for her, as I know my father wouldn't take care of her. He wouldn't be concerned about what happens to her if I'm not here.

Her face grows fuzzier and my head lulls to one side, darkness dragging me into the abyss.

"Maxim," her voice sounds far off as I drift away, knowing I'll fight death as long as I can for her.

LIVIA

I pace up and down the waiting area, getting pissed off glances as I do, but I don't care.

Maxim has been in surgery now for an hour and still no news. The bullet hit the brachial artery and shattered the edge of his humerus, so they're trying to get all the fragments out and stop him bleeding.

Fear like nothing I've ever felt floods me every second that ticks by. I can't lose Maxim, even though I wanted to throttle him when we first got married. He's my world, my rock. Without him, I have nothing.

"Mrs. Volkov?" A doctor says, drawing my attention to a surgeon in bloodied scrubs.

I rush over, heart hammering so hard I can hardly hear anything around me. "Is he okay?"

He nods. "Yes, he's out of theater and stable. We removed all the bone fragments that could have caused an issue and the bleeding has stopped, but we want to keep him in for a few days, of course, to monitor him."

I swallow hard, my throat constricting in relief, as all I want to do is cry. "Can I see him, please?"

"Of course, follow me."

He leads me through the swing doors and through to a small private room where Maxim is lying asleep on the bed. "He's a little drowsy from the anesthetic, but he should be coherent."

"Thank you, doctor," I say, walking into the room.

Maxim's eyes open the moment I enter, and he smiles lazily. "Hey, printessa."

"Hey," I say, feeling the tears trickle down my cheeks. "I thought I was going to lose you."

He shakes his head. "Did you really think you'd get rid of me that easily?"

I walk toward him and sit down on a chair next to the bed, clutching his hand. "I've never been so scared."

"Well, well, didn't think my feisty little princess would ever worry about me." He tilts his head slightly. "What changed?"

"Everything," I murmur.

He nods as if he understands. "Indeed. I have felt the change too, moya lyubov."

"It was my fault you got shot," I say, knowing the guilt has been almost as unbearable as the worry. "If I'd worn flats—"

"Don't you dare blame yourself for this." He grinds his teeth. "Blame my father."

"Why? What did he do?"

Maxim shakes his head. "He made ridiculous demands and then forgot to get us out before he scheduled a hit on Remy's cargo."

"What demands?"

He sighs. "He didn't want to give up Imalia. The guy has totally fucking lost it."

"I don't understand. Why agree to the meeting if he isn't willing to negotiate with the woman he holds as leverage?"

"Good fucking question." Maxim winces as he shifts in bed. "Fuck, whoever shot me got me good."

I swallow hard. "It could have been worse."

"Has my father visited?" He asks.

I shake my head. "He rang me about twenty minutes ago to check up on you and I had to tell him I hadn't heard anything and that you were in surgery, but he said it's too risky for him to visit."

He shakes his head. "Figures. Even if I were on my deathbed, he wouldn't be here."

"Surely that's not true."

He narrows his eyes. "Did you know he shot my sister less than three months ago? He tried to kill her and landed her in this hospital."

"Shit, and I thought my father was fucked up."

Maxim's jaw works. "After my mom died, he changed, and that's when he started being more abusive, not that he was a saint before, but it wasn't as bad." There's a glint of sadness in his eyes. "He never went as far with Viki, since he had to preserve her skin for her future husband, but with me…" He breaks my gaze, glancing down at his hands. "He would say scars make a man."

"What made him the way he is?" I ask.

He meets my gaze, shrugging. "The same brutality as a child. He has more scars than I do and he told me I was getting off light compared to him as a child."

"Brutality breeds brutality," I mutter, knowing that statement is more true than I can explain. My violent desires and needs to maim never would have existed if my father did not ingrain it into me as a child. The anger and desire to fight against the man abusing me.

"Exactly," he breathes, sighing heavily. "You're the only person I've ever spoken to about my scars." There's such fire in his eyes as he watches me. "I think perhaps fate brought us together, even though you resisted it to start with."

I roll my eyes. "That's because you're cocky and think you can boss me around."

He smirks. "I still believe I can."

"You'd think you would have learned by now." I cross my arms over my chest. "When have I ever let you boss me around?"

"I can think of a few times more recently when you've been more pliable." He licks his lips. "For example, when I forced my cock down your throat before we left for the casino."

"You can be a real pig, you know?"

He nods. "I know, but being totally serious, I think I needed you to fight me. Hurt me." His Adam's apple bobs as he swallows, looking unsure about what he's going to say next. "I've been unchecked for so long, my violence spiraling out of control. You fighting me helped ground me, if that makes sense."

I nod, as it makes perfect sense. "It does." I suck in my inner cheeks, unsure about sharing my inner most demons with this man. "The pills I took helped suppress that side of me."

Maxim doesn't look surprised by my admission. "I guessed that much when you broke my hand."

Guilt floods me as I remember how the aggression poured out of me that day. It was untamable. "Yeah, I'm sorry about that. When you took me to that place, you uncaged a monster."

He shakes his head. "Not a monster, a beautiful, powerful queen." He reaches for my hand with his good one and squeezes. "My queen."

My throat aches and I shake my head. "How can you say that when you know how dark I can get?"

He raises a brow. "You don't think that same darkness lives in me, too?"

I know it does, but my father always made me believe men like him want sweet and innocent women. "Yes, but men want their women sweet and innocent." I bite my lip, feeling vulnerable at what I'm about to say. "Even you expected me to be pliable and easy to force into submission."

"I'm fucking glad you weren't. That's never what I wanted or needed. I think that's pretty fucking clear, considering how in love with you I am."

I swallow hard, trying to ignore the pain clawing at my chest. Although I told him I loved him in the back of that van and he said it back, I wasn't sure he truly meant it, considering he had been shot and wasn't totally lucid.

"I never thought I was capable of loving anyone other than my mom and Rizzo," I say, biting my bottom lip. "Until we met, and even then, I thought I'd probably kill you before our first year anniversary."

He chuckles, shaking his head. "I thought you would as well."

"What I'm trying to say is I'm pretty sure I love you, as I'm not sure what else this crazy, intense feeling could be."

Maxim beckons for me to get closer. "Come here."

I do as he says, shifting onto the side of the hospital bed and wrapping an arm around his waist, careful not to hurt him. "I was so scared while you were in theater." I hold him tighter, knowing that losing him would tear an irreparable hole inside of me. "Never do that again."

"Right, because I chose to get shot while we ran from Morrone's fucking casino," he says, sarcasm dripping from his tone.

I gaze into his eyes. "I shouldn't have worn the heels."

He shakes his head. "I would have got hit whether you were wearing them or sneakers."

"Don't lie to me." I press my lips to his, inhaling his scent as I do. "I would have never been able to live with myself if you had died," I breathe against his lips. "You're my world."

He smiles, nipping my bottom lip with his teeth. "You really have changed your tune since we met, haven't you?"

I tilt my head. "Haven't you?" I ask.

He nods. "Yes, as you're my queen." He kisses me, wincing as he moves. "My princess. My equal."

I sigh and lean into him. "So I'm no longer your slave and captive?" I ask.

He smirks. "Oh, you're that too when it suits me."

I laugh. "Even a bullet couldn't stop you from being an asshole, hey?"

He nips my earlobe in warning. "Watch it, printessa."

I slip off of the bed and out of his grasp, folding my arms over my chest. "Or what? You're not exactly in a position to be making threats."

His jaw works. "My injury isn't here forever, so don't get any ideas."

"Perhaps it's my perfect chance to torture you the way you tortured me for six days," I say.

"You wouldn't dare."

I raise a brow. "Watch me." I move toward the bed

and reach under the sheets, grabbing his already hard cock under his hospital gown. "So hard for me," I muse.

His eyes narrow. "Don't you fucking dare tease me, Livia."

"It's alright, you have one free hand to finish yourself off." I slide my hand up and down his cock four times before releasing it and trying to remove my hand.

He grabs it with his good hand, eyes flashing with fire. "You fucking get back under that cover and put your hot little mouth on my cock before I make you regret ever touching it," he growls.

I smirk and yank my hand free, shaking my head. "No, it's about time you see how it feels to be denied something you want so badly." I turn around to leave and glance over my shoulder, hitching the skirt of my dress up and pulling my ass cheeks apart so he can see how wet I am. "I'll see you tomorrow, baby. As visiting hours are over."

He growls like an animal as I walk out of the hospital room, feeling oddly satisfied to get my own back on him. After all, he locked me up for six days and tortured me. One little taunt isn't going to hurt. And if it does, it means he'll punish me, which is what I crave, anyway.

There's a lightness in my step as I walk out of the hospital, knowing for the first time in my life everything is going to be okay. The darkness inside of me is no longer something to fear. It's a part of me, and Maxim has taught me how to embrace it.

30

MAXIM

*L*ivia packs my shit into a holdall, looking sexy as hell as she moves around the room in her little dress, which makes me harder than stone.

Five days in this hellhole and I'm beyond ready to leave.

"Thank fuck I'm getting out of this place today."

Livia shakes her head. "It's not that bad here."

"Not that bad? Have you seen the food they've been bringing me?" I ask.

She crosses her arms over her chest. "Yes, but you haven't been eating it. I bought you meals every day."

"Yes, for lunch, but the other two meals have been shit and I'm bored out of my mind." I grab the skirt of Livia's dress as she moves past the bed with my good hand, yanking her toward me. "Plus, I'm ready for you to ride me at home like a sexy cowgirl." I release her

329

skirt and pull back the sheets so she can see how ready, as my cock bulges against my hospital gown, which is wet where I've leaked precum.

She bites her bottom lip, shaking her head. "You know the doctor has prescribed you bedrest. He said strictly no strenuous activities."

I smile, noticing the way Livia's cheeks flush at the bulge and her lips part. "It's not strenuous if you do all the work."

She sets her hands on her hips, which draws attention to her beautiful figure, which only makes me harder. "You were shot in the shoulder only five days ago, Maxim."

I roll my eyes. "And I'm on a fuck load of painkillers, so I'm as high as a kite and ready to fuck."

I see the flash of desire in her eyes, even as she fights it. "Stop talking like that."

I tilt my head. "Why? Am I convincing you to hop on and enjoy the ride?"

She bites the inside of her cheek, looking at me furiously. "You're not the only one who's horny, so shut up."

That only convinces me to push harder, as I keep the sheets peeled back and release my cock beneath my hospital gown. "Then hop on and relieve yourself, baby."

She releases a frustrated sigh. "Here?" She asks, glancing at the door, which has glass panels in. "What if someone sees us?"

"So what?" I say, stroking my painfully hard dick with my good arm. "I'm so ready for that pretty little cunt of yours."

Her cheeks deepen in color as she glares at me, her thighs clenching in response to my dirty talk. "Fuck it," she says, walking toward me and getting onto the bed.

She straddles my legs, and I slide my good hand under her dress and groan. "No panties?"

She bites her lip, looking guilty. "I kind of hoped you might want me to ride you at some point, so every day I turned up without them on."

"Fuck," I groan, feeling her wet heat against my hard length.

She sets her hands on my chest and pushes me down. "Lie back and relax. I don't want to fuck up your recovery."

I groan as she rolls her hips above me, coating the length of my cock in her wetness. She's wetter than ever, poised to fuck me in a public hospital. "Do you like the idea of fucking in public, princess?" I ask.

Her lips purse together, and she gives me an irritated glance. "Ever since you licked me to climax in the lobby of that wellness center, I fucking crave it."

I laugh, loving how angry she is about that. "Good, because I want to fuck you where anyone can see us, so people know you belong to me."

"I don't belong to anyone," she says, as she grinds her clit against my shaft, chasing her own pleasure.

I roll my eyes. "Are you still trying to convince your-self of that?"

A whisper of a smirk tugs at her lips, but she doesn't answer me. Instead, she reaches for my cock and wraps her delicate hand around my shaft, lifting her hips to line her entrance up with the head of my cock. She hovers there, holding my gaze. "Tell me what you want."

I grind my teeth, struggling to accept my position right now. Physically, I can't take control because my shoulder is fucked, but it doesn't change how badly I want to. "Fuck me. I want you to ride my cock until you come apart, making a mess of the hospital bedsheets."

Her eyes dilate as she moves suddenly, impaling herself on my dick in one swift motion.

I grunt, and she moans. Both of us are desperate for this after five days of being apart. It's so damn diffi-cult to resist the urge to take control and grab her hips, even though I know I'd do too much damage to my shoulder. Instead, I rest my good hand on her hip, feeling her movements as she thrusts up and down over my cock.

Livia's eyes snap open when she feels me tighten my hold, digging my fingernails into her skin. Her tight muscles are still wrapped around me as she comes to a stop, leaning forward and pressing her lips to mine. "No touching."

I swallow hard, realizing that right now Livia has all the fucking cards. "Don't be a tease, baby. You may have the power now, but once my shoulder is healed, I'll make you pay, so tread carefully."

Excitement flashes in her eyes. "You should know by now that threatening to punish me is like dangling a fucking piece of meat in front of a starving lion."

I laugh, because she's right. "Hmm, because the idea of me carving your pretty little skin up once I'm healed and then licking the blood off of you isn't off putting?"

Her breath hitches as she moves again, the idea making her too needy to resist. "You better had as soon as you're able," she says, holding my gaze.

I groan, digging my fingernails harder into her hips. "I can't wait."

She fucks me harder now, her eyes rolling back in her head as she imagines our twisted fantasy.

I watch her in awe as she moves her hand across her body, pinching her hard nipples through the fabric of her dress and moaning. I grind my teeth together, enjoying the show as she chases her pleasure with no thought of anything else.

She's the most breathtaking women I've ever seen, especially when she's like this. Full of red hot desire as she takes what she wants from me.

A flash of movement outside the door draws my attention, and I notice a couple of nurses sniggering at the door. "Looks like we have an audience, baby."

Livia's eyes shoot open as she glances toward the door, moaning when she sees the two women watching.

"Let them watch." Her hips roll harder as she meets my gaze, looking at me like some sexy siren that's got me under her spell.

"You're fucking perfect," I breathe, moving my good hand up to cup her throat and applying pressure. "I know how much you love me choking you." I flex my fingers, tightening my grasp. "Let's give them something to talk about."

Livia's eyes flash with a challenge as she bounces more viciously on my cock. Her body working in fluid movements as she pulls down the front of her dress, freeing her firm breasts.

I groan at the sight of her hard nipples pointing right at me, wishing I had the ability to sit up and suck on them. When I'm healed, I'm going to spend hours buried in her to make up for this bullshit. "Play with those nipples for me."

She does as I say, reaching up and rubbing her fingers over the sensitive peaks, moaning as she does. Her head falls back in pleasure. "Fuck, I'm so close, Maxim."

"Good," I growl, tightening my grasp on her throat. "Play with your clit and make yourself come on my cock," I demand.

Her body tenses as she moves her hand down her stomach and then rubs her clit, moaning as she does. "Oh fuck, yes!" she cries, as her orgasm shatters through her and she trembles around my dick, her muscles tightening around me.

She fucks herself through it, bobbing up and down on me so forcefully she demands my release, too. I snarl as I come apart inside of her, bucking my hips upward to meet her movements as I spill every drop.

We remain like that, rocking into each other long after our mutual release. Our audience has dispersed from the doorway after watching us fucking like we'd didn't give a shit. I stare up at my beautiful wife, feeling pure adoration for her.

"I think they've gone away now," I say.

She smirks at me. "Well, the show is over."

I inhale her beautiful jasmine scent and groan. "I wish it wasn't. That was so fucking hot." I look into her eyes. "I think we both have a thing for sex in public, don't you?"

"Perhaps," she says, yanking the top of her dress back over her beautiful breasts and sliding off my still semi-hard dick. "It's time to get you out of here."

I slide my legs out of the bed and Livia grabs a pair of boxer briefs, kneeling in front of me. "Probably not the wisest position unless you want me to fuck you again."

She rolls her eyes. "How else am I supposed to help you dress?"

I clench my jaw. "Naked and pressed against that fucking window in the door while I fuck you from behind."

She laughs. "Stop messing about and lift your leg up for me."

When I don't move, she forcefully yanks my feet off the floor and slides my boxer briefs on. All I can think about is fucking her, day and night. It's a sickness. Maybe I need to go to rehab for sex addiction.

She pulls my boxer briefs up and I grab her hand when she's almost all the way up.

"Careful, printessa. You really are asking for another fuck."

Livia shakes her head and steps back. "Handle it yourself. We can fuck as much as you want at home."

"Is that a promise?" I ask.

She nods. "Of course."

I groan at the thought, perhaps recovery isn't going to be so bad with my own sexy nurse to ride me whenever I want.

She slips my pants on half way up my legs, allowing me to pull them up the rest of the way. Once I'm dressed, she slings my holdall over her shoulder and helps me out of bed.

I stretch slightly, wincing at the aching pain radiating through my shoulder. "The doctors have prescribed me painkillers, but I don't think I'll get them," I say, glancing nervously at Livia.

Her brow furrows. "Don't worry about me, Maxim. I don't need them anymore."

"Why is that?" I ask, intrigued as to how she can stop suppressing that side of her all of a sudden. A side she despised.

"Because you've made me realize I don't need to

hide that part of me anymore." She squeezes my hand. "And when I'm with you, the darkness isn't something to fear, if that makes sense?"

I nod, because it does. Since I've been with Livia, the darkness inside of me doesn't seem to drown me the same way it used to. "It makes perfect sense."

She smiles as we walk toward the exit of the hospital, ready to start the rest of our lives together. It may be fraught and dangerous, as tensions between the Morrone family and ours have never been higher. Add the Callaghan family to that and we're in the middle of a time bomb waiting to go off, but all I know is I'll protect Livia with my life, and hope we make it through.

For the first time, I actually have something worth fighting for

31

LIVIA

*M*axim walks into the apartment, smiling.

It's been five weeks since the Morrone's men shot him in the shoulder, but he's healing well. He's back to business as usual, as the war between the Russians, Irish and Italians has intensified since our escape from the Morrone family casino.

"I have a gift for you, moya lyubov," he says.

"What kind of gift?" I ask, standing to greet him.

He shrugs. "Come and see for yourself." He holds his hand out and I take it, glancing at his shoulder.

"How's your shoulder?" I ask.

"It aches, but the doctors say the aching should go away in a few weeks."

Maxim leads me into the elevator, pressing the basement level call button. The elevator jerks as it moves downward.

"Where are we going?" I ask.

He yanks me against his side. "No questions. Be patient."

I tap my foot against the floor of the elevator. Maxim is being cryptic and I don't like surprises. When we get to the parking level, he doesn't head toward a car, instead he drags me into the torture chambers, making my heart rate speed up.

He stops outside a door and I swallow hard, anticipating what I'll find on the other side. "What happens next is up to you, moya lyubov." Maxim pushes open the door and all the air whooshes out of my lungs.

My father sits in the center of the room, bruised and bloodied. Thankfully, Maxim kept his pants on, as that's not a sight I want to see. I glance at Maxim. "What about your father and his alliance with him?"

"I told you I could convince my father. You have to tell me how far you want me to take this, as I'd do anything for you." He grabs my hand and kisses the back of it. "He hurt you. He hurt your mom and your brother. I understand if you only want me to hurt him and then let him go, or if you want me to go all the way."

I stare at the pathetic excuse of a man who broke me in irreparable ways and know there's no chance of forgiveness, not after the way he fucked my mom's life up. "All the way," I mutter, meeting Maxim's ice-blue gaze.

His eyes flash with respect as he nods. "I agree

wholeheartedly. He has no right to breathe the same air on the same fucking planet for the way he hurt you."

I raise a brow. "You like to hurt me."

He shakes his head. "I don't hurt you. I inflict pain that you crave, which is different. I'd never tear you apart the way he did."

"I know," I say.

Ever since the first day we met, despite his cold, indifferent ways, I knew he wasn't like my father. We are the same. It just took me a little while to recognize that.

"Do you want to watch?" He asks.

I nod.

"Are you sure?"

"Certain. I may have promised my mom I wouldn't be the one to end him, but I'll witness it, because I need that, Maxim." I squeeze his arm. "I need it so badly."

He nods, eyes full of understanding. "Okay, baby."

I think he's the only person on this earth I'd ever admit that too, but after all the trauma I went through as a child, the endless beatings, it's only fair I get to witness my husband put him through just a small amount of the pain he inflicted and end his life.

I walk in and come to a stop in front of him, rage flaring in my veins. "Hello, Father."

His eyes snap open at the sound of my voice. "Liv, what is this?"

I glare at him, hatred infecting my heart. "What is this? It's retribution." I walk around him. "Payback for all the shit you put me, Mom and Rizzo through."

His nostrils flare. "It's all a lie that I poisoned your—"

I slam my palm into his face, just like he did to me in front of Maxim and Spartak the day I met them.

He snarls, showing his true colors. "Keep your filthy hands off of me."

Maxim steps forward, holding a long, thin knife. "Don't worry, she will be. I can't promise that I will, though."

"What the fuck is going on?" His eyes widen as he stares at my husband. "Your Bratva and my organization have an agreement. You can't tie me up like an animal."

Maxim smirks at him. "Can't I? I'm married to the heir of your empire and if something happens to you, the Volkov Bratva gets everything." He steps closer. "So give me one good reason I shouldn't kill you?"

His eyes widen, shifting between me and my husband. "You can't be intending to kill your own father?" He splutters.

"Unfortunately not, since Mom made me promise I wouldn't kill you."

His shoulders sag in relief as he shuts his eyes.

"But that doesn't stop Maxim from doing it for me, while I watch and enjoy the agony he puts you through."

His Adam's apple bobs as he swallows hard. "Listen, Liv—"

"No, I'm done listening to you." I step closer to him

and look him right in the eyes, those dark eyes that haunted my dreams for years even after I grew up. "You beat me as a child and Rizzo. You abused my mom, and you fucked with her health for years by slipping her drugs. There's no way you deserve to live."

The fear in my father's eyes is what I've wanted to see since the first day he beat me and Rizzo and yet it doesn't satisfy me enough. I need to see him bleed.

"Over to you," I say, giving my husband a nod.

Maxim smirks. "I always enjoy torture, but it's much more thrilling that I get to torture a man who harmed you, moya lyubov." He grabs my father's hand and slams the end of the knife into his fingertip, making my father scream at the top of his lungs.

I smile, surprised he opted to use the same torture method I used when we tortured Daniel. Maxim thinks I'm insane for telling him what he's doing for me right now is sweet, but he doesn't understand how badly I've longed for this day.

He pulls the knife out and sticks it into his middle finger on his other hand, enticing another shrill scream.

I never thought the day would come that I'd see my father in the pain he deserves.

Maxim continues until he's slammed the knife into each fingertip and my father is panting for oxygen, blood dripping down his hands.

"Where should I cut next, printessa?" Maxim asks, his ice-blue eyes finding mine.

I shake my head. "Where ever you want." I want to

watch my husband at work, admire the darkness that I love so much inside of him. "I want to see the real you at work."

His nostrils flare and he nods, walking over to the table, which has a lot of implements on. He picks up the same large serrated knife I chose to use on Daniel.

He twirls it by the hilt, walking back to stand in front of my father. "So, Vito. I hear you like to beat your own children," he says, placing the knife against my father's throat and pressing. "Only a coward beats children." I notice a bead of blood where Maxim presses the knife as it trickles down his bare chest.

"Please, don't do this, Liv."

"It's Livia, not Liv," I snarl, irritated that even to this day he ignores my wishes. I've never liked the name Liv, but he always shortened it now matter what I said.

"Sorry, Livia. Please don't do this." He pleads at me with his eyes, like the coward he is. "You're my daughter."

"You should have thought of that before you beat me and Rizzo so often." I place my hands on my hips, glaring at him. "Or before you taught me how to torture and maim enemies, because every single cut I inflicted on our enemies, I imagined it was you I was making bleed," I spit.

He's about to speak again when Maxim says, "Enough bullshit." He slams his fist hard into my father's jaw. "It's time to make you bleed."

My heart swells at the anger he holds toward this man, anger because of what he put me through.

I watch as Maxim slides the knife through my father's skin. He goes deep enough to make him bleed, but not too deep that he'll bleed out too fast. It's like watching an artist at work as he carves him up, making beautiful lines of red blood spill from the man I've hated for so long.

I feel a heavy weight lifted from my shoulders, even though it's not be inflicting the pain.

"Please," he begs, tears streaming down his face the same way they used to stream down mine when he beat me until I could hardly move. I feel no remorse as Maxim ignores him and steps back, admiring his masterpiece.

"You're a piece of shit, Vito." He spins the blade by the hilt again, blood splattering off of it, and then he lunges forward, slamming the knife deep into my father's right leg. "A piece of shit that deserves this and so much more." He pulls the knife out, blood arching into the air as it spurts rather fast out of his leg.

I sense he hit a major artery, which means this torture won't last much longer. His scream is so fucking satisfying, though.

Maxim does the same to his other leg, as my father's head lulls to the side. He's losing his strength.

"Please, Livia. Make him stop," he begs, as he meets my gaze.

I glare at him, knowing there's not a thing on earth that could force me to stop this. "Never."

He swallows hard, staring down at his bloodied legs. "Why are you doing this, Maxim?" my father asks, turning his efforts to my husband as the blood covers his chest. "She's a filthy little liar and a whore, you shouldn't list—"

Maxim reacts so fast I hardly see it happen. One second my father's talking, the next, Maxim has carved open his throat, and he's choking on his own blood.

I soak up the image, as this is the moment I've longed for. To watch him die and bleed and suffer how he made everyone I love suffer all our lives.

It came a bit too fast, as I would have enjoyed watching him suffer a little longer, but I know Maxim reacted because of what he was saying about me.

I rush toward Maxim and grab hold of his lapel, kissing him with all the love and gratitude I feel. My broken knight in shining armor has silenced my biggest demon. The reason I couldn't sleep for years at night, woken by terrible nightmares.

The knife he was holding clatters to the floor, as he grabs me with his bloodied hands, lifting me as he carries me toward the wall.

I moan as my back hits the hard brick. "Fuck, Liv. You make me so fucking horny after I kill someone," he breathes. The words seem to remind him *who* he just killed. "Shit, are you okay?"

I tilt my head, looking into his eyes. "I'm more than

okay. You killed him." I kiss him again, biting his lip as I do. "I fucking love you more than anything." Tears prickle at my eyes as I hold him so tight, knowing that I've never felt gratitude like this. "I feel like a weight has been lifted."

Maxim twirls me around, kissing my lips. His face splattered in my father's blood, but I don't care. Call me sick. Call me depraved. We're two broken people who have found solace in each other. Two broken people who exist in a world of brutality and violence and have embraced it as part of who we are.

I'll never apologize for it or hide it again. Not now that Maxim has made me realize it's a part of who we are, love it or hate it. There's no running away from yourself.

32

EPILOGUE

*F*ive months later…

      I wander down the streets of Catanzaro, reminiscing about my childhood here before it took a dark turn. There was a time I recall where our family was almost happy, but after the discoveries five months ago, I'm glad my mom is safe and away from my father. All along, he was the one with the mental problems, not my mom.

I just visited her in her new apartment and she's doing great, now she's no longer being slipped drugs that make her condition worse. When the doctor told me at the hospital, I've never wanted to kill my father more. Thankfully, my husband handled it since I promised my mom not to touch him. After returning to Catanzaro shortly after to inform his men, who still hadn't agreed to move, they were all relieved by the news that he'd gone 'missing'. The Bianchi mafia answers to the Volkov

Bratva in Chicago, working as an offshore branch of our organization, with Maxim and me at the helm, which means we have to visit Catanzaro frequently.

Maxim sits at a small table outside my favorite cafe, reading a book. We've been here for seven days now and he's blending in like a local. He even took the time to learn some Italian so he can converse with the servers.

I'm not only here to visit my mom, but we've both booked into a healing retreat, which is supposed to help you talk about past trauma. Neither of us expects to heal from our abuse as kids, but it can't hurt. We don't want to end up like my mom and dad, broken beyond repair. Rizzo is due to us out here with a friend in one week, which I'm excited about, as he will have finished his senior year at The Syndicate Academy.

We can be together in our hometown as a family, away from the toxicity that was my father.

I sit down opposite my husband. "Well, fancy seeing you here."

He smiles and sets his book down. "Indeed, strange, considering we agreed to meet here."

I raise a brow as he grabs his coffee and takes a sip. "How is she?"

"My mom's great today." I lean back in my chair. "She's better than she's been in years and is even going dancing tonight with a few old friends."

Maxim's eyebrow rises. "Friends, hey?"

I shake my head. "I'm happy for her. She's got a life. Even if it's late, it's better late than never."

The waiter approaches. "Ciao Livia. Cosa posso portarti?"

"Uno grande caffè latte, per favore."

He smiles. "Al momento."

I reach across the table as he leaves and clutch my husband's hand. "Thank you for agreeing to this vacation."

He tilts his head to the side. "I needed to get away, too."

I swallow hard, knowing Maxim isn't taking his father's recent actions well. Particularly his decision to marry one of the Morrone family's relatives, a relative who he took captive against her will, but that's a different story.

"I know." I take in my surroundings and the lively street. "I miss this town."

A smirk twists his lips. "I can see why. This place is nothing like Chicago."

"I thought you like Chicago."

The waiter returns with my drink and sets it down in front of me.

"Grazie," I say, taking a sip and shutting my eyes at the delicious taste. "You can't deny the coffee is divine compared to Chicago."

Maxim watches me for a while before commenting. "I do like Chicago, but I see the appeal of this place."

He glances around the streets. "It has a friendlier atmosphere, happier too, I guess."

"Does that mean you'd come here on vacation often?" I ask.

He raises a brow. "Now, now, Livia, don't get ahead of yourself. I don't think my father would be too pleased if I keep jetting off on vacation, do you?"

"You are working while you're here too, overseeing the new operation," I point out.

Maxim drains the rest of his coffee and sets his cup down with a thud. "I thought we might spend the afternoon on the yacht. What do you think?" There's a glimmer of mischief in his ice-blue eyes, which appear so striking in the midday sun.

"Hmm, I wonder why you'd choose to spend time on the yacht?"

His smirk widens. "Privacy."

I lick my bottom lip, knowing that for a while I've wanted to give him something he desires. Something I feel he has earned along with my trust. "Maybe I'll let you do what you've wanted to do for a while."

He straightens, eyes darkening. "Don't tease, moya lyubov. Otherwise, I might have to take it forcefully." His hand disappears under the table as he tugs at his cock, flooding me with need.

"I'm not teasing," I say, keeping my expression neutral. "I want you to take it."

He growls, standing from the table and chucking a twenty euro note down. "We're leaving now," he says.

I swallow hard at the ways his pants are straining over his massive bulge from talking about anal. Maxim took everything from me, but he allowed me to keep that to give to him when I was ready, and I'm ready now.

I pout at him. "But, I haven't finished——"

He seizes a fistful of my hair and yanks me out of my chair, unconcerned by the fact that many people in the cafe are staring at us. "Don't test me, moya lyubov." He tugs me against him and whispers into my ear. "You can't tell me to fuck your ass and expect me to wait while you drink your fucking grande caffè latte."

I love the way it sounds when he says Italian words in his Russian accent. "So rude," I reply.

He chuckles. "I'll make you one on the yacht, after I've taken your anal virginity." He captures my hand and yanks me away from the cafe down the street, leaving people gawking after us.

The yacht is based at my family home's private marina at the edge of the city, which is walking distance, but Maxim is too eager to walk. He flags down a cab and says the address in Italian to the driver.

"We could have walked."

He throws me a sharp look. "You could have walked." He grips my hand, forcing it over his rock hard crotch. "I would have been uncomfortable."

I roll my eyes. "Your dad was right on our wedding day. You're like a horny teenager who can't control himself."

He growls and grabs my throat, angling my face up to him. "Don't push me to punish you right here in the back of this cab while the driver watches," he breathes.

My nipples harden and my body sets on fire at the prospect of doing anything in the back of this cab. It's sick how deeply I want him to make good on that. "Do your worst," I spit.

He growls and grabs a fistful of my hair, unzipping his pants and pushing my mouth over his cock.

I gag the moment it hits the back of my throat, my pussy soaking my panties as he takes what he wants in front of the driver.

"Ignoraci e ti pagherò il triplo," Maxim grunts, thrusting his hips toward my face and thrusting into the back of my throat.

He just told the driver to ignore what we're doing and he'll pay him triple his fare.

Saliva spills onto Maxim's suit pants, but he doesn't care, fiercely thrusting like an animal in heat, fucking my throat with rapid jerks. He's after one thing and that's his release.

I groan around his shaft, slipping my hands beneath my skirt and playing with myself. I'm so fucking wet that a squelching sound fills the back of the cab as I dip three fingers inside myself.

"Fuck, you are so wet that I can hear you fucking your own pussy," Maxim grunts, jerking my hand out of my skirt and sinking my glistening wet fingers into his mouth. "My dirty little princess," he breathes, sucking every drop off.

I moan as he returns to thrusting his hips up into my throat, pushing so far I gag and almost throw up on his cock.

He senses he pushed too far and eases up, groaning. "I'm going to cum down that pretty little throat, and I want you to swallow every drop. Do you understand?"

I can't speak, so I give a slight nod of my head.

He groans. "Good girl."

I move my hand back under my skirt and rub my sensitive clit, moaning around his shaft as he picks up the pace. The public setting is all it takes to increase my desire as I feel myself tip over the edge before Maxim, moaning aloud around his cock.

"Fuck," he grunts, thrusting once more and then spilling his cum down my throat. "Such a good girl coming for me with my cock in your throat," he groans, pumping into my throat repeatedly as he spills his seed down my throat.

I swallow, trying to keep up with him, but there's too much as it spills onto his pants and my lips.

He stops thrusting into the back of my throat and his cock flops out of my mouth, but doesn't soften as he slides it back into his pants and does up the zip.

The driver is beetroot red color as I sit up straight and look at him in the mirror. He keeps his eyes on the road in front of him, but he's struggling not to look back.

I lick my lips, making sure I lap up all of his cum and sink against Maxim, who kisses my lips.

"Fuck, it didn't work. I'm still hard as stone thinking about your ass." He grabs my hand and makes me feel how hard he is.

At that point, the driver pulls up to the gates of the family home. I'd offered my mom the house after my father disappeared, as she'll never know the truth about what Maxim and I did, but she said there were too many terrible memories in that house. I have to agree with her, which is why we're putting it on the market before we leave. That's why we moored Maxim's yacht in the private marina and we're staying on that instead.

"Per favore, puoi lasciarci qui?" I say.

The driver nods, still not looking back. "Si."

We get out of the car and Maxim pays the driver triple, as he promised. It's amusing to see how fast he speeds away from us, in shock at both of our brazen attitudes, but I can't find it in me to care. Maxim has taught me to embrace sex in a way I never believed I could, and that we can get away with anything.

He leads me down the drive toward the marina and straight onto the boat, sighing in relief as he drops his pants and boxers to the floor, stepping out of them. "You deserve a punishment for teasing me with that tight little asshole of yours while I can't take it in a cafe."

I curl a strand of hair around my finger. "I thought you'd be happy to take it."

He comes toward me, unbuttoning his shirt as he undresses. "Oh I am, moya lyubov." He grabs the back of my dress and tears it open, scattering the buttons across the living room floor. "I'm not a very patient man." Roughly, he pushes the fabric down and then leans down to bite my hard nipples one by one.

I groan, wanting more pain.

Even as we attempt to heal, I know that part of me will always exist. The desire to both endure and inflict pain, but I'm just lucky I found a man who longs for the same. A man that doesn't shy away from my darkness but embraces it, nourishes it.

"Let's go to the bedroom," he breathes into my ear, biting my earlobe hard.

I groan and allow him to lead me into our bedroom of the yacht.

"On all fours on the bed, now," he instructs.

I give him a heated glare, but get on the bed because I'm as eager for this as he is.

Maxim makes a guttural sound behind me, one that threatens to strip me bare.

I shudder, waiting for him to make a move. My heart pounds so hard I can hear it thudding against my rib cage in a steady rhythm.

Maxim's rough hands part my cheeks and he rubs the tip of his cock through my soaking wet pussy. "Are you ready for my cock in your ass, moya lyubov?"

I bite my lip. "Yes, so fucking ready," I breathe.

He kneels down behind me and thrusts his tongue

against the sensitive passage, setting my body on fire with need. "I can't wait to feel it stretched around my cock, but you've been a naughty girl making me wait all this time, forcing me to prepare you for months," he growls.

My nipples tighten as he's right. I've been teasing him, knowing how badly he wanted it and denying him the opportunity for a long while, even though I wanted it too.

"How should I punish you?"

I tremble, wanting him to hurt me, to provide me with that release I so often crave.

"All I have to say is the word punish and your pussy gushes," he says, bringing his flat palm down against my arousal and making me squeal. "I love the way you crave pain, moya lyubov."

He bites my left ass cheek hard enough to leave teeth marks and then does same the right, making me groan.

And then he gets up and grabs a bottle of lube off the nightstand, as we'd been playing with some toys the night before. I swallow hard, knowing that despite working through larger implements, Maxim is far bigger than any toy I've used.

The thing is, I don't fear the pain; I crave it. I sense the more it hurts, the better it will feel. Maxim squirts some of the cold liquid onto my sensitive hole, sliding a finger inside as he works the lube inside of me.

I clench my thighs, knowing that the moment his

cock is inside of me, I'll last a few seconds. Slowly, he works two fingers inside of me and then three. The sting of stretching such tight muscles coupled with the sensation of being finger fucked sends me over the edge as I come unashamedly squirting on the duvet. It happens whenever I have something in my ass and I come.

"Oh, fuck, baby, I love the way you squirt," Maxim groans, leaning down to lap up my cum. He adds a fourth finger, dipping them up to his knuckle inside of me.

"Fuck," I breathe, struggling to imagine what it will feel like when he buries his thick cock inside of me. "Stop messing and get it in me," I pant.

Maxim spanks my ass hard. "Who's in charge?"

I bite my inner cheek. "You are."

"That's right." He grabs the lube again and squirts some on his dick, and I watch him between my thighs, spreading it on his the thick, velvety length, salivating at the sight.

My thighs quiver in anticipation as he lines the head of his cock up with my tight virgin hole.

He thrusts forward, working an inch inside of me as I scream out.

"Relax," he purrs, reaching around to rub my clit as he rocks his hips back and forward gently, working inch after inch into the tight space. "That's a good girl," He praises, rubbing my clit harder and faster. "You've swallowed every fucking inch."

I groan, feeling fuller than I've ever felt before in my life. "It hurts so good," I breathe, loving the sting and pleasure that morphs into the most delicious sensation I've ever experienced, and he's not even fucking me yet.

"You ain't felt nothing yet, baby." He digs his fingertips into my hips and pulls his cock almost all the way out of me before thrusting in so hard it feels like he's trying to tear me in two.

"Fuck!" I scream, struggling to make sense of my jumbled thoughts.

Maxim doesn't ease me into it. He's brutal and ruthless as he thrusts his cock in my ass. "You are such a good girl, taking every inch of my cock." He palms my ass cheeks in his hands, pulling them wider and pistons his hips in and out, fucking me like an animal. "I love watching every inch disappear."

"Stop talking and fuck me," I hiss, glancing over my shoulder at him.

His eyes flash and I know he's taken that comment as a challenge. "With pleasure." He yanks me upright, his cock buried in my ass, and walks me over to the window of the yacht, slamming me chest first against it. "Why don't we let the world see what a dirty little slut you are for my cock in your ass?" he breathes, slamming into me with such force I can hardly keep my knees from buckling.

Maxim holds me, though, making sure I can't fall. His hard muscles keep me upright as he breaks me apart against the glass, threatening to ruin me and make me all at the same time. It's all so overwhelming, the sensation of his cock stretching my ass like never before.

There's no gentleness, as my prince lays his claim, taking what I've denied him for months. Gentle isn't a part of our vocabulary. Both of us crave brutality, even with sex, and I wouldn't have it any other way.

His hot and heavy grunts against my ear with every thrust sends me closer to the edge, as he presses my body so tightly against the glass that my clit rubs against it, driving me to grind myself against the window. I don't care who sees. Right now, I'm not in my right mind.

I'm lost in the dirtiness of what we're doing, loving the way pain and pleasure merge as one. And then he wraps an arm around my throat, choking my air supply the way he knows sends me over the edge every time. It's all too much to process, so fucking good I feel like I might have died and gone to heaven. I want my release, but I never want this to end.

"I want to feel that ass milk my cock, baby." He tightens his hold on my throat. "Come with my cock in your ass for the world to see," he growls, biting my shoulder so hard I'm sure he pierces the skin as he licks the wound, tasting my blood like a fucking animal.

A silent scream tears from me as my mouth drops open, but nothing comes out. A flood of stars burst behind my eyelids as they clamp shut. Tremor after tremor chases through my body as the most intense orgasm I've ever had hits me like a tsunami of pleasure. A gush of liquid coats my inner thighs as I squirt like I've never squirted before.

He snarls as he releases my throat, sliding them down to my hips and brutally fucking me through my orgasm.

I shudder, unable to work out if I'm still riding the same orgasm or if he's sent me over the cliff edge again. The pleasure is so intense it's almost unbearable. Half of me wants it to end and the other half never wants it to, which is so conflicting.

My husband groans as his release hits him, his entire body shuddering against mine as he fills my ass with cum, exploding deep inside of me.

I slump against the glass, knowing if it weren't there, I'd be in a messy pile on the floor.

Maxim's powerful arm slides around my waist and he hoists me away from it, dragging me toward the bed.

We both fall onto it together in a tangle of limbs, chuckling. "Fuck, that was crazy," I mutter, wincing at how sore my ass feels.

"Crazy good, or crazy bad?"

I glance at him, rolling my eyes. "What do you think?"

"Judging by that fucking intense orgasm you had, I'm going to say, good?"

I nod and rest my head against his chest, holding

him close. "I know that I don't say this enough." I swallow hard. "But I love you, Maxim."

He smiles down at me. "I don't say it enough either, but I love you too." He kisses me, biting my bottom lip as he pulls away. "We're just two twisted people who found our salvation in each other, and that means more than any words we say to each other."

A few stray tears escape and trickle down my cheeks, as that's how I feel. Without him, my life had no meaning. He's made me realize that just because I'm broken, it doesn't mean I'm ruined. We still have our lives ahead of us and we can live each day to the full, together.

THANK you for reading Evil Prince, I hope you enjoyed Livia's and Maxim's story.

The next book in the Chicago Mafia Dons Series is Brutal Daddy, and follows Imalia's and Spartak's story.

Brutal Daddy: A Dark Captive Mafia Romance

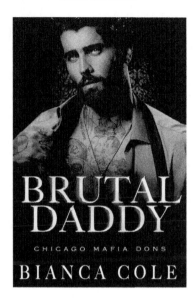

I'll die before I call him daddy...

Within hours of reaching Chicago, I'm taken.

Strung up in front of the most dangerous man in Chicago.

Spartak Volkov expects me to cower to him and give up my family.

He wants my submission.

He wants me to betray the people I love.

He wants to use me to end the war.

None of that scares me, though.

It's the sick desire in his eyes when he looks at me.

The way he calls me baby girl.

The scariest part of all, the way my body reacts to his touch.

The man is not right in the head.

He's dark, depraved, and everything I shouldn't want.

And yet, in his capture, I feel protected and wanted.

His brutal ways are addictive and I fear I'll never want to leave.

I vowed to never call him daddy, but he's peeling back my layers and laying bare my deepest and darkest desires.

Perhaps we're not so different after all…

ALSO BY BIANCA COLE

The Syndicate Academy

Corrupt Educator: A Dark Forbidden Mafia Academy
Romance

Cruel Bully: A Dark Mafia Academy Romance

Chicago Mafia Dons

Merciless Defender: A Dark Forbidden Mafia Romance

Violent Leader: A Dark Enemies to Lovers Captive Mafia
Romance

Evil Prince: A Dark Arranged Marriage Romance

Brutal Daddy: A Dark Captive Mafia Romance

Boston Mafia Dons Series

Cruel Daddy: A Dark Mafia Arranged Marriage Romance

Savage Daddy: A Dark Captive Mafia Roamnce

Ruthless Daddy: A Dark Forbidden Mafia Romance

Vicious Daddy: A Dark Brother's Best Friend Mafia
Romance

Wicked Daddy: A Dark Captive Mafia Romance

New York Mafia Doms Series

Her Irish Daddy: A Dark Mafia Romance

Her Russian Daddy: A Dark Mafia Romance

Her Italian Daddy: A Dark Mafia Romance

Her Cartel Daddy: A Dark Mafia Romance

Romano Mafia Brother's Series

Her Mafia Daddy: A Dark Daddy Romance

Her Mafia Boss: A Dark Romance

Her Mafia King: A Dark Romance

Bratva Brotherhood Series

Bought by the Bratva: A Dark Mafia Romance

Captured by the Bratva: A Dark Mafia Romance

Claimed by the Bratva: A Dark Mafia Romance

Bound by the Bratva: A Dark Mafia Romance

Taken by the Bratva: A Dark Mafia Romance

Wynton Series

Filthy Boss: A Forbidden Office Romance

Filthy Professor: A First Time Professor And Student Romance

Filthy Lawyer: A Forbidden Hate to Love Romance

Filthy Doctor: A Fordbidden Romance

Royally Mated Series

Her Faerie King: A Faerie Royalty Paranormal Romance

Her Alpha King: A Royal Wolf Shifter Paranormal Romance

Her Dragon King: A Dragon Shifter Paranormal Romance

Her Vampire King: A Dark Vampire Romance

ABOUT THE AUTHOR

I love to write stories about over the top alpha bad boys who have heart beneath it all, fiery heroines, and happily-ever-after endings with heart and heat. My stories have twists and turns that will keep you flipping the pages and heat to set your kindle on fire.

For as long as I can remember, I've been a sucker for a good romance story. I've always loved to read. Suddenly, I realized why not combine my love of two things, books and romance?

My love of writing has grown over the past four years and I now publish on Amazon exclusively, weaving stories about dirty mafia bad boys and the women they fall head over heels in love with.

If you enjoyed this book please follow me on Amazon, Bookbub or any of the below social media platforms for alerts when more books are released.

Printed in Great Britain
by Amazon

18509423R00222